A DROWNING IN SWANSON LAKE

A
DROWNING IN
SWANSON LAKE

Scott Gertner

Copyright © 1997, 2003 by Scott Gertner.

Library of Congress Number: 2001118937
ISBN :   Hardcover   1-4010-3258-3
          Softcover   1-4010-3257-5

All rights reserved. No part of this book may be reproduced or transmitted in any form or by any means, electronic or mechanical, including photocopying, recording, or by any information storage and retrieval system, without permission in writing from the copyright owner.

This is a work of fiction. Names, characters, places and incidents either are the product of the author's imagination or are used fictitiously, and any resemblance to any actual persons, living or dead, events, or locales is entirely coincidental.

This book was printed in the United States of America.

To order additional copies of this book, contact:
Xlibris Corporation
1-888-795-4274
www.Xlibris.com
Orders@Xlibris.com
12500

For always believing ...... to
my wife, Deb, with love.

1

It was in the time before war, when penny candies and quarter movies anchored our lives, and jellybean violet and tangerine butterflies shimmered like blown tattered wisps of crepe, delighting in their birth and in the assumption of their own immortality. The years were longer then, long enough to accommodate one's dreams. I lived in that time and beyond, staring through the night blackness into a world as infinite as my own. It would be years, many years it seemed, before I understood my world then was as fragile as the butterflies, which were already disappearing, and as ephemeral as the penny jawbreakers and double feature movies. The Cold War with its Cuban missile crisis, and threats from the Soviet leader Khrushchev to bury us, assaulted me in ways I was not prepared for. If wisdom followed age, I felt confident I would not be blindsided again. I prepared myself for anything, and soon became convinced of my newfound sophistication. That is, until the sudden disappearance of Ollie Magnusson, when again the lines of real blurred. I don't believe I refused to see what was occurring. I just missed the clues. Plain and simple.

The town of Swanson Lake lay a few hours and years from New York City. The name spawned unrealistic expectations, and likely contributed to the influx of its earliest inhabitants. But there were no swans, there never were any swans, and the lake seemed more like a pond with aspirations. The people that first settled the area two hundred years before were likely the same crowd that gave Greenland its name. Yet we always searched desperately for an explanation that might give dignity where none existed. The more exotic our origins, the more important we felt. Doc challenged my skepticism.

"I'm tellin' ya, Hal. Most people don't know history, especially their own. I'm not sure about the swans, but there was a lake . . . . It just eroded . . . . Then the vineyards . . . . well, that's all past history."

Doc presented his opinion with the confidence he gave to his diagnoses. But, in fact, very little was known about our three square mile area, and despite the periodic roundtables about the origins of the town's name, one speculation seemed as valid as the next.

Television and newspapers were important then, but not nearly as important as what Opal thought and said. Opal is Ollie's sister, and for most of my growing up, whether or not she found me handsome or brave or funny, was all I cared about. The older men would talk about the "commies" while I obsessed on a Duke Snyder homerun or my new Willie Mays baseball card. Nothing it seemed could disrupt the rhythm of our lives. That is, until the day Ollie disappeared.

Opal, Ollie, and I met under inauspicious circumstances. It was at a church picnic where I flaunted my newly acquired ability to walk, to the dismay of my father. When he wasn't holding my hand or eyeing me directly, I managed a few steps of freedom before being yanked back into confinement. One such moment occurred when Dad struggled with an ear of buttered corn, allowing me the quick escape and the opportunity to meet Opal. Introducing myself the best way I knew, I tried pushing a stone through her left ear in an attempt to watch it exit from the right one. Her squeals brought an abrupt end to my courtship efforts and a pummeling from Ollie who was, unfortunately, as mobile as myself, and much stronger. After the three of us were separated, I earned a "deedee", a double demerit, Dad spanking my bottom hot before humiliating me further by strapping me back into the stroller. I liked Opal, I liked her a lot, and assumed she would recognize that in my bizarre expression of affection.

I hated Ollie after that and waited to get even, but being two years older, he always managed to stay taller and stronger than myself, no matter how fast I grew. I stayed away from him and gave him no reason to hit me, especially since my expressions of affection for Opal became more civilized. I shared my crayons and cookies, and even let her win at *jacks*. Soon thereafter Ollie would give me the baseball cards that came with the chewing gum, without me having to flip for them. In time, we all played together and became inseparable. In cowboys and Indians, we all were one or the other, never having to make the difficult choice of killing each other. We became best friends in no time, and although Ollie initially tagged along to insure his sister's safety, he now did so because we enjoyed each other's companionship.

🐾 🐾 🐾

I awaited Saturday with such anticipation, it made Friday night sleeping a struggle at best, and an ordeal ordinarily. I tossed about like a just caught fish until the smells of Dad's percolating coffee inaugurated a new day. Saturday was the day Mr. Magnusson took me and Opal and Ollie into Brewman. He gave us each a dollar to distribute flyers advertising his wife's fruit pies and canned offerings for that week. We did this after delivering the previous week's orders. I hated when Mrs. Magnusson made the strawberry rhubarb pies and the mint jelly, their popularity such that it meant more work and less time for ourselves. But an extra pie or one too damaged to sell provided us with an extra treat, Opal's Dad letting us divvy up the spoils. We sat in the back of his pickup truck as Mr. Magnusson drove us up and down the streets. He gave Opal and me the important responsibility of delivering the food and collecting the money, leaving Ollie with the less accountable task of distributing the flyers. When we finished, the three of us went to Fanny's for some licorice wheels and a *lime Rickey*. With the leftover change, we either went to the movies or played miniature golf. Mr. Magnusson later picked us up in front of Fanny's, after his errands were done, and after we had nothing left from our dollar.

The ride home never seemed as much fun as the ride in. Not only had our much-awaited day ended, we felt too tired to even speak. Even Ollie just sat and stared. It was very different on the ride in. We not only read aloud the old, rusty metal signs that still remained along the roadway, "Get *Kist* Today. *Kist Soda*", *Bayer Aspirin*-Safe for Aches and Pains. Does Not Depress the Heart", and "*Omar*-Turkish Blend Cigarettes. Twenty For 15c", Opal and I listened to the chatterbox that brought us news and gossip updated since the previous week's trip. Miles before approaching a particular farm, Ollie volunteered a new piece of information.

"The Jameson barn fell . . . . killed two hogs."

And sure enough, as we passed the farm, Opal and I looked at the collapsed barn. We didn't know how he knew about this since he had no occasion or means to get into Brewman by himself. But farm after farm provided new revelations.

"Mr. Stohler died . . . . His wife is selling . . . . "

And a mile up ahead.

"Mrs. Hardy is leaving her husband . . . . He had a fair."

Ollie's information would later prove to be accurate.

"I swear, Ollie, you probably know which cows is gonna calf in the coming year."

He deliberated a few moments before responding to Opal's remark.

"I think so . . . . "

He then nodded more assuredly.

" . . . . But I'll know soon enough."

I looked at Opal and we coughed into our hands to conceal our laughter. I had read about people like this in the *Hudson Star Gazer*. They knew which things would happen to people way before anyone else did. I couldn't remember what they were called. Opal reminded me.

"Ollie a psychic? . . . . "

She laughed.

A DROWNING IN SWANSON LAKE 11

".... I don't think so."

"It's possible, Opal."

"Then he would be predicting everything.... No, he's not one of those."

Then Opal realized a possibility.

".... Oliver Magnusson! If you been hitchhikin' out here by yourself, you'll get the strap for sure."

She looked into his face for any reaction, but he just lifted his head into the wind as a dog might. However, the mystery was finally solved one day in town. We went to Ronnie's for a soda when we overheard Blue Armondsen tell Ronnie information we would later hear from Ollie, and in the same exact words. Opal and I understood that when he wanted, Ollie listened better than most people.

༄ ༄ ༄

The movie theater in Brewman featured *Around The World In Eighty Days*, a movie I wanted to see ever since Dad bought me a *Viewmaster Viewer* with the color slides of France and Italy. I relished the opportunity to see even more countries as I followed David Niven in his hot air balloon. For twenty-five cents, *The Ambassador* showed the main feature, a *Three Stooges* feature length comedy, four cartoons, and a ten-minute silent slapstick marathon where audience members could win prizes if the number on their ticket stubs matched the number of the winner in the race. I once won a model airplane kit Dad put together for me, and Opal won a paint by numbers watercolor set. Ollie never won anything because his ticket was long gone before the race began. I offered to hold it for him, to keep him from losing it, but he always refused. It was his ticket, he insisted, and no one would take it from him. However, since he really didn't care about the race or the prize, his unguarded ticket eventually found its way to the floor or to someone else's pocket. His toys came mostly from the outside. A rock, an empty soda can, a tree branch-all provided his entertainment. I admired him for that, for the imagination he had in slipping in and out of characters to become a warrior one day, and an adventurer the next.

However, even Ollie strayed occasionally from his reliance on outside diversions. He would often spend most of his allowance on packets of baseball cards, despite his dislike for the cards that "got in the way" of the thin, flat squares of bubble gum. He then exchanged his cards for the gum in my packets, and each of us walked away the winner. But Ollie's prize grew in size and noise as he stuffed slab after slab of gum into bulging cheeks that cracked and spewed huge bubbles. He looked like the cartoon character of the wind and I half expected him to blow Swanson Lake clear across the border to Vermont. On rare occasions Ollie refused to give up his cards, choosing instead to replace or add to the ones on his bicycle spokes. These created the sound of an anemic motorcycle, and coupled with the gold streamers on his bicycle handles, he imagined himself Marlon Brando in *The Wild Ones*. Ollie enjoyed playing the renegade, although his appetite for daring challenges would become increasingly more worrisome in the years ahead.

Yet for now, the three of us were together, and Opal and I only worried about who would win the relay race on the slapstick marathon. Neither of us won a prize that day and we emerged from the lobby into the blinding, disorienting sunlight. Soon I saw a soft breeze inflate an empty potato chip bag and carry it over our heads and across the street. I thought about the movie again, imagining me and Opal in a hot air balloon traveling all over the world, staying in any city we pleased and for as long as we liked. When Stan later threw away an empty straw apple basket, I took it home and attached an old sheet to it. I then invited Opal to join me as we traveled from one European capital to another. As we sat in the container, I penciled in a mustache to resemble David Niven's. She laughed.

"You don't have to do that. You're much handsomer than him anyway."

At that moment I knew eighty days with Opal would never be enough. I was thinking more in terms of a lifetime.

2

Ollie's predilection to play "chicken" became a source of hysteria for me and Opal. On the ride into town, he often stood just as we reached a low overpass, only to duck an instant short of having his head smashed like a walnut. Opal and I sometimes had to pull him down and put our full weight on him as we approached. But Mr. Magnusson's words still had the power to reform Ollie, if only momentarily, and his curses and threats reminded his son of the dire consequences that awaited him if he survived. However, once back in town and away from his father, Ollie continued his daredevil exploits unchecked. He dodged in front of cars, darting unseen from behind parked ones. His only response to his near death and the driver's expletives was to laugh like a funhouse clown and tap dance a few steps to his good fortune. Opal and I thought this might change after a tragic accident occurred one day in Brewman.

The *Mr. Softy* ice cream truck had its usual throng of school children buying frozen rockets and orange sherbet pops during the lunch recess. Suddenly, one of the boys ran from a classmate after stealing his ice cream cone. "Old enough to know better", as was later said, he failed to look as he ran across the street. An oncoming car hit him, barely hard enough to knock him down.

13

David Warren stood up, appearing only a little dazed, although he soon sat down at the urging of the adults nearby. When an ambulance came and carried him away, no one could know that the swelling in his brain would prove fatal even before he reached the hospital. I wondered what lesson Ollie would draw from this, hoping he would see it as God's way of serving him notice. And for a week after that Ollie did suspend his escapades, David's death managing to inject him with a dose of caution. However, on the eighth day Ollie resumed cavorting with fate, this time bringing a renewed vigor to his efforts. It began with a partially successful attempt to cannonball himself from a barn roof into a snow bank. Aside from an underlying piece of branch that skewered his thigh like a shish kebab, costing him a few inches of flesh, Ollie limped and grinned in the aftermath. Opal and I then considered the possibility that Ollie knew something we didn't. Perhaps he celebrated and basked in the knowledge God considered him worth saving, despite the dark thoughts he harbored, and the self-destructive behavior he exhibited. Opal and I, desperate for answers, satisfied ourselves we had moved a bit closer to understanding Ollie. But it did little to help us discover Ollie's whereabouts when he disappeared years later. I soon learned that Ollie's disregard for death began and ended with himself. Opal and I had been walking behind him on a dusty road a mile outside of town when Ollie stopped at the old abandoned shack up ahead. We saw him bend down and then let out the most horrifying scream, all the while pointing to something in his hand. We assumed he injured himself, and we sidestepped the tangled vines, rusty cans, and broken glass to see the cause of his anguish. He stared at his half open fist, saying nothing and not moving. Opal said he might be having one of those seizures her nana used to have. But speculation died when Ollie opened his fist to reveal a small dead toad, its body likely flattened from a succession of bicycle tires. Then Ollie drew the toad to his lips where Opal and I, thinking he planned to eat it, screamed for him to stop. Ignoring us, he attempted to blow into its mouth. At first I assumed it was a pitiful attempt at mouth-to-mouth resuscitation, although I soon understood Ollie had his sights on something far greater. He tried to inflate the flattened toad in order to return it to the living. It worked in the cartoons and I knew he relied on that precedent for his action. When his patient failed to recover and jump off his hand, Ollie began to sob. But a minute or so later, a smile replaced his tears as he placed the toad into his pocket.

"It sometimes takes awhile for him to wake up again."

Opal and I said nothing, realizing the futility in trying to reason with him. We simply watched Ollie add some grass to his pocket, knowing it would become a blanket to keep the toad warm and comfortable until he awoke. But when it finally became obvious to Ollie this would not happen, the frog's odor making our eyes hurt, Ollie relented and buried it. He recruited Opal and me as pallbearers, which we undertook gladly in order to retire the stench. All through the service, Opal and I looked at each other for more clues, for anything that might help us understand him further.

But if Ollie's behavior often wandered beyond the explicable, his beautiful alto voice brought him a certain normalcy. His voice made him ideal for the doo-wop rock 'n roll songs the three of us sang on the way to town to catch our school bus. Opal and I were his backup and we performed the whole range of Shirelles, Five Satins, and Beach Boys hits. "Soldier Boy", "In The Still Of The Night", and "Surfer Girl" reverberated across the withered vines as we sang to our audience of raccoons, deer, and squirrels. We imagined them waiting for our daily concert to begin, and we always serenaded them with a half dozen well rehearsed and, we assumed, masterfully sung tunes. Ollie always performed his role of lead singer with such authority that Opal and I did all we could to keep from laughing at his seriousness. He was at the *Fillmore* or the *Loews*, in the spotlight, the headliner, and he savored every moment. Opal and I were delighted for him and for the momentary calm that seemed to overtake him and dispel his restlessness. He had now become someone else, someone that even he could like, if only for a short while.

Ollie and I often met death in the games we played, in the shootouts during our cowboys and Indians adventures or in the struggle with pirates, but we never expected anyone to actually die. And we certainly never expected to cause someone's death.

One late afternoon when Ollie and I became bored with skimming stones across the pond, we decided, no, I decided to try something new with a piece of wire we found. A cold kept Opal at home and her absence allowed my devilish instincts to go unhindered. I instructed Ollie to hide behind a bush holding one end of the wire while I hid behind the bush across from him holding the other end. We would let the wire rest on the ground until someone passed by, then suddenly pulling up on the wire to trip him. I thought my plan brilliant and we eagerly awaited our first victim. I ruled out adults and girls, the consequences being too great. But one of our frailer male classmates, someone we knew couldn't pummel us, seemed the ideal victim. No sooner had Ollie and I taken our places behind bushes when Nels Nelgren bicycled into our trap. A fellow bus mate, his small, thin stature and good-naturedness qualified him for the prank about to occur. Feeling sure we would all get a good laugh from it, I gave the signal to Ollie. When the bicycle's front wheel went over the wire, we pulled hard, and Nelgren somersaulted over the front of his bicycle. I expected him to just fall off the bike, not fly through the air like a spastic *Superman*. However, he landed on a patch of thick grass and I waited for him to jump up and curse and scream at us. Except he didn't move. I waited, but he lay there motionless. Ollie came out from his spot and we walked cautiously towards the body.

"Be careful, Ollie. He's playin' for sure."

I picked up a stick and approached Nelgren. I poked him gently to draw a reaction. But nothing. Then I tried tickling him, but he lay still. I couldn't see him breathing.

"Is he dead, Hal? Did we kill him? . . . . "

The words felt branded into my brain. "Dead" and "kill" were still sizzling. "Did I break his neck?", I thought. I never considered this possibility. Nelgren still did not move. I would have given anything for him to get up and beat me silly. I would have deserved it. Now all I could look forward to was years in *Sing Sing* or *Attica*, waiting for the day when they would shave my head and strap me into the electric chair. Ollie would be spared. I would tell them he had nothing to do with it. I heard Ollie's voice.

" . . . . Did we really kill him?"

I nodded and then we both started to cry. My tears weren't for Nelgren as much as they were for the punishment that awaited me. My concern soon shifted to a possible witness and I looked around. Seeing no one, I pulled Ollie.

"Let's get outa here!"

We ran all the way. Just before Ollie and I parted, I made him promise not to tell anyone about what happened. He nodded. I wasn't satisfied.

"Say you promise."

"I promise . . . . But shouldn't we do something?"

"Yes. We have to pray real hard."

"Pray for what?"

"That no one notices he's missing."

Ollie thought for a moment.

"Won't his parents notice it?"

Ollie had become smarter than I. I could not think anymore.

"Okay, then just pray for us."

Ollie still looked confused when I left him. I said nothing at dinner, eating little, before excusing myself with a headache. I rushed upstairs to begin my night of praying. I did feel sorry for what I did, I promised God I wouldn't do it again, and if He would just make it turn out all right, I would become a missionary somewhere in Africa. Suddenly the phone rang. I answered it on the first ring so Dad wouldn't pick it up and hear the news from someone else. I paused before I said hello. I expected Sheriff MacCauley. It was Opal.

"Ollie told me what happened. Shame on you, Harold Moffat! . . . . You can be very stupid!"

Her words stung.

"He promised he—"

"Is that all you care about, that Ollie didn't keep his promise? He cried all evening, Hal. He said the two of you killed Nels Nelgren . . . . "

I was surprised at how calmly she said that. Then she continued.

" . . . . We know how he likes to exaggerate . . . . how bad was Nels hurt?"

I remained silent.

" . . . . Hello?"

"I don't know. I can't say for sure."

I was lying to both of us.

"And you just left him? You didn't get any help?"

"I was scared . . . . but I didn't see blood or anything."

I hoped Opal would not see through my half-truths, even as I understood that did not matter anyway. Her abhorrence after discovering the complete truth would dwarf what she felt at that moment. I couldn't talk anymore, unwilling to lie further, and unwilling to hear her anger and disappointment.

The next morning I awoke to the nightmare that refused to go away. I wanted to stay home, but Dad already stood at the stairs waiting for me. I expected the worst. Sheriff MacCauley would either be waiting for me at the bus stop, or pull me out of class to interrogate me and obtain a confession. When Dad dropped me at the stop, I tried not to look at anyone or anything. I focused on the ground and the steps needed to reach and board the bus. I no sooner stepped onto it when I heard my name called. I looked up and nearly fainted. Facing me, with a huge grin, sat Nels Nelgren. He now laughed at my open mouthed expression.

"Sure was hot last night. Good and sweaty. Get any sleep?"

He laughed again. I took my seat next to Ollie, Opal still sick.

"He ain't dead, Hal. Isn't that good?"

I smiled. I couldn't be angry with Ollie for breaking his promise and I certainly couldn't be angry with Nelgren for living and inflicting a punishment as severe as I ever received. I deserved that and more. I knew Nels would be satisfied with the revenge he exacted and would let the matter drop. My entire body now relaxed and I felt grateful he survived. As we approached the school, I thought about my prayers and wondered what my life as a missionary would be like.

3

If ever two people existed with too much time on their hands, it was Stan and Doc. They had become living synonyms for the word "idle". One day, on the way home from school, Ollie, Opal, and I had just gotten off the bus and were headed home. I ran ahead to buy some baseball cards at Stan's grocery, figuring they would catch up to me after I finished my ritualistic shaking and sniffing of the packets to determine which most likely contained the players I needed. I hated to be rushed during this process, and so I went ahead to allow myself some extra time. As soon as I turned into Stan's doorway I stopped abruptly, sliding and nearly slipping on a piece of wilted lettuce. Doc sat slumped in his chair, snoring, his balls of chin resembling a triple scoop ice cream. Stan stood behind him holding a fishing pole and dangling a line with a chunk of Genoa salami hooked to it. Doc's favorite lunchmeat floated an inch from his bulbous nose. The tiny red veins on Doc's nose always reminded me of a plastic see-through model of a body part, the blood vessels clearly visible and ready to be examined. And as this facial incongruity competed with his markedly uneven eyebrows, the impression one received was of a face that had been taken apart and reassembled by an amateur. Stan winked at me and I felt glad he included me in on the joke. Opal and Ollie soon approached and I put my finger to my mouth to quiet them. They approached cautiously, and although I had to bite my hand to keep from laughing, Ollie couldn't quite stifle the giggle that warbled in his throat. I covered his mouth and Stan glared him into silence. Then he returned to his project. The salami made Doc's nose twitch, interrupting the rhythm of his snoring. When Stan moved it even closer, Doc wet his lips. Now it was I who couldn't contain himself, and I burst out laughing. That startled Doc, who upon awakening and seeing something floating less than an inch from his eyes, jolted suddenly and nearly fell to the floor. Only his last second grab at the counter kept him upright. Stan's eyes bulged, his mouth sprayed saliva, as he emitted a laughter resembling a hacking cough. Ollie and I had tears streaming down our face, although Opal seemed less amused. I knew she considered these childish boy's pranks, but I couldn't stop laughing until I saw Doc's face become as red as one of Stan's undercooked roast beefs. I saw what lay ahead and I pulled Opal and Ollie away before we would be seen as co-conspirators. A few steps into the street I heard Doc's voice.

"You son-of-a bitch! Are you outa your mind?! You damn near poked my eyes out with that stunt!"

"Stop playin' to the balcony, Doc. It was a harmless prank."

"Harmless, my ass. I could have fallen and cracked some bones! I could've broken my neck!"

Stan either realized the possible seriousness of what he did, or he pretended to.

"Yeah, you're probably right . . . . I went a little too far . . . . Sorry, Doc. I wasn't thinkin'."

"Well . . . . don't let it happen again . . . I mean it."

Although I had expected Doc to pounce on Stan's comment about "not thinkin', I did not feel disappointed. Doc's warning was amusing in itself. Despite his contrite admission, I knew Stan already began planning his next bit of torture. Doc knew it, too.

ß ß ß

Stan suffered from a bad case of dandruff, especially in the winter months, creating the impression of someone who had been dipped head first into a vat of confectioner's sugar. Rarely ten minutes went by before Stan began tearing furiously at his scalp in his attempt to relieve the unbearable itching. For a few brief moments he would close his eyes, smile, and enjoy the momentary relief. He didn't see, or care to see, the avalanche of white flakes and dead hair that parachuted from his head onto the uncovered donuts and coconut marshmallow squares on the counter in front of him.

"Your little hobby is gonna get us into trouble."

But nothing Doc said mattered. Minutes later, as though prodded with a pitchfork, Stan would again begin the ripping and scraping of his scalp. He considered his finger nails inadequate for this purpose and employed alternative, more powerful, weaponry. During the summer months, Stan's arsenal included wadded up pieces of aluminum foil to scratch his mosquito bites bloody.

"I'm scrapin' the itch outa them," he would say, proud of his accomplishment. But the foil did not suit his hairy scalp. Instead, he used a toothpick to target and spear specific itch spots. Often this created small sores around his hairline that resembled an outbreak of chicken pox or measles. This toothpick then became sacramental, it being given special and exclusive rights to serve both his scalp and teeth. He always kept it in his shirt pocket and I almost expected it to have its own case and monogram. Doc warned Stan about the danger of infection, but since Doc's alternative remedies had failed, everything from prescribing olive oil shampoo to wearing a Yankee baseball cap with the hair wet, Stan continued the one treatment that worked. However, as the scabs became larger and more painful, Doc felt confident about his chances of persuading Stan.

"You're infecting that thick head of yours. Pus 'll form and creep slowly into the nooks and crannies of your brain . . . . like advanced syphilis, but of course without the up side of getting that disease."

I heard that disease mentioned on *The Untouchables* and I asked

Dad about it.

"You get it from being bad."

That made sense, since Al Capone died from it. Now Stan had something like it, and I kept trying to figure out what specifically he did to deserve it. A number of things qualified, although the pink and sore nose he gave me and Ollie from his "gotcha nose" pinch seemed certain to recommend him

Doc's warning apparently succeeded in getting Stan to reconsider his habit. Other people's health might be inconsequential, but Stan considered his own a different matter. He looked at Doc with one eye, unsure if his seemingly farfetched diagnosis was possible.

"Are you foolin' with me or just demonstratin' you never really finished medical school?"

"Do as you wish. You have been warned."

Since Doc maintained a serious expression far longer than their jokes allowed for, Stan grew so worried his forehead formed trenches. Soon he took the toothpick from his pocket and looked at it.

"Even I know a mouth is full o' germs. I'll grant you that, sure enough. And just in case you're on the level with that pus stuff and my brain, I'm willing to change my habits . . . . "

Stan threw away his toothpick, Doc looking at me and smiling. It wasn't often either of them convinced the other of anything, let alone something as important to Stan as this. Doc appeared ready to savor his victory when Stan went and took a box of toothpicks off the shelf and placed it next to him by the cash register. He retrieved one from the box and began scratching with it.

" . . . . It's not that much money. I can afford a clean one each day. It's stupid to risk catchin' something from a dirty toothpick."

Stan attacked his scalp more furiously than before, confident he had now remedied the situation. Doc looked at me, unsure whether or not he was being toyed with. I provided no help. There seemed to be just enough sense in what Stan said and did, to make me think he might be serious. Doc shook his head, muttered something about Stan and "a baboon's butt", and went outside to chew on his cigar. I stayed behind, hoping Stan would share the joke with me and I would feel more adult because of it. But he didn't, because he had been serious, after all. As I watched him stab and rip at his scalp, I thought of a wild chimpanzee with a demented sense of self-grooming.

☙ ☙ ☙

If Doc's medical skills were questionable when he was in his prime, they became more suspect when he reached his late sixties. Years of bad health and the natural aging process played havoc with his judgment, so that his diagnoses grew into models of contradiction. Headaches graduated to brain tumors, muscle stiffness became polio, and just when you began mentally planning your funeral, he would dismiss what he said and assure you all was okay. His assurances were worthless, and you left feeling far worse than when you came. The illness or injury might heal, but Doc's words still haunted you and kept you uneasy about your future. People in town dreaded the prospect of needing immediate emergency care, and some, like Dad, ruled out Doc under any circumstances

"My skin would have to bubble and drop off my bones like the meat on a boiled chicken. And even then I'd sooner drive to Brewman to see a real doctor."

I remembered Dad's reassuring words the day my injury required immediate attention. Ollie and I stood back to back, trying to push the other away and cross over a branch we laid between us. We exerted our full weight and strength to keep each other from crossing that line. Suddenly, Ollie stepped aside. I fell back a few feet before falling on a broken *Coke* bottle and cutting my leg. Unaware of my injury, he laughed hysterically.

"I guess you won, Hal. I guess you won . . . . "

He soon stopped when I got up, blood oozing from my calf, just below the back of my knee.

" . . . . Jeez, Hal. There's blood comin' out from ya."

Opal had been lying on her back, staring up at the sky. At the mention of "blood", she leaped to her feet. The cut didn't hurt that much, but I had fallen hard on the glass and I knew the gash was deep. Blood continued flowing.

"Did you do this, Ollie?! . . . . "

Before he could explain, she continued.

" . . . . Never mind, now. I'll deal with you later. We better get Hal to Doc right away."

If the sight of my own bleeding scared me, the mention of Doc petrified me.

"It'll stop on its own, Opal. I just need a *Band-Aid*, that's all."

Even I didn't believe that, so Opal's words were no surprise.

"Are you crazy? Just look at how much you're bleeding . . . . "

I could feel the blood running down my leg. Opal took off her belt.

" . . . . Here. Tie it so the bleeding stops."

I saw it done hundreds of times in the westerns and when I pulled it tight enough to stop the flow, I felt like a real cowboy. I wore my wound proudly. My bravery ended when we began walking and I remembered our destination.

"Maybe you're right, Opal. My leg is bad. Maybe we should go to Dr. Myers in Brewman. My Dad will take me."

"It'll take too long. We'll stop at Doc's. We have to pass him anyway."

With that comforting recommendation of Doc's abilities, "we'll have to pass him anyway", I limped my way to the slaughterhouse. Opal and Ollie supported me, my arms around their shoulders, as I tried not to put too much pressure on my leg. We still had a mile to walk and I didn't know how long the belt would do its part. When we entered the town, I began feeling dizzy, partly from the loss of blood, but mostly from the sun and the anticipation of what lay ahead. When we arrived at Stan's, to my disappointment, Doc sat in his usual perch like some overstuffed watchdog. His face tore away at his favorite sandwich—a huge chunk of Italian bread stuffed with Genoa salami, Swiss and blue cheese, lettuce and tomato, and green olives. I watched him make this sandwich countless times, to the annoyance of Stan.

"For Chrissakes . . . . you got half the deli case in there."

"Only half?"

Doc would then add a few more slices of meat or cheese.

Eventually, Stan restricted his complaints to a scowl or to an incoherent mumble. As I now watched the tomato drippings stream down Doc's chin, I worried about the timing of my injury. Eating had always been his act of worship, and I would now commit sacrilege by interrupting him. I dreaded having him angry and resentful while he treated me. But when he saw me, and the blood that began dripping, he put down his sandwich. I felt relieved Stan wasn't there to see the mess I created. I took a napkin from the counter and began wiping the floor.

"Never mind that. Just step over here . . . . I see you boys were roughhousing again . . . . "

I walked over to him.

" . . . . Come on, come on. I don't have all day. Let's see it . . . . "

He wiped his hands on his pants in preparation for examining my wound. I hesitated a moment before rolling up my pants leg. I didn't look at the cut, choosing instead to stare at the pest strip that dangled above me while I waited for his verdict.

" . . . . A good gash. Deep. What you fall on? . . . . "

I told him.

" . . . . Better than a rusty can . . . . yeah, this one's a bleeder. Good you used the belt. Smart thinking. Blood loss is serious business . . . . "

I became more nervous with each passing second, and I thought I might faint if I didn't soon sit down. But Doc's breath, which had been wafting towards me, arrived full strength just as I turned to look at him. When he then also yawned, I felt grabbed, shaken, and slapped back into total consciousness. Satisfied he had seen all he needed to, Doc got up and went behind the counter to get his black bag. He moved slowly, with no more urgency than if he was getting a *Slim Jim* or a pretzel stick.

" . . . . We'll fix you up as good as new. You're lucky it missed an artery . . . . "

I felt relieved and I could see Opal smile. Ollie appeared fascinated with Doc's bag and watched intensely as he removed gauze and rubbing alcohol from it. I was further relieved that Doc treated me right there, instead of in the room upstairs he reserved for his more serious cases.

" . . . . Now this'll bite . . . . "

Before I could react to his words, Doc began cleaning my wound with the rubbing alcohol. I felt the pain shoot clear to my temples and I would have screamed if Opal had not been there. I bit my lip, closed my eyes real tight, and pretended I was lying in the grass next to her with our shoulders touching. But I could not keep the tears from welling in my eyes as Doc rubbed and dabbed my gash with his gauze. When he finally bandaged it, and I considered the ordeal over, I savored my machismo. Until Doc spoke again.

" . . . . No need for stitches that I can tell. It should heal fine . . . . Of course, the deep wounds are tricky . . . . There's lots that go on underneath . . . . But we'll keep an eye on it, don't worry . . . . "

Doc then walked over to his sandwich and made a face that seemed a cross between indigestion and annoyance. I thought my injury might have ruined his appetite. But he continued on the same tract as before.

" . . . . Germs are the problem. I cleaned it good but you can never be sure . . . . "

He kept trying to convince himself of something. Then he did.

" . . . . No use in taking chances. Dirt is dirt. I better give you a tetanus . . . . Yeah, I better give you one of those . . . . "

I hated needles. I turned my back to Opal, sparing her the sight of a coward who began wincing even before Doc speared my muscle. But Doc's ramblings numbed me to the physical pain, only to replace it with a more potent mental one."

" . . . . Infection, gangrene . . . . no . . . . nothing to fool with. A nasty business . . . . we can't have that, can we?"

He smiled and I couldn't be sure if he actually expected an answer. I had heard "gangrene" before, when Dad talked about his mother's diabetes. She had gangrene and they had to cut off her leg.

"Gangoreen?! You think I have that?!"

Doc laughed.

"No, no. I'm making sure you don't get it."

Opal became curious.

"What turns green?"

I answered before Doc could.

"Your leg. And then they cut it off."

She gasped. Ollie couldn't contain his excitement.

"Then you'll be a pirate for real!"

Opal looked as though she were about to cry, when Doc intervened.

"Hal doesn't have gangrene and he isn't going to get it. And that's that."

I wasn't convinced and neither was anyone else. I just wanted to leave, and would have, if I still didn't feel responsible for the blood on the floor. I bent down to wipe it when Opal took my napkin and thrust it at Ollie.

"This is your job. You played a part in this."

Ollie knew better than to argue with his sister when she was both angry and right. He cleaned up the mess in his usual careful attention to details, rubbing each spot repeatedly.

"That's enough, Ollie. You already spent more time cleaning that floor than Stan did over these past seventeen years. Even you couldn't get it to shine . . . . "

Surprisingly, Ollie heeded Doc's words and didn't try to polish the floor to ballroom perfection. I thanked Doc and we started to leave.

" . . . . Tell your dad he owes me a lunch . . . . "

Before we could get through the door, he added,

" . . . . Now don't worry. It'll be fine . . . . but you'll let me know if something doesn't look right . . . . Just in case."

I wanted to throw a package of *Twinkies* at him, but I just nodded and went home. Opal took my arm and told me how brave I had been, although I didn't feel brave. In fact, I felt scared, and each day I lifted my bandage to check on my wound. It began to heal, although not quickly enough. And the skin seemed to have a greenish tinge that Dad claimed were my veins. But I still felt suspicious and I drove Dad crazy until he promised to take me to Dr. Meyers. However, before my scheduled appointment, the gash healed. In fact, my leg revealed no trace of my injury. Despite all that, for months afterwards I worried about the part you couldn't see under the skin, the germs Doc talked about, and the gangrene just ready to erupt and ravage my body.

4

If I never wanted the Saturday trips into town to end, I certainly never expected them to end so soon and so abruptly. Mr. Magnusson halted his weekly trips when a batch of his wife's custard pies was improperly prepared and a round of salmonella struck Brewman. No one died, although many victims prayed they would. Opal related the tales of horror that made its way to our town and to the embarrassed Mr. Magnusson and his disgraced wife. Even Sheriff MacCauley investigated.

"It was horrible, Hal. He made her feel like a criminal, like she done it on purpose . . . I never saw Ma cry so hard or so long . . . . "

Opal then cried. I wanted to say something, although I didn't know what. Her mother was such a nice lady and I knew it had to be an accident. That's what I told Opal.

" . . . . But it don't matter, don't you see? Ma cared so much about her cooking, about what people thought. She was so proud of what she could do . . . . "

Mrs. Magnusson had always enjoyed having me over for dinner. She hung on every one of my gestures, facial expressions, and words while I devoured everything she placed before me. Her cooking made a person feel special, and my telling her that pleased her immensely. Now Opal began describing a different woman from the one I knew.

" . . . . She just sits and says nothing . . . . and she doesn't cook no more . . . . Daddy is doing everything, waiting for her to come out of it, but she doesn't . . . . She just sits by the window and laughs at nothing in particular."

Even after Sheriff MacCauley cleared her of any wrongdoing, rumors began to spread that were laughable if they weren't so mean spirited. One claimed she went crazy and spent her days painting yellow spots on the dead mice she found in the traps. Another said she once tried to mix ground glass in her husband's coffee, but he discovered it just in time. Opal and Ollie were often the first to hear this slander, and they felt helpless, as we all did, to stop it. However, since the accusations grew increasingly ridiculous, approaching the same level of outlandishness as the one about the local postmaster sneaking the polio virus into the glue in postage stamps, most people stopped giving credence to them and anything else pertaining to the incident. And if one or two still persisted in believing them, just as one or two still refused to lick their postage stamps and elected instead to sponge them with a wet tissue, the residents of Swanson Lake and Brewman considered the issue forgotten. However, no one really expected the act of forgetting to become permanent, as the reemergence of a previous scandal showed.

The food poisoning incident ended Mrs. Magnusson's cooking days and, in turn, my dinner invitations and additional time with Opal. But the Magnussons now had more on their mind than my welfare. They had to answer the charge that Mrs. Magnusson tried to kill Ollie while pregnant with him. It was a charge leveled not by the courts, but worse, by her neighbors. Ollie shrugged off the story as "dumb", not believing his mother would try and hurt him.

"She loves me, Hal. She said so . . . . That means they're wrong . . . . "

He paused before bringing up some more proof.

" . . . . How come I ain't dead if she wanted me dead?"

I couldn't answer that, nor did I know what to say that might comfort him. I just didn't know enough about it, or more honestly, I didn't understand what I did hear. But I had to try, at least for Opal's and Ollie's sake, and so I went to the wisest person I knew.

"They're bringin' that up again? . . . . "

Dad shook his head.

" . . . . People are always tryin' to outdo each other in cruelty . . . . "

I half expected him to dismiss it as just meanness, or tell me I needed to get older before I would understand it all. He surprised me.

" . . . . It's time that nonsense got put to bed . . . . And I know just who can do it."

I grew excited at the possibility of meeting someone even wiser than Dad. For those few moments I imagined packing my bags and journeying to a mountaintop where a guru sat cross-legged, with only the whites of his eyes visible as he looked heavenward. But my hope for enlightenment crumbled more and more with each step Dad I took towards Stan's. It finally disintegrated when we approached Doc. By himself, reading the newspaper, my disappointment conjured up the image I once saw in a documentary about an unskilled diamond cutter. I expected my search for answers to be shattered into worthless dust. He looked up when he saw Dad and me.

"How do you like them Russkies? . . . . "

He began pounding the newspaper with his finger.

" . . . . They beat us to outer space and soon they'll beat us to the moon . . . . I thought with Ike at the helm their days of spying were over . . . . "

Dad tried to interrupt, but Doc ignored him and continued.

" . . . . They did it with the bomb and now this . . . . Nothing and no one is safe anymore from that bunch . . . . no one . . . . "

When Doc fizzled out on that subject, Dad brought up the other.

"I wanted to ask you about the Magnusson boy."

Doc laughed.

"Don't tell me you just noticed something peculiar? . . . .
What's he into now?"

"Not now . . . . during the pregnancy."

"That's old news. Move on."

"The gossip mill is working overtime again . . . . But you know
most of the details."

Doc became defensive.

"I had no part in that . . . . in either birth. And you know that."

"I know."

Doc pulled out a piece of food between his teeth before
continuing.

"She wanted a midwife like she was used to in the South . . . .
crazy . . . . and woulda used one here if she had found any I
don't get it."

"Get what? She used a doctor."

"Yeah, but not me . . . an obstetrician. Talk about overkill . . . .
You'd think people woulda told her about me and that she had a
skilled professional ready and able to do the job."

"I'm sure they did . . . . "

Doc and I looked at Dad, who now tried to make the best of
his verbal blunder.

" . . . . but you know how pig headed people are . . . . even
when the best choice is in front of them."

I knew Dad had to pinch himself hard to keep from laughing.
I expected Doc to dismiss the words as patronizing and insincere.
To my amazement, he accepted them.

"Exactly. That's just part of human nature . . . . And that's
why I hold no grudge . . . . I mean, if I got angry at every person
who . . . . "

Then Doc stopped and glared at Dad, who appeared
preoccupied.

" . . . . If you don't plan on listening, just say so . . . . "

"Sorry, I was just thinkin' about somethin' else . . . somethin'
I h eard . . . "

"Ah, something you heard . . . . then it couldn't be anything I
said."

A DROWNING IN SWANSON LAKE   33

Dad ignored him.

"Didn't she take something with Ollie? .... They're now sayin' she took some English drug.... the ... lid... "

"Thalidomide?"

"That's it."

"Not so.... wasn't even available then. Besides, that caused physical defects, not.... what Ollie has.... No, the only thing I heard was she did a bit of drinkin'.... likes her bourbon. But as far as ending it, she coulda done that.... she coulda done that sure enough if she wanted ... no.... I don't think so.... "

He paused a moment.

".... Of course, the drinking coulda been her solution to something she couldn't deal with at the time.... hard to tell without knowing how much she actually drank.... Then we would know her intentions.... and that certainly is one possibility."

Dad nodded, pretending to understand all or most of what had just been said. Doc now looked at me, as though realizing for the first time I had been there.

"Should he be hearing this?"

Dad came to my defense.

"He knows not to repeat it. Don't you, Hal?"

I nodded, although I didn't need to. Once again Doc touched both ends of the probable, eliminating the chance to draw any real conclusions. I could not repeat what made no sense to me. As far as I was concerned, Doc simply traded one rumor for another. On the way home, I asked Dad what he thought.

"It's hard to know.... but she deserves the benefit of the doubt."

I felt cheated.

"Yeah, but Doc said she overkilled Ollie. Don't that mean what they said is true?"

Dad stared at me for, what seemed, a long time. I did not expect a quick answer to a difficult question.

"Sometimes you make even less sense than Doc.... and that takes some doing."

Dad's reaction made it clear I misunderstood something important. I decided to keep my next question simple.

"I just meant, do you think Mrs. Magnusson did something bad?"

He looked at me again, this time recognizing my words and their meaning.

"No . . . . I don't believe so."

That still didn't reassure me. It was a non-answer that didn't stop me from wondering, even after the rumors finally died about her, and a new one arose about the baker, Mr. Maxwell.

5

Before *Ho-Hos, Ding Dongs, Yankee Doodles,* and *Devil Dogs,*
there were the whipped cream charlotte roux, fresh fruit strudels,
and dark chocolate drizzled butter cookies from Ben Maxwell's
bakery. It's not that these packaged cakes didn't exist. They simply
could not compete with Mr. Maxwell's infinitely more satisfying
temptations. Only Ollie, who enjoyed ripping apart the cellophane
wrappers as though they were Christmas wrapping paper, and then
sucking the cream that stuck to it, preferred Stan's shelf varieties.
It almost seemed unnatural, until you remembered it was Ollie
and then it somehow made sense.

After the school bus dropped us off, Opal and I stopped in for
an afternoon treat. Most of our schoolmates made their purchases,
then ran as though chased. Ollie, however, felt too uncomfortable
to enter the bakery at all. Instead, he chose to meet us at Stan's.
Sometimes he would just ignore our request and keep walking or,
occasionally, provide an excuse logical only to him.

"He has sissy hair . . . . and his teeth looks like Indian corn."

Mr. Maxwell had naturally curly, licorice black hair which
Ollie somehow thought looked feminine. I disagreed, although I
did agree with his description of the teeth. But I didn't know why

that would keep Ollie from going inside. I asked, but received no explanation. Just another excuse.

" . . . . He talks funny."

Mr. Maxwell had an accent foreign to Swanson Lake and America. Opal went on the attack.

"Talks funny? So does Ma. What does that have to do with anything?"

Ollie just looked at her. I tried a different tact.

"Ollie. Mr. Maxwell is such a nice man. You don't have to be afraid of him."

"I ain't afraid!"

"Then come inside with us."

He made a face before reluctantly following us. I knew he saw this as a distraction from getting to Stan's and buying his *Twinkies*. Despite my and Opal's attempts to persuade him to try the fresh bakery items, he refused.

"I don't like them."

"You never tried them."

"I don't like the way they look."

Opal looked at me, not believing how anyone could not like the array of colors and shapes in the display case. I could see Ollie struggling not to look at them, staring down at the floor and moving around the sawdust with his feet as he waited for us to make our selections. His behavior puzzled me, although something he said later helped me to finally understand more about his reluctance to enter the store and buy something.

"There are too many colors . . . . too much to pick . . . . I might pick the wrong one."

The choices overwhelmed him, threatening to unsettle the choices he already felt safe with. He couldn't take the chance of either liking something and having to decide between it and his old reliables, or not liking it and then having spent the money he saved for the packaged cakes. So he chose to ignore it all, shuffling his feet as I picked out the biggest oatmeal cookie and Opal bought her charlotte russe. Mr. Maxwell piled the whipped cream a mile high, or so it seemed, and when her lips enveloped the cherry on top, her nose made a full impact collision with the cream. Her nostrils, now stuffed white, prompted Ollie and me to laugh so hard, Mr. Maxwell returned from the back room to see the cause of the commotion. Opal's face became the color of the cherry she just ate. She removed the cream from inside and above her nose with her finger, a grin revealing her intentions to smear it on us. Ollie and I ran from the bakery. Opal chased after us. I did not stop to pick up the cookie I dropped, declaring it a casualty of war and a small sacrifice for eluding her attack. When I felt my safety assured, I turned around to see Opal only a few steps behind her brother. Suddenly, Ollie stopped short and shoved her hand up to her face, where cream lay in clumps on her forehead. Ollie laughed even harder than before.

"Ollie, I'm gonna cut you up and fry you like fatback."

Ollie laughed and taunted her, and Opal made a start as though to chase him again, but decided to finish what remained of the cream and cake still in her hand. I wanted to return to Maxwell's to get another cookie. Ollie became impatient.

"Aw c'mon, Hal. Buy your cookie at Stan's."

"You guys go ahead. I'll catch up to you."

Opal and Ollie went on ahead. As I walked back to Maxwell's, I could hear Ollie screaming. I turned to see his face sporting a big glob of whipped cream. This time Opal did the laughing. I entered Mr. Maxwell's shop and the dangling bell let him know he had a customer. He came to the front.

"So? You come back or you have a twin brother. Which is it?"

I smiled.

"I dropped my cookie."

"Doesn't surprise me the way you two were laughing so . . . . "

I thought he might be angry for the noise we made and I was ready to apologize. But he continued.

" . . . . It's nice to hear . . . such laughing."

His eyes then became as dark as his hair. He stared and said nothing. I didn't know what to do except reach in my pocket for a nickel to buy another cookie. When I handed it to him, he looked at it as though unsure what it was.

"For the cookie. Another oatmeal, please."

He pushed my hand away gently.

"You dropped your cookie. You didn't eat it . . . . wouldn't be fair to charge you for something you didn't enjoy . . . . I'll make the sidewalk pay me the nickel."

He gave me another cookie and I put my money back into my pocket. I thanked him and left. But something gnawed at me. It had to do with the way he looked, not his appearance, not what Ollie described, but the way he looked at me and everyone else. It made me realize how little I knew, anyone knew, about him.

Benjamin Maxwell came from out of nowhere to live in Swanson Lake. To hear Stan tell it, one could only conclude aliens dropped off Mr. Maxwell on their most recent visit to earth.

"It's mighty fishy the way he just appeared one day outa the blue."

Doc laughed.

"Ain't that how most people appear? Or do they prepare everyone for their arrival with messengers on horseback?"

He laughed again.

"I'm not sayin' that. You know I'm not sayin' that. But we usually find out where someone's from, sooner or later."

"Maybe he burrowed up from the center of the earth."

"I can't talk serious with you . . . . And you blame me."

"Okay, fine . . . . So Maxwell likes his privacy, so what?"

"I don't like it."

Except for knowing he lived above his bakery, Mr. Maxwell kept everything about himself secret. He would ask me about my school work and my favorite baseball players, always offering to help me with my homework. Yet he never talked about himself, even when I wanted to know.

"Did you grow up around here?"

"Do I sound like I did?"

I knew it was a stupid question. I also knew he saw right through me. But I wanted to find out if Stan had been correct.

"But if you're not from around here, are you still . . . . from around here?"

He looked at me as though I were the alien.

"I don't know what you say . . . . I am from many places and no place at all."

Now I became the confused one. I tried the less direct approach.

"Were there trees?"

"Trees? Ha! No, no. No trees. No light . . . No air."

It seemed Stan had been correct all along. As far as I knew, light and air existed everywhere . . . . that is, everywhere on earth. I now looked closer at him to discover anything I might have missed. No antennae jutted from his head, and his skin and hair seemed too real to be just a disguise for a green crusty creature underneath. Everything looked the way it should have, although this provided no real assurance. Each week *The Hudson Star Gazer* revealed photographs of Martians disguised as humans. Dad always poohpoohed those stories, although I could not dismiss anything that might explain Mr. Maxwell's sudden arrival from a place so foreign to anything I knew. However, I gave him the benefit of the doubt and considered him far more likely a spy than a creature.

Stan's periodic warnings about spies in our midst seemed to have some basis in fact. Even the legitimate newspapers printed FBI warnings about communist infiltrators, whom Stan liked to refer to as "filthy traitors". Now I had the means to get closer to Mr. Maxwell and uncover his secret life. Throwing away my childish decoder ring, I vowed to become a full fledged government agent in pursuit of a truth that would make me a hero to both Opal and Swanson Lake. I couldn't wait to impress her with the mission I planned to undertake.

"Shame on you! Spying on someone who's so kind to you . . . . You're the spy, not him."

I felt glad we had walked far enough from town for anyone to hear her accusations. I never expected to switch places with Mr. Maxwell and become Swanson Lake's "filthy traitor".

"Sure he's nice, Ope, but maybe it's just a front. That's what I wanted to find out."

I thought my position reasonable and expected Opal to at least consider it.

"I'm very disappointed . . . . to even think such a thing . . . . You disappoint me, Hal."

That word always stung, but especially now. My new career ended before it began, and my hopes for heroism dashed. But I would try and salvage Opal's opinion of me and, in so doing, allow me to assuage the guilt that had begun oozing through me.

I knew only something extreme would return me to Opal's graces. So I promised to apologize to Mr. Maxwell for what I had intended to do. If not heroic, my action would certainly be judged "noble". Opal's responses had become too unpredictable, so I prepared myself for either praise or a guffaw.

"That's a wonderful idea . . . . a confession will make you feel better . . . . And he couldn't stay mad too long . . . . especially since you never actually followed through with betraying him . . . . "

I no longer felt so sure about the wisdom in apologizing for something I did not do. Mr. Maxwell knew nothing about my plans, and never had to. I wanted to reconsider my offer. However, before I could renegotiate, Opal spoke.

" . . . . It takes a lot of courage, Hal . . . to do that. I'm proud of you."

I managed a smile, knowing now I could not break my promise. But if Opal's reaction had been positive, I felt much less confident about Mr. Maxwell's.

When I entered the bakery, Mr. Maxwell was eating one of his foul smelling meat loaves. Although they rivaled Stan's in odor, Mr. Maxwell's were expected to smell bad. Made from fish, he loved to tease me.

"Here. I saved you a piece. I knew you would be hungry."

"No . . . . thank you."

"You're the loser then . . . . "

He put a big piece in his mouth, closed his eyes, and smiled.

" . . . . Mmmmmm."

He opened one eye to see my reaction. I tried, unsuccessfully, not to contort my face.

"I'm sorry. I didn't mean to . . . . "

He laughed.

A DROWNING IN SWANSON LAKE   41

"Oh, you're a good boy . . . I can tell these things. And you're a smart boy, too . . . . "

I felt glad he didn't know me that well. He looked at me.

" . . . So? You've come for a cookie, I take it."

For the moment I had forgotten why I came. Now I wasn't so sure I wanted to tell him.

"No, uh yes . . . . Sure."

"Sounds like you're not so sure. I know you didn't come for my gefilte fish sandwich."

That was the word I couldn't remember, along with ingredients I didn't care to.

" . . . . So? It's a secret why you come?"

I wanted to confess, and yet I didn't want him to hate me. I wasn't sure I could have it both ways. I proceeded slowly.

"When someone does something bad . . . . or thinks something bad . . . . should they tell others?"

I had hoped to preempt the need to go further. Mr. Maxwell put down his sandwich."

"Such a serious question . . . . "

To my disappointment, he began to nod slowly.

" . . . . yes . . . . yes . . . confession is good . . . . although a conscience is much better. Then you don't have the bad thoughts that make you want to do the bad things in the first place."

I knew I was in trouble. A confession would have been difficult enough without it also revealing my lack of conscience. He must have read my expression because his next words attempted to vindicate me.

" . . . . You're a good boy, I can tell."

I looked away, not wanting to hear another untruth. I wanted Mr. Maxwell to stop focusing on me and change the subject completely. Better yet, I wanted him to ignore me and return to his work. But he did neither. When the silence became intolerable, I looked up to see him still there, and looking at me.

"This must be a very bad thing this someone did, to make it so hard to talk about."

"It is."

"But that's when the talking is even more important . . . . before the heart becomes like stone."

I still could not tell him, although I thought I had a compromise that would please him.

"Maybe it's better to tell God first."

I expected to be patted on the head for my devotion to Him. Instead, Mr. Maxwell slammed his hand on the counter.

"God?! What God?! . . . . The One who's dead? . . . . "

My eyes widened at news I had not heard, nor could believe. Yet for a few brief moments I felt relief in knowing the Sunday worship would no longer be necessary. Then the look, the eyes, that unsettled me before, scared me now. Mr. Maxwell's stare froze him into someone I did not recognize. I could no longer look into the blackness that was his eyes. I wanted to leave behind what upset me, and would have, had his words not intervened.

" . . . . I'm sorry I yelled like that . . . . No . . . . you're right to believe . . . . I shouldn't speak for you . . . . "

He threw the rest of his sandwich into the garbage.

" . . . I've got work to do . . . . We'll talk some other time."

I didn't know what I said to upset him. But I had an idea that might make amends.

"What?! You want to invite who to dinner? . . . "

Dad's hearing suddenly failed him.

"Mr. Maxwell . . . . He's alone and all."

"That's not my problem."

"You two might become friends."

"I ain't lookin' for new friends . . . I've got plenty o' grief from the ones I got."

"Then go in to buy something. He makes great oatmeal cookies-"

"The next time he buys a couple of hammers, I'll return the favor and buy his cookies."

"C'mon, Dad. Can't you just stop by?"

"You his agent? Tryin' to get him new customers?"

"No, it's not that."

"Sounds like it to me."

Dad continued to swat away each suggestion, either through stubbornness or suspicion, thwarting my attempts to regain Mr. Maxwell's goodwill. I worried he would still be angry with me and not allow me to enter his bakery. I not only wanted his forgiveness for what I thought, and then for what I might have said, I didn't want to jeopardize our relationship. I liked getting all the attention. It made me feel special, even if I earned it by default. But just as I concluded my previous suspicions undeserved and unjust, Mr. Maxwell revealed something too strange and important to ignore.

"I never noticed it before."

Dad rubbed his chin.

"I think I know what it is. Let me ask Doc . . . "

I didn't want anyone else to know, especially Stan.

" . . . Don't worry, Hal. He's out building his shelter."

I then remembered that Stan spent part of every afternoon constructing his atomic bomb shelter, ready to withstand the Russian attack he regarded as inevitable. Premier Khrushchev's threats to bury us scared most everyone, but only Stan took it seriously enough to reinforce a ten by fourteen hole with concrete and steel.

"Go ahead and laugh. When that poison dust settles over everything, and you're either barbecued or gaspin' for air, I'll be tucked inside safe and sound with my *Playboys* and feasting on dried beef and beans . . . . And I'll let none of ya inside."

Doc smiled.

"With you eatin' beans, I'll take my chance with the poison gas outside."

Dad and Doc laughed. But Stan's warnings always scared me. Despite Dad's assurances that an atomic war would never happen, I learned in current events that it could. Now Mr. Maxwell compounded this fear with the secret code tattooed to his arm. I waited for Dad and Doc to confirm my suspicions and devise a strategy for dealing with it. Finally, Dad told him what I thought I saw.

"Really? I woulda never guessed. I mean, I figured he was from over there, but never in one of those things . . . . horrible . . . . "

He shook his head.

" . . . . those numbers will always haunt him . . . . always bring him shame."

"I'm sure he never expected anyone to see them. Hal caught a glimpse of them this morning."

I had been anxious to give testimony about the secret blue code I discovered when Mr. Maxwell raised his shirt sleeves to chocolate dip his butter cookies. But if I didn't understand what Dad and Doc discussed, I knew from the lack of urgency I had done Mr. Maxwell a disservice yet again.

When Doc's head dropped to his chest and Dad began poking at donuts he considered too disgusting to buy, I assumed no more would be said about Mr. Maxwell's tattoo. I regretted not having the chance to hear something additional that might clarify what I already heard. And when Stan suddenly charged in, I recognized the futility in staying any longer at the grocery. However, before I could leave, Stan's comments resuscitated the discussion. I never expected his ignorance to provide me the opportunity to learn more.

"Damn instructions'll kill me before I get to finish . . . There's a conspiracy somewhere in this."

Stan slammed the instructions down on the counter. Startled, Doc raised his head and continued from where he left off. It reminded me of someone kick starting a stuck record in a juke box.

"That's more than a physical scar, sure enough."

He looked out into some distance as though he had just pronounced a new philosophical truth.

"Who's that? . . . "

Doc looked at Stan, still a bit groggy.

" . . . Who has a scar?"

"Weren't you listening? . . . Maxwell . . . . the numbers on his arm."

Stan's eyes widened. I no longer cared he would find out if it meant

"Numbers? . . . . "

Stan grinned. He almost sang his next words.

". . . . I knew it. I told you so."

Dad now looked at him.

"Told us what?"

"That he was an agent . . . . A commie agent . . . . Why else the secret numbers?"

Doc shook his head.

"You moron . . . . "

I hoped no one saw me flush red. Doc spoke to his partner as though to a child.

" . . . . The numbers are from those camps . . . . Concentration camps . . . . the ones the Nazis used for the Jews . . . "

"He's a Jew?"

"I suppose, I don't know . . . . the Gerries sent a lot of other people there, too . . . . gypsies, communists—"

"So he could be a double curse. Jew or commie or both . . . . He certainly looks both. And come to think of it, I think he's on one of those post office wanted posters. I swear he is."

"You swear. And what a reliable eye witness you've proved to be."

"What does that mean?"

"You forget the Chinese doctor from Manhattan that passed through here?"

"That was years ago."

"And you swore she always waited on you at The China Lantern in Brewman."

"I can't help if she had an exact double."

"Yeah, right."

"Don't get so high and mighty. So I made a mistake."

"And you're mistaken now."

"How can you say that?! That's the dumbest thing I ever heard!"

"Then listen to yourself more. You'll be amazed."

Dad attempted diplomacy.

"No one knows anything for sure."

"We know he's a Jew and a commie. And I'm bustin' my chops to build protection against something his kind gave to the Russians . . . . "

Doc and Dad looked at each other. Stan went on the offensive.

" . . . Who's the moron now? . . . . The Rosenbergs . . . . the ones they executed for giving the bomb to the Russkies . . . . Just connect those big red dots and you'll see what I'm talkin' about."

Stan paused as though waiting for Dad or Doc to acknowledge his wisdom. Doc looked at him.

"Stan, remind me to check the *Sears* catalogue . . . . see if we can order a sponge to soak up the idiocy spilling out your ears."

Dad and Doc looked at each other, smiling at the joke that drove Stan away in anger. I then expected them to turn their attention on me, someone guilty of the same stupidity as Stan. But they just smiled, laughed, and reveled in the humiliation they knowingly brought to Stan, and unknowingly brought to me.

When I failed Mr. Maxwell for the second time, I decided it would be the last. I would learn as much as possible about him from what he said and didn't say. I wanted especially to learn more about the camps Doc mentioned, and even though I couldn't trust myself not to ask dim-witted questions, I would take my chances with Mr. Maxwell.

I continued staying away until I felt comfortable enough to lie about my absence. I also no longer wanted to confess suspicions and accusations I considered unforgivable and hurtful. On the day I decided to return, the time in school and the bus ride home became unbearable. I could already taste the warm oatmeal cookies hours and miles before I reached the bakery. But when I finally approached it, I could see only darkness inside. I assumed a power outage the cause and would gladly buy the day old of any cake or cookie he had. When I knocked and no one answered, I went to Stan's to wait out the blackout and Mr. Maxwell's return.

As I passed Ronnie's restaurant and Dad's hardware store, everyone had power except Mr. Maxwell. I could even see the lights on in Mrs. Crabtree's across the street. It seemed unfair to punish Mr. Maxwell for well deserved punishment for me, although I didn't know why he would have to suffer as well. Mr. Maxwell's lost income converted to more profits for Stan, who somehow found a reason to complain about his good fortune.

A DROWNING IN SWANSON LAKE   47

"If he woulda told me before he took off, I coulda ordered more stuff. I sold out by noon . . . . That's a lot of money we lost that coulda been made."

"Why should he tell you?"

"Professional courtesy."

"Like the kind you would have given him?"

I had worked myself into a craving for something sweet. With the bakery closed, my only other option rested four feet from me. But the donuts looked picked over, sneezed on, and more. I went over to the candy rack. I continued listening.

"They have their funny holy days . . . He's probably begun some pilgrimage. Don't ya think?"

"How do I know? Let the man take a day off, for Chrissakes . . . . I wish you did."

"Maybe I would if I could trust your fat ass not to sleep or eat all day."

"Trust me. Go ahead. I dare ya."

When the discussion about Mr. Maxwell quickly disintegrated into a display of mutual belittlement, I made the easy escape.

The next day I returned to the bakery, still closed, and with no sign of Mr. Maxwell. I had no alternative but to return to Stan's. This time, however, I hoped to hear useful information. I reasoned that, as mayor, Doc would have access to the latest and most important news in town. When I approached the grocery, I observed Doc sniffing an empty wrapper from a chocolate bar. He looked at me, the wrapper still glued to his nose.

"Like perfume . . . . what a gift from the gods . . . . Do you know where chocolate comes from, Hal? . . . . "

I didn't come for a quiz. And I didn't know the answer. I shook my head.

" . . . . Well, they don't come from candy bar trees . . . . "

He burst out laughing. He probably thought I still played *Candyland.*

" . . . . Beans . . . . lovely cocoa beans . . . . And you know where—"

"Mr. Maxwell's store is still closed."

"So I hear . . . . A bit unusual . . . . no word, no note. Of course . . . "

He paused.

"What? Of course what?"

"Could've pinned a note inside, on the door, and it just fell to the floor."

"Can we look?"

You want me to open his shop?"

I nodded. I knew he could if he considered it an emergency. He once did this when Dad, doing some late night bookkeeping in his store, detected a foul smell coming from Ronnie's restaurant. Suspecting a gas leak, he called Ronnie. When she didn't answer, Dad had Doc drive in to open the restaurant. The source of the odor turned out to be one of her exotic meals slow cooking in a crock pot. Now Doc could use his emergency powers again and open the bakery. He folded his candy wrapper and placed it into his shirt pocket for further sniffing.

"Stan'll kill me for leaving the store unattended."

"We'll tell Dad to watch out."

As we passed Dad's store, we saw him with a customer. Doc knocked on his window, pointed to Stan's, and mouthed his request. Dad nodded, but looked confused as to why Doc and I would be going anywhere together. I didn't remember ever walking with Doc, and I would have remembered if I did. For every three steps I took, he had yet to negotiate one. His weight and his bad knees made walking an effort, and made walking with him a torment. I tried to walk as slowly as he did, but couldn't. So I took a few steps, turned around and waited, took a few more steps, waited, until we eventually reached the bakery. Doc panted as he took out a handkerchief to wipe the sweat pouring from his face and neck.

"Might as well just shove me inside a clothes dryer and be done with it . . . . the damn heat."

There was no bench nearby for him to sit on, and I looked around for anything that might support his weight. Except for some empty flour and sugar cartons that were more likely to start singing than to hold up Doc, nothing sturdy could be found. He decided to lean against the bakery glass and took some deep breaths. He looked at me.

" . . . . I needed a workout anyway . . . . did I ever tell you I was in the Olympics?"

"No."

"That's good, because I wasn't . . . . "

He smiled at me. It wasn't much of a joke, although I smiled back. Then he straightened up, pressed his face against the glass, and cupped his face with his hands to better see inside the bakery. He banged on the window.

" . . . . Hmmm . . . no answer."

I felt I was in the presence of a very stupid Sherlock Holmes. I became annoyed, and only after I spoke did I become aware of my disrespect.

"I already told you that! . . . . That's why we gotta go inside."

Doc looked at me, partially taken aback by my rudeness and partially by the obviousness of my suggestion.

"Of course . . . . under the circumstances . . . . "

He took out a large set of keys, searching for a particular one. Then he opened the door, turned on the lights, and called out.

"Anyone here? Maxwell? . . . . Ben? Are you here?"

I wondered if Doc thought Mr. Maxwell had just been hiding all this time, a sort of perverse game of hide and seek. Getting no response, Doc walked slowly to the back, cautiously looking around him. One possibility that occurred to me, and likely to Doc, was a scenario involving foul play. I imagined Mr. Maxwell a kidnapping victim or worse, perhaps for something he knew, or for something he concealed in the bakery. And neither Doc nor I could be sure the perpetrators had left the premises. I grew frightened. I no sooner finished rehearsing all the details of my escape plan when Doc's panic stricken voice bellowed from behind a door leading to the back storage area.

"Oh, my God! . . . "

I froze.

" . . . Stay back, Hal! . . . "

He didn't need to say it twice. But my quivering legs had

become useless. I waited for Doc to appear and say something, anything, that would keep me upright. Loud, heavy breathing now heralded his return. Holding a handkerchief over his nose, he appeared on the verge of vomiting. He soon wiped his face very slowly, almost as if he were afraid to wipe away his features.

" . . . Whew!"

He then stared at something behind me. I turned around quickly, yet saw nothing. I looked at Doc.

"What's wrong?"

My voice jolted him. He seemed to forget I could speak.

"It's Ben Maxwell . . . . he's dead."

"For real?!"

"Of course for real."

"Then we better get outa here. We don't wanna get murdered, too."

He looked at me.

"Murdered? . . . . He wasn't murdered."

I felt somewhat relieved.

"But he didn't look sick."

Doc didn't answer me. He covered his face again and walked hurriedly back to the room where he found Mr. Maxwell. Soon an odor as strong as blackness began to envelop me, suddenly choking out the air like the stench of ammonia. Feeling as though I swallowed clumps of hair, I would have gagged had I not run from the bakery. Once outside, I bent over, struggling to regain my normal breathing.

"You okay? . . . . "

Doc stood in the doorway.

" . . . . It's a little tough to take, isn't it?"

"It felt like a punch to the stomach."

"You got off easy . . . "

He then walked back inside to use the phone. I stood in the doorway, where I could both breathe and hear. Doc asked for Sheriff MacCauley and waited a few seconds before speaking.

"Hi, Bill . . . Henry Wyatt . . . . I'm at the bakery and . . . . no, no, I ain't buyin' donuts. It's serious, Bill . . . . Ben Maxwell, he owns the place . . . . apparent suicide . . . . well, no. I didn't

look but it . . . . fine, fine, then decide for yourself . . . . I'll be
here . . . . Okay."

I had never heard that word used outside of movies. Then it
struck me that a note would be found blaming the one person
who betrayed him. I didn't know whether to stay and pretend
ignorance or run away before the sheriff arrived. As I had done two
years earlier with the Nels Nelgren episode, I rejected the fugitive
life and chose instead to take my chances. Doc stood with me just
outside the doorway.

"What did the note say?"

Doc looked at me.

"I didn't see a note."

"But if its suicide, there gotta be one."

"Are you in cahoots with the Sheriff? He just said the same thing."

Doc grew testy, but I persisted.

"Then how do you know it wasn't murder or something?"

"I'll tell you what. When MacCauley gets here, I'll introduce
you and the two of you can work as a team."

I didn't want to talk to the sheriff.

"That's okay . . . . I wanna stay outa the way."

"Maybe you should go home . . . . or stop at your dad's."

I had to know everything. I lied.

"He was my best friend. I want to stay."

"Your best friend? . . . . "

He gave a short laugh.

" . . . . I don't think Ollie and Opal would appreciate that."

"Well . . . . the best grownup friend . . . . after Dad . . . . "

I looked at him and realized.

" . . . . and you and Stan."

He smiled, saying nothing. Just then Sheriff MacCauley pulled
up with another man. I had only met the Sheriff once before,
when he asked questions about Mrs. Magnusson. He was tall and
had especially long legs and arms that seemed like stretched rubber.
The other boys called him Sheriff *Gumby,* the name I tried not to
think of as he walked up to me and Doc.

"Got yourself an assistant I see."

"Jack Moffat's boy, Hal. He's a smart one. Thought you could use him."

I wanted to kick Doc. Sheriff MacCauley looked at me.

"Sure, could always use some good help . . . . "

Although I smiled from nervousness, I relaxed somewhat when I considered how sufficiently imbecilic my unnatural grin must have appeared. I hoped that would disqualify me as his potential deputy, and even more importantly, as a suspect.

The other man now retrieved a black case from the trunk, nodding to Doc as he went inside. The sheriff called after him.

" . . . . Prints all around . . . . "

Then to Doc.

" . . . Graham . . . Forensics . . . . He'll need to know everything you touched."

"Only the door knob . . . . and the face and neck . . . and arms . . . . just to confirm death and check for obvious wounds."

"And from that you ruled out foul play? . . . . "

The sheriff laughed, revealing a broken top tooth.

" . . . . I hope you're better with your medical opinions."

He laughed again. Doc's eyes narrowed to slits.

"Look, right now I can't say for sure what he died from. But no injuries tells me it's likely either suicide or natural causes . . . . I'm going with suicide because of his age . . . . only forty one according to his driver's license."

I found it difficult to believe Mr. Maxwell had only been six years older than Dad.

"And you eliminated poisoning . . . . why?"

"I didn't eliminate-"

"And what about the possible wounds under the clothes you didn't remove?"

Doc looked at me and I knew if I had not been there, he would have said far more to the sheriff than he did now. The veins in his neck and nose had never been so pronounced. Even Stan never succeeded in provoking Doc to such a degree.

"I did not do an autopsy! It's a judgment call based on my experience and expertise."

Sheriff MacCauley's face threatened to collapse in laughter, although he succeeded in remaining serious. Mr. Graham's call to the sheriff defused the situation.

"Be right there! . . . . Wanna come, Doc? The boy stays here."

That suited me. I never saw a dead body and I certainly didn't want to see someone I once knew. I remained at the doorway, straining and failing to hear the conversation inside. An ambulance arrived, its siren off, and two men carried a stretcher inside.

"In the back."

I enjoyed my newly acquired celebrity status as I directed them to the storage area. People now began congregating. I wanted them to ask me questions, even if I couldn't answer them. I felt important being the friend of someone who just died. I saw Dad step outside his store and wave for me to come over. He hated going too far, fearing he might anger his customers. But I had to know what the sheriff and others found, and I would not leave until I did. Continuing to ignore his wave as well as his call, I willingly accepted the consequences for this knowledge. Soon Blue Armondsen approached.

"What happened?"

"Not sure . . . . but Mr. Maxwell is dead."

"Dead?"

That word whispered its way from person to person, a hushed echo soon transformed into a shrill repetition of "who?" which reverberated like a chorus of frenetic owls. Some people pointed, others pressed their faces against the window to catch a glimpse of the activity inside. I wanted to tell them the death occurred in the back room and it would be impossible to see anything, but I became fascinated watching their necks strain and heads bob like corralled turkeys. Soon the sheriff emerged, Doc and Mr. Graham a few steps behind. Silence followed immediately after.

"Better you get the truth than malicious gossip . . . . "

Sheriff MacCauley had a deep voice that commanded attention. Dad considered him an excellent campaigner, winning elections more from his speaking ability than from the actual job he did.

" . . . . Ben Maxwell was found dead in his store . . . . an apparent suicide . . . "

Doc stood erect and beamed, as though waiting to be praised for his diagnosis. The crowd erupted in sighs, tongue clicking, and head shaking. Sheriff MacCauley raised his hand.

" . . . . And until an autopsy is done and I know more, I won't attempt to speculate or answer any more questions now. Thank you."

He had not taken two steps when a volley of questions assaulted him.

"Who found the body?"

"How long was he dead?"

"Did he leave a note?"

I expected the sheriff to ignore this one, as he did the others. But he nodded, mumbled a "yes", and then a "no comment" to a question about the note's contents. He and Mr. Graham pushed their way to their car as questions continued to be machine gunned at them. I also elbowed my way to the car, hoping the sheriff might toss the crowd another bone and reveal the note's contents. However, he said nothing further, and used his siren to maneuver through the cluster of people. Only when the two ambulance attendants emerged with the sheet covered body of Mr. Maxwell, did the crowd become silent again. They, like me, simply watched the body being loaded into the ambulance like so much baggage, hoping to catch a glimpse of something that might suddenly and miraculously clear up the mystery surrounding his death. I felt sad, although I wondered why I didn't feel sadder. Perhaps I wanted to believe I would still see him somehow. As the attendants were about to close the back doors, Mr. Maxwell's arm fell off the stretcher and dangled. I could see the tattooed numbers. I jumped back, as did a few others, who thought the body still alive. The attendants laughed at our reaction.

"Show's over, folks."

With that, one of the attendants tucked Mr. Maxwell's arm back under the sheet. As the ambulance drove away, I knew that dangling arm would haunt me for years, especially after I understood fully what the tattooed numbers meant.

With the sheriff and ambulance gone, the crowd dispersed.

A Drowning In Swanson Lake   55

Doc had already begun walking back to Stan's and I ran, although not very hard, to catch up to him. I did not want to confront him about why he lied about the note, although I had to assume it had something to do with me.

"Did he write a lot, on his note?"

"Not much."

We walked in silence for a minute or so.

"Did he say what made him do it?"

Doc looked at me, pulling his head back. My directness surprised him.

"No one knows the dark thoughts that breed within a person like so many worms . . . . devouring his spirit . . . . until it is too late."

"I hope I don't get worms . . . . "

Doc looked at me and smiled. When he didn't answer, I persisted.

" . . . . Did Mr. Maxwell have worms? Is that why he died?"

Doc looked at me, his expression now quite serious. Then he squinted, as though trying to see answers a half mile ahead.

"Maybe you're closer to the truth than you know."

"Did the note mention worms?"

"I can't tell you what it said."

"Because you didn't read it?"

"Because it's a private matter, that's why."

I had to satisfy myself with that for the time being. I tried believing that if Mr. Maxwell had mentioned me, Doc would have told me. We now passed Dad talking on the telephone, my wave drawing no response. I knew spaghetti and meatballs, his favorite dish, would be my peace offering for ignoring him before.

Stan had, by this time, returned to the grocery. I knew Doc would tell him everything after I left. However, just before Doc went inside he turned to me.

" . . . . Sometimes a person has to talk."

He said nothing more and I left before Stan could begin attacking Doc for leaving the store unattended.

When the medical examiner completed the autopsy a few days later, I not only found out how Mr. Maxwell died, I earned myself a nickname as well. Browsing through as many comic books as possible before Stan blasted me for "freeloading", a phone call allowed me extra time to both read and eavesdrop. Stan answered it.

"Stan's . . . . Oh, hi . . . . Fine . . . . Of course. Where else would he be? . . . . No, no . . . good timing. He's between meals. You have a few minutes yet . . . . "

He laughed. Doc made a face.

" . . . . Sure thing, Sheriff . . . . Give him a few moments to lift his head off his chest and wipe the drool from his lips."

Doc grabbed the phone.

"Yeah, I see, huh-huh . . . . okay . . . . and what did I say? . . . . yeah, right . . . . short memory . . . . okay . . . . thanks for calling . . . "

He handed the phone back to Stan.

"Do I know my stuff or do I know my stuff?"

"You know your 'stuffing', that's for sure."

"Wise guy . . . . I am truly a medical man of the highest caliber . . . . "

Stan remained silent.

" . . . . How come you're not saying anything."

"It sounds like maybe you did something right for once . . . . I'll give you a freebee."

"Good. Then listen up. MacCauley just confirmed my diagnosis, a diagnosis based on no more than a few minutes of skilled observation . . . . Dilated pupils . . . mouth lesions . . . . yes, the trained eye of a master."

"Lucky guess."

"Jealous, are we? . . . . I said poison and it was poison."

"You also said a sleeping pill overdose . . . . or did I not hear you?"

"I did not say that. No one listens to me."

"The smart ones don't."

"Fine. Then I'll just keep quiet and not waste my breath on someone so obviously resentful of my accomplishments."

I wanted Doc to reveal more details. I knew I didn't need to encourage him to continue. No one did. Doc would not allow mere insults deter him from crowing. When he spoke a few minutes later, he sounded as though he had just been asked a question.

"Yes . . . . Rat poison . . . . Horrible, horrible way to go."

"I think I sold it to him, too."

"A slow death . . . . incredible suffering."

"*Drano* woulda been quicker . . . . the way that stuff bubbles through the plumbing."

Doc looked at him.

"You're a callous s.o.b."

"I don't pretend to like someone I don't. I always hated him and his God forsaking communist views."

"His views?! The only thing you ever knew about him, and even that you're not sure of, is you sold him a can of rat poison!"

"I know enough–"

"This conversation is over!

Stan had not managed to bring Doc's veins to the surface, the way Sheriff MacCauley had, but he did succeed in upsetting him far more than usual. Doc walked outside and pretended not to hear Stan.

"Stop being such a baby . . . . I got a right to my views . . . . Fine, stay out there . . . I hope it rains . . . . jerk . . . . jeez, for Chrissakes, come in . . . . I'll fix you a sandwich . . . "

Stan had exhausted the full range of his arsenal, to no avail. I felt abandoned with few options. I could make a sudden dash to the street, hide behind the cereals and hope he had forgotten my presence, or I could just act nonchalantly. I chose the latter.

" . . . . You still here? I thought you left ten minutes ago."

I quietly cursed my choice.

"I'm still here."

"You finish all the comic books?"

"Almost . . . . I mean I already read them anyway."

"Yeah, here . . . How long were you hiding?"

"I wasn't hiding . . . . I was just quiet, that's all."

I could have added I also stood motionless and took slow, quiet breaths.

"I'm too used to seein' you. You're becoming unnoticeable . . . . "

"Who's unnoticeable?"

Doc now returned, falling immediately into his chair.

"Couldn't stay away, huh?"

"I'll take that sandwich you promised . . . . The usual . . . . but extra on the Genoa and the blue cheese."

"Now I can't hear you."

"Fine. I'll make it myself."

"Stay!"

Stan went to make the sandwich, Doc calling to him.

"So who's unnoticeable?"

"Certainly not you. We're lucky anyone can see inside the store with your beluga torso up front."

"Me . . . . Stan says I'm unnoticeable."

Doc slapped his knee and laughed.

"That you are. When did you come in?"

Stan answered for me.

"Been here all the time."

"Well, you certainly are unnoticeable . . . . like the layers of dust *some* people get used to."

Stan came to the front.

"I don't see any dust here."

"That's my point . . . . "

Doc turned to me.

" . . . . Maybe we should call you 'Dusty'. What do you think?"

I smiled.

"Sure."

Despite the way I earned it, I loved a nickname a cowboy or baseball player might have. When I told Dad, he said I could keep the name as long as he could still call me Hal whenever he wanted. And Opal, who usually didn't like nicknames, thought it sounded "far out". Only Ollie objected, jealous he didn't have a nickname, and pouted until Opal and I decided on "Cat" for the nine lives he appeared to have.

In the days immediately after Mr. Maxwell's suicide, I devised a plan to get into the bakery and search its back room. I grew too curious about the information contained in the note, and hoped I might discover something to explain the mystery surrounding Mr. Maxwell's life. I ruled out "breaking and entering", choosing instead the approach that worked before.

"What in heaven's name for?"

"I once lent him some baseball cards . . . . a stack of them."

"Baseball cards?"

"Yeah . . . . He liked the Yankees . . . . I thought I could get them back."

Although Doc looked at me suspiciously, he gave me the benefit of the doubt.

"Well, where are they? How do you know they're even there?"

"He promised to give them back . . . . I saw him take them to the back storage area."

I winced at my obviousness.

"Are you fibbing? Because it's a terrible thing to be a fibber."

I raised my right hand.

"No, honest injun."

"Well . . . . I'm only givin' you a few minutes."

When we entered the bakery, a pungent odor smacked us. It only grew worse when we entered the storage area. Doc went to the small window level with his head.

" . . . . I left this open a crack . . . . didn't do much good. The smell of death still lingers like . . . . well, the smell of death . . . . "

He reached up and opened the window some more.

" . . . Remind me to close this when we leave. We don't need a flood on top of everything else . . . . "

I half listened to him. My eyes had already begun telescoping everything around me.

" . . . Well, go ahead. I don't have all day . . . . "

Doc went to sit on the window ledge out front, giving me forty steps and at least a minute's warning. As I moved about the room, nothing seemed out of the ordinary. There were bags of flour, buckets of flavored icings, and numerous muffin tins and cookie sheets. But in the corner, at the back of one of the tables, lay a small framed black and white photograph. I picked it up to get a closer look, and it meant nothing to me until I recognized Mr. Maxwell. Young and handsome, he stood next to a woman almost as pretty as Macy Magnusson. Next to her stood two boys, both about my age. No one smiled. "Frankfurt, 1942" had been scribbled in the border along the bottom.

" . . . That doesn't look like a baseball card! . . . "

Doc's booming voice almost made me drop the photograph. I was about to return it to the table when Doc took it from me. He stared at the photograph for a few moments before he spoke.

" . . . A bad place to be then . . . Germany . . . . Europe . . . . killing and more killing . . . . saw this the other day . . . . I'm sure they died in the camps . . . . "

I wanted to examine the picture further, to search the faces for answers to the questions I had about the camps and much more. But Doc grew antsy and wanted to leave.

" . . . . Let's go. He must have thrown them out by mistake."

"I know they're here . . . just a few more minutes."

He sighed.

"Fine, but any more snooping and we're leaving. Got it?"

I nodded, then waited for him to return to his stool. I hurriedly and quietly opened every drawer. I had decided my mission required risks, and I would continue searching until I found out all I could about Mr. Maxwell. Finally, in the last drawer, I found something. On top of a layer of navy blue satin rested a folded piece of cream colored cloth with strange writing. I assumed it was a fancy tablecloth, although nothing else in that drawer suggested it had been used for that purpose. Next to the cloth lay a black book, its pages edged in red, with the same strange writing. The book's middle squeezed a cap, similar to the pope's, only it was knitted like the dresses in Mrs. Crabtree's shop. I wanted Doc to explain this, and a reprimand seemed a fair price to pay.

"Finished? . . . About time."

"I can't find my cards . . . . but I found this."

He saw the open drawer and groaned.

"You had to open everything? . . . . after what I told you?"

"I didn't know where to look . . . . He coulda put them anywheres."

Doc became angry.

"I don't appreciate being dragged here under false pretenses . . . . How would you like me to tell your dad?"

I had kept my plans secret, especially to Dad. He didn't like snoops or "busybodies". And he certainly didn't like liars. I apologized to Doc, almost begging him not to say anything. Although he finally relented, my reputation had been permanently tarnished.

" . . . . So? What is it?"

I handed him the folded cloth. He nodded.

" . . . . Ah, yes. This is one of those ceremonial cloths Jews wear . . . . around their shoulders like a shawl . . . . "

He picked up the book.

" . . . . Yeah . . . . Here's the Hebrew bible and the skull cap they wear . . . . Pretty exotic stuff, huh? . . . "

He didn't wait for an answer. He put everything back in the drawer and closed it.

" . . . We've poked around long enough. Let's go."

"What will happen to that?"

"Good question. The store and everything else belongs to his next of kin . . . . whoever that is. But I got a feeling they won't find anyone."

Doc was right. Even after an extensive search through newspaper announcements, Sheriff MacCauley concluded no next of kin existed. The county then took over the bakery, trying to sell or rent it without success. Dad said no one would ever feel comfortable in a place where a suicide occurred. Finally, after almost a year of standing vacant, the county demolished the bakery, planted some trees and flowers, and added a few benches and walkways to create a small park. Only a small marker in one of the cement walkways confirmed that Ben Maxwell or his bakery ever existed.

As we walked back to Stan's, I could not contain my curiosity.

"Did the note-"

"-Are you still on that? Mind your own business. It's got nothing to do with you. It's got nothing to do with anybody we know."

I felt relieved. I also said nothing, not wanting to jeopardize the opportunity to ask him other questions. When I felt he had calmed down, I proceeded cautiously.

"When Mr. Maxwell left the camp, how come he didn't bring his family with him?"

Doc stopped and looked at me as though I had just dropped my pants.

"Do you know what you're saying? . . . . "

I thought I did.

" . . . . Do you know what concentration camps were?"

"You said they were bad places. So why didn't they all leave?"

"They were not just bad. They were evil, horrid places . . . . Slaughterhouses . . . . Very few survived them . . . . and you see what that did to him."

It took me a moment to understand.

"They killed his family? . . . . even his sons?"

"The Nazis didn't care. And once they killed them, they incinerated them in ovens-"

I laughed. Doc glared at me.

"-You think that is funny?!"

"You said ovens . . . . because Mr. Maxwell was a baker . . . . "

Doc placed his hand on my shoulder.

"Hal . . . .

He paused. I might have reminded him of my new name had he not appeared so somber.

" . . . . do you understand I mean ovens that burned corpses down to ashes?"

I began to perspire.

"Sit down and put your heads between your legs . . . . Look, maybe I shouldn't be telling you all this . . . . "

I didn't care that I still felt queasy. I wanted to know more.

" . . . You still look a little pale."

"I'm okay . . . . really."

"We'll talk about it later."

"I want to talk now."

My transformation into a whiny brat, and an impudent one at

that, convinced me I had sacrificed any further discussions with Doc. But surprisingly, he smiled.

"I forget you're only seven."

"Eight."

"Stop by later, when your dad is there. We can all discuss it."

I felt relieved he had given me a second chance, even if it meant having Dad discover the extent of my ignorance about something so important. I had already surpassed my quota of stupid questions, and I did not want to see Dad's disappointment in every new one I asked.

Seeing Dad and Doc chatting later that afternoon in Stan's, I welcomed my opportunity to learn more about the concentration camps. My geography teacher had often talked about how the village elders became the source of wisdom and knowledge, and all the villagers were encouraged to seek out the truth from them. Therefore, despite my initial reluctance to expose my ignorance, I decided I would not hesitate to ask all my questions. However, I reconsidered my decision when I saw Stan enter the grocery through the back alley door. If I thought Dad might contribute something with a question or a bit of information Doc neglected to mention, I felt certain Stan would only interfere and disparage everything about Mr. Maxwell. I went to Ronnie's for an egg cream, hoping by the time I finished he would leave to work on his fallout shelter. A half hour later I returned, Stan still there, and in a heated argument with Dad and Doc.

"Don't tell me you believe that. That theory is as stale as-"

Dad finished it for him.

"-one of your breads."

Stan ignored Dad's remark and Doc's belly laugh.

"Swanson Lake was named for a Mr. Swans, who left the property to his son. It's only common sense."

Doc clapped slowly and in rhythm.

"The town historian has spoken."

"Better than the village idiot."

Stan hooted at his own retort and seemed to wait for anyone, Dad, me, or even Doc, to congratulate him for his cleverness.

Hearing nothing, he chuckled again as if to remind us of his wit. But this only opened the way for Doc to go on the offensive.

"You do know the village idiot always laughs to himself, the way you just did . . . . "

Dad's laugh drew Stan's anger.

"How come you laughed at that? . . . Mine was funnier."

I heard enough. The elders in this village were not going to give me the answers I needed. But I knew someone who talked like Mr. Maxwell, who probably knew something about these camps. However, I would have to wait four more days, until the next visit from our cleaning lady, Mrs. Morrison.

If it weren't for Greta Morrison's missions of mercy every other week, there would be no way to get to the bathroom without a map or compass. Dad was a great one for putting off anything he could, and since neatness never felt natural to him anyway, Mrs. Morrison entered a world of chaos, pure and simple. I had given up trying to undo what Dad did, and instead relied on her visits to return our home to respectability. She always sighed when she arrived, as though somehow forgetting who lived there and what awaited her. Maybe she secretly hoped Dad would reform, but it never happened.

"I never hear such a thing . . . . where the earthquakes hit only one house . . . . "

She shook her head.

" . . . . It's such a pity. No?"

She liked to joke about it, but it had to be frustrating to know all her hard work disintegrated as soon as the door closed behind her. I always wondered why she came back, but Dad said she had no choice. Married to an American soldier stationed in Germany after the war, they returned to America where he contracted cancer and left her to fend for herself.

"We're doing her a favor, Hal. Otherwise she probably wouldn't get by."

I knew what Dad meant, although it seemed absurd to imply that we, and not she, had engaged in an act of charity. Dirty dishes and glasses remained where originally placed, becoming shrines to the previous week's meals. Newspapers were strewn about to become coasters for still more dishes and half eaten foods. But the specialty of the house had been Dad's laundry ethic. Each day's dirty clothes became signposts leading from the bathroom shower to his bedroom. By week's end, when Dad exhausted his supply of clean clothes, he recruited into active service all that lay scattered on the floor around him. Only those clothes failing his remarkably lax standards of his "sniff test" were spared the indignity of further service. This meant even the underwear he wore over several hot July days could be forced to reenlist. All this created an aroma like the breath from Ollie's dog-a touch of mildew, a hint of sewer, and a smattering of sour milk. I certainly played no small role in this, but even I had limits on how much revulsion I could tolerate. Not Dad. My suggestion that we straighten up a bit always met with the same response.

"We're not gonna take away her livelihood . . . . wouldn't be right."

Similarly, Dad considered himself Ollie's benefactor, rewarding him occasionally with the opportunity to bring order to the jumble and clutter in his store's inventory.

Mrs. Morrison always dove into her work with furious determination, wise enough not to stop for lunch and risk losing the momentum and desire to continue. Her quick, jerking movements also provided her with the robotic efficiency she needed. I tried to be absent when she cleaned, partly from the guilt I felt, and partly from not wanting to interfere with this miracle worker who made living respectable again. The house became so transformed that for the few hours before Dad returned from work, I had a window of opportunity to invite Opal over to play board games and pretend Dad and I lived just like normal people.

On the day I decided to be present, I endured the tedium of watching her vacuum, polish, and vacuum. When the house became quiet again, I followed Mrs. Morrison into the kitchen. Pretending to look for something to eat in the *Frigidaire,* I soon focused on her activity at the sink. She rolled up her sleeves to rinse some rags and I readied myself to ask about the concentration camps. But I saw nothing. No numbers, no letters—no tattoo. I moved closer, hoping she would turn her arms so I could be sure. Then her arms dropped to her side as she turned toward me.

"You don't like to play? She's so beautiful outside."

"I was about . . . . to do that."

She smiled and nodded, waiting for me to leave. I just stood there.

"So?"

"Mr. Maxwell, the baker . . . . did you know him?"

With the mention of his name she shook her head and repeated the same words.

"Terrible, terrible . . . . a terrible thing."

"Did you know him?"

"Only seeing him when I pass . . . . I bake for myself."

"No, I mean did you know him a long time ago?"

She looked puzzled.

"In Germany? . . . . "

I nodded.

" . . . I didn't know he was even from there."

"He was."

I somehow expected the confirmation of that to jog her memory and get her to realize she did know him after all. Her question encouraged me.

"From what city do you say he comes?"

I felt proud I could remember the city, even if the name made it impossible to forget. Despite that, I almost spurted out "hot dog".

"Frankfurter."

She chuckled.

"Frankfurt . . . . yes. I live there for a few years only."

"So maybe you knew him."

"She's a big city . . . . No, I don't know him."

I grew frustrated.

"Are you sure?"

"Am I sure? . . . . I think I would know this. No?"

I wanted to tell her I had no answers, only questions.

"Were you in the war, too?"

"Of course. We all were. You cannot hide from it. The bombs they come, and then they come some more until it is raining bombs and there are fires everywhere and there is no air to breathe. . . . The firestorms are everywhere in Dresden. . . . "

I wondered how she had survived, but she answered that before I could speak.

". . . If I was not home, to hide in the root cellar, I would become dead like my sister and mother. . . . They die a horrible death."

Her voice broke. She stood still, staring down at the floor. I hesitated before speaking again.

"Mr. Maxwell's family also died. . . . "

She looked at me.

" . . . . That's what Doc said."

"And for me and Mr. Maxwell, the war . . . . she never would stop . . . . The memories never end . . . . It is no wonder he does this to himself . . . . I wish now I spoke to him, the both of us so much similar."

"But how come you don't have the blue numbers on your arm like him?"

Mrs. Morrison froze, dropping her rags. She then shook her head as though answering another question.

"It was bad for everyone . . . . worse for some maybe . . . . I don't know."

I thought she would clarify what she meant, but she burst into tears and ran to the bedroom. Her reaction both startled and confused me, and although I did not know why I made her cry, I would have apologized for doing so. But after a few minutes of waiting for her to return, and after hearing her hiccup some sobs, I decided to leave. I told myself Mrs. Morrison would no more be angry with me than I would with her. I had depended on her for answers and she, like the other adults I asked, had disappointed me. I finally understood I could not rely on anyone, other than myself, for the answers I needed.

For the next week, I stayed after school and read everything the library had about the war and the concentration camps. Contained in the pages of my reading were answers to questions I asked and didn't ask. Each afternoon the librarian, Miss Latham, had to shove me out at closing, each time with another book I spent the evening and most of the night reading with a flashlight under my covers. I didn't want Dad questioning me or trying to give answers that were half truths. His response that "the war was over and done with", too easily dismissed information whose importance became more and more obvious through my reading. So I searched for the truth in the encyclopedia and in the history books. The photographs and eye witness accounts spoke the true horror of the war and the Nazi concentration camps. Admittedly, I didn't always understand what I read, and the books couldn't tell me if Mrs. Morrison, as a German, had anything to do with murdering Mr. Maxwell's family. Nor could they tell me what Mr. Maxwell thought or felt each day thereafter. But I did come to understand why my visits always seemed so much more important to him than they were to me. I could have shared my comics, showed him my homework, and even tasted the fish meat loaf he always wanted me to try. I could have done all of that. I became furious with Dad and Stan for their suspicions about him, and angry with myself for believing them. After Mr. Maxwell's death, when all Dad could say was, "I guess we'll now have to settle for Stan's packaged cakes", I hated him. I wanted to tell him Mr. Maxwell was much more than that, much more than he or Stan, and I would demand they apologize for everything mean they thought and said. But I knew I had no right to demand anything, at least not until I finished wrestling with my feelings of guilt and disloyalty.

My nighttime reading continued religiously. That is, until the nightmares began. The recurring image of charred disfigured corpses, their twisted, grotesque faces capturing their final screams, their last seconds of fear and horror, became intolerable. I dreaded falling asleep. Finally, I decided to end what had become so disturbing, satisfied in the belief I had learned all I wanted and needed to know about this subject.

A DROWNING IN SWANSON LAKE 69

If the rumors about Mr. Maxwell bothered me, I wondered how Ollie could shrug off the ones about his mother. It took a colony of ants to reveal I had been mistaken.

Passing the shed one late afternoon, I stopped to watch an army of ants devour a chunk of green caterpillar. A slimy mucous gravy oozed from what remained of its body, reminding me of the okra Mrs. Magnusson once served and which I almost served back. Waves of ants rushed to envelop the caterpillar, oblivious to the danger above them. I saw them as Nazis overtaking an American supply depot, and myself as the god ready to annihilate them. I took my nearly empty soda can and filled it with some standing water from a puddle nearby. As I began to pour from above, I watched the unsuspecting soldiers scatter or get washed away from the torrential rains. I began to refill my can when I heard a voice.

"Don't hurt 'em, Hal."

I turned and saw Ollie. Tearing off a piece of *Twinkie,* he placed it precisely where I initiated my onslaught. We watched the surviving ants return, devouring the cake as they did the caterpillar.

"They look like chocolate jimmies . . . . A *Twinkie* with jimmies . . . . Don't it, Hal?"

"It does."

I watched as Ollie put down another piece of cake, as though to make amends for what I did. But I had not yet abandoned my campaign of destruction, already eyeing a branch a few feet away. I toyed with having those fingers of God smite a few escaping enemy soldiers, when Ollie's words again restrained me.

"People are mean . . . . meaner than animals . . . . "

I felt sure he meant me. I was ready to defend my actions or apologize, although I had to do neither.

" . . . . They're wrong about Ma and they know it."

Realizing the true cause of Ollie's distress transcended ant hills, I took comfort in knowing I played no part in causing it. But it also bothered me to see him upset. Ollie rarely gave anyone an inkling of what he was really feeling, and I felt honored. I also became self righteous once I knew his comments didn't refer to me.

"Of course they're wrong . . . and cruel. At least animals don't wanna be mean . . . . if they can help it."

I wasn't sure what I meant exactly, although it sounded right. Ollie looked at me, saying nothing. He then strategically placed his last piece of cake. Suddenly he sneezed. Either from not having a tissue or refusing to use one, Ollie bent over to discharge the mucous from his nose. The wind almost blew it back into his face before carrying it just far enough to land on the ants. I wondered which natural disaster to equate that with, although the ants tunneled their way through it and began to treat it as another gift.

"I think they like that better than the *Twinkies*."

"No more snot balls, Ollie . . . . "

I had no intention of becoming its next recipient and began my walk home. Ollie followed and we said nothing for about a quarter of a mile. Then he stopped suddenly and grabbed my arm. I turned to look at him.

"But some animals can never be mean . . . . no matter what."

His statement seemed to come out of nowhere, until I realized he was responding to the remark I made earlier and which I already forgot.

"All animals can be mean . . . . even if they don't wanna be."

"Uh-uh . . . . Not dogs."

I thought I'd borrow one of his expressions to make my point. "That's stupid."

"It's not . . . dogs won't eat you, no matter what."

I laughed.

"You mean "bite you . . . dogs won't bite you"."

"No, they'll bite if you hurt them first . . . . but they won't eat you no matter what."

"If they're hungry enough, they will. Even people do that."

"But never dogs . . . . I even read it."

"And it said that?"

"I mean it, Dusty. This man lived by himself and he had a dog, but then no one saw them for weeks . . . . until his neighbor called the police . . . . and they found the both of them dead . . . in skeletons . . . . It said the man's heart attacked him."

A DROWNING IN SWANSON LAKE   71

"So that don't prove nothing."

"But don't you see? The dog starved, too. He coulda ate the man and lived, but he didn't . . . . cause he couldn't do it."

"That's all bunk. You saw that in the *Hudson Star Gazer*. Right?"

He nodded. I tried to imagine the photographs they would have included with the article.

" . . . . That's not a real newspaper, Ollie. It's all just made up stuff."

"Uh-uh. Ask Stan."

"I don't gotta ask him."

I wanted to tell Ollie how I also accepted Stan's version of world events, his proof always drawn from articles in the *Hudson Star Gazer*. But he also needed to know that I had since learned neither Stan nor the newspaper should be believed or trusted. I might have told him if I thought he could keep this secret.

"Because you know it's true?"

I grew tired of arguing.

"That's right, Ollie . . . "

He stood there beaming.

"I told you so . . . . And that's why animals are higher than us?"

I could not let that remark go unchallenged.

"Higher than us? You mean superior?"

He nodded.

"You even said people would eat people if they gotta . . . . You did."

I resented becoming his student. But I knew I had him trapped.

"So rats and mice and wolves wouldn'ta eaten that man in the newspaper? They're animals, too."

He hesitated.

"Then I meant . . . . only dogs."

"But you said animals . . . . Which is it!?"

He whispered.

"Dogs."

"All dogs . . . . like the one in the newspaper? . . . . "

He nodded.

" . . . but that newspaper lies about everything . . . . So then it can't be true about the dog . . . . And it can't prove dogs or any other animals are superior to us."

I realized I had been yelling. I stopped and waited for Ollie to challenge me again, but he didn't. He couldn't. He exhausted his intellectual capacity early on, with the first few points he made. Maybe he tried to tell me animals were his proof God still existed, just as people had convinced Mr. Maxwell He no longer did. And maybe Ollie needed to believe that when people failed him, when I failed him, he could always depend on the nobility within the animals around him. But I didn't listen to any of that. Instead, I bullied someone whom I least needed to bully, someone who only wanted to prove he also believed in something. As we walked silently to our homes, I wanted to say something. But I felt too ashamed and humbled to speak.

6

Every Sunday morning a number of us attended prayer service in Ida Du Page's living room. Although they included genuine worshippers, Mrs. Crabtree and Adelaide Benton the prime examples, most, like Dad and me, showed up just often enough to maintain our Christian status. On a morning as crisp as the apples that sweetened the air and made Ida's homemade cider the reward for attending her service, Dad and I made one of our appearances. Most of us were Episcopalian or Lutheran, but Swanson Lake was too small to support a church, any church, so Ida volunteered her home. Now in her early seventies, Ida had given up drink for religious drunkenness. She became our resident clergy, although with few births and fewer marriages or deaths in recent years, she had little to do except take meals to a few shut ins and oversee the Sunday service. She ran the service like a Quaker meeting. We all sat in silent prayer until one of us felt moved to speak. After almost an hour, Ida stood up and summarized the gist of what all of us had been praying. The Lord only knows how she knew this, but she spoke with such authority we accepted it. All I know is she never spoke to anything in my prayers. When I was younger, I assumed my prayers were too soft to hear. As I grew older, I knew my thoughts were too sacrilegious to repeat. So I often spent much of the hour dwelling on Ida's creased, leathery skin, or Mrs. Baker's huge chin wart that seemed ready to explode at any moment and drench us all in pus. But those physical imperfections captured less and less of my attention as I focused exclusively on perfection itself. That's when Opal attended, and replaced God and everything else.

Dad didn't mind going to the service once or twice a month. At least not in the beginning.

"A lot better than the fire and brimstone hoe-down I remember as a kid . . . . Give me peace and quiet . . . . How I hated being yelled at . . . . "

However, years brought a certain confidence, even arrogance, to Ida and her sermons, and Dad grew increasingly tense because of it. I first noticed it after one of her more impassioned displays of moralizing.

"Were you praying for the Negroes?"

"What Negroes? What are you talking about?"

I knew someone had to be praying for them if Ida spoke about it. I thought it might have been Dad because he sat the closest to her.

"Ida talked about Negroes and a little rock and . . . . interrogation."

"She did? When was this?"

"Just before . . . "

I then became curious about prayers so intense, he could ignore Ida.

" . . . . What were you praying about?"

He looked at me and hesitated, before answering.

"You don't repeat prayers. It's a private conversation between you and God . . . "

If Dad seemed pleased with his answer, I felt disappointed. He always said we should not keep secrets from each other. I reminded him of that.

" . . . I have to watch what I say around you . . . . "

He smiled, but I still wanted an answer. He looked at me.

" . . . But don't tell anyone, okay? . . . . "

I nodded.

" . . . . Scout's honor?"

"Scout's honor, or hope to die."

He leaned over and whispered.

"I was thinking about the store's inventory and what I needed to order next week . . . . But I shoulda been praying. That's what we're here for. Right?"

I nodded again. Dad did not want to waste an opportunity to provide a moral lesson, although he had already taught me what I needed to know. I too would not let praying intrude on my daydreaming. As with the notes he sent my teachers to excuse my lateness, Dad's confession exempted me from the act of prayer. However, it did nothing to explain what I had heard, and Dad had not.

"Ida's a do gooder, Hal. She thinks everything needs changing, even if it ain't broke."

I became confused.

"Are Negroes broke?"

Dad laughed.

"Very good, son . . . Most are, to be sure . . . . I'll have to remember that."

I didn't know what I said that was so funny. I tried again.

"She said we're mean to them . . .

"Oh, for Chrissakes. She reads one newspaper article about Negroes in Little Rock . . . . Ida should just leave well enough alone . . . . and quit preaching her political babble . . . This is a church for God's sake."

"But are we mean to them?"

"What she's talkin' about is a thousand miles away. Did you ever see me mean to one? Were you ever mean to one?"

I shook my head. I had once seen one in Brewman, hosing down some dumpsters in back of the *A&P*. Opal and I stared for awhile, then left without saying anything to him. We mentioned it to Mr. Magnusson.

"Stay away from them . . . . and any like him."

Opal and I guessed he had been in jail and we promised her

father we would keep away from him. Now Dad was saying the same thing.

"They're happy where they are and we're also happy where they are . . . . so there's no need to bother with one another."

In current events I eventually learned more about the historical event Ida discussed, and about integration, the word I had misunderstood in church. When I told Dad what Miss Hargitay taught us about the issue, he called her a "radical" and her teaching "blasphemous".

"That nonsense has no place in a classroom . . . . She's no better than Ida."

He threatened to go and speak to her, although he reconsidered when I assured him I did not agree with, or even believe, what she said. Actually, I could have been more truthful and achieved the same results. I just didn't care about a situation so removed from my life. In that respect, Dad had been correct.

If Doc went to church each week, it seemed more from a desire to exercise his mayoral power and duties than from any deep religious conviction. At the close of each meeting, Doc stood up and opened the floor to any town matters. The group of twenty or so worshippers guaranteed him a captive audience. Only Doc took his job seriously. He first proposed the idea of a mayor in order to enhance Swanson Lake's respectability.

"Isn't it time we gave ourselves some credit? . . . Being unincorporated makes us a nobody, the poor cousin no one sees or talks about . . . . But a real town with a real mayor, now that's something we can feel proud about . . . . and something we can make happen."

Since it didn't actually affect anything one way or the other, people nodded, shrugged, or just kept quiet when Doc named himself Swanson Lake's champion and first mayor. But his ambition appeared to have no limits when he expanded his mayoral role to include tourism.

"New York Cheddar is famous, a world class cheese admired near and far . . . . It brought wealth and prosperity to the citizens of the Herkimer valley, and beyond . . . . And look what the upstate

A DROWNING IN SWANSON LAKE

77

vineyards had done for that area, despite our own unfortunate attempts to duplicate it. But an idea will come to us, something so perfect we can't fail, because Swanson Lake has a gold mine we just haven't discovered yet . . . . "

Doc paused, more to catch his breath than to make a point. He soon continued.

" . . . . Just think what it would mean . . . . to be known for something special . . . . the fame and prestige of it . . . . the Empire State's most amazing success story . . . . and it's all within our grasp . . . . "

Dad stifled a giggle. He seemed disappointed the room didn't erupt in belly laughs, and a stampede to the front door never materialized. In fact, thirty nine eyes remained focused on Doc.

" . . . . We obviously don't have to reach a decision today . . . . although if you have any ideas, please share them now . . . . Remember. We control Swanson Lake's legacy and the way history will look upon us."

Doc waited. When it finally looked as though he might have to adjourn the meeting, a voice like gravel in a coffee grinder, crashed through the silence from the back of the room. It seemed perfectly suited for a face whose black eye patch draped her right socket, the result of a horse riding accident.

"I'm knee deep in the finest pony manure. Make a great peat or for plantin'."

Adelaide Benton's suggestion produced a few snickers and Doc's diplomatic response that "we table that proposal for now". He encouraged us to consider other possibilities.

"Think. Think . . . . What makes us special?"

Either finally recognizing nothing did, or exhausted from the service and Doc's speech, the others sat silently and struggled to keep from yawning. Doc looked elsewhere for help.

"Maybe if we prayed . . . "

Then he closed his eyes, soon opening them when he sensed his call to prayer had been ignored. Doc sighed.

" . . . . Okay, okay. It's been a long morning . . . a lot to think about . . . It'll come in time, you'll see."

And it did, but not in the way anyone expected.

Dad had not planned on attending service the following week, except that his annoyance with Ida Du Page's "radical political outbursts" had festered into a full blown rage.

"She's a menace and needs to be watched. I, for one, won't let her get away with nothing . . . . Nada . . . . If she so much as utters a syllable about Negroes or anything political, I'm gonna tear into her and tell her where to put her lollipop views of the world . . . . We've come for church and nothing else."

I had looked forward to seeing Dad challenge Ida's pompous and self-righteous pronouncements. But that all changed a few minutes after the service began, when Mr. Magnusson and Opal entered. I knew not to underestimate Dad's proficiency in embarrassing those he targeted, and those unlucky enough to be present or related. I considered waiting outside. Then I tried thinking about anything that would keep me from listening. Nothing came to me. I realized I could not abandon Dad, despite the shame and humiliation his insults would earn for us. So I sat, stared at the floor, and hoped for the best.

Sunday's service proceeded as usual, with the same seven or eight worshippers rising to speak. When an hour had passed and no one appeared to have anything more to say, Ida took her cue and stood up. All of Dad's body stiffened. Then all of my body stiffened. I could hear him reach into his pants pocket for his notes about the separation of church and state. I picked at a fingernail as Ida spoke.

"If we look to the Spirit that is within each of us, to the Christ that is within our hearts, we will not waver from what is right . . . . nor shirk from our Christian responsibility. The world's evils need addressing, and we don't have very far to look . . . . "

Dad began squirming, his breathing becoming noticeably more rapid. I did not have to look at him to see his face. The lip he began chewing, the sweat above his eyes, and his twitching left eyebrow, had become his battle face. Even the gulps he took, the hard swallows that sounded like dropped chunks of rock, became predictable in his anger. I gripped the top of the empty chair in front of me, closed my eyes, and prepared for the explosion and shock waves.

" . . . . the way we treat our neighbor, the way we talk to our family, will say more about us and our commitment to Him than any Bible passages we might quote or empty concerns we might speak . . . . I too am guilty of this hypocrisy but know that there is hope as long as our hearts stay open to Him and His voice . . . . "

Then I heard nothing except Dad's breathing, which soon became quiet and measured. I slowly looked up. Ida had begun the handshaking that ended our service. Dad's body slumped back into its relaxed state, a satisfied smile stretching his face. He whispered into my ear.

"God musta told her to knock off that other stuff . . . "

He stood up and stretched.

" . . . Let's get some of that fresh air."

He put his arm around me as we went outside. Dad then looked around, and in a soft voice, continued his instruction.

" . . . . Ya see the difference from last week? Today she kept on the subject. You become a good Christian by being nice to your neighbors and praying to Him. That's the heart of it all . . . . But when she gets into marching and protesting and all that, she's just being a troublemaker . . . . And that's why God finally stepped in today . . . . to remind her what He expected."

Dad's belief in divine intervention would suffer a major disappointment the following week when Ida resumed her customary rhetorical attacks. Her ranting about how "the two evils, fascism and communism", put America in danger of becoming one because of our fear of the other, climaxed with a call to "fight for God against the evils men make". Dad would leave that service shaking with rage, calling her "a traitor to her country" and no better than the "colored instigators down South". He would also vow never to return as long as "that agitator is in charge". But he and I had not yet attended that service. For the time being, Dad could savor the victory of him and God over Ida.

Doc soon approached and engaged Dad in a conversation about

Swanson Lake's "cottage industry". I only half listened as I looked for Opal.

"I might be a little ahead of my time on this . . . . thought I'd give everyone a few extra to mull it over."

No sooner did Doc finish his sentence than Opal came up to me. She frowned.

"How come you're mad at me?"

I had no idea what she meant. Then I realized.

"I didn't look at you because . . . "

I stopped. She waited for me to continue.

" . . . . I'll tell you later . . . but I'm not mad. Honest."

"I never saw you try not to look at me."

"I'm sorry . . . . I won't ever do it again. Scout's honor."

Her smile gave me the opportunity to change the subject.

"You wanna go butterfly hunting?"

She shook her head.

"Too many bees . . . . I hate bees."

Doc suddenly spun his head completely around, as though he was part puppet.

"Bees? Honey bees? . . . "

And so began Swanson Lake's road to fame and fortune, as Doc saw it. If the others seemed mildly enthusiastic at the beginning, they became increasingly apathetic when asked to help implement the details of the honey production and marketing.

Doc next tried a more personal approach, talking one on one to anyone willing to stop and listen. He always reminded them that this opportunity could "wither like our vines", unless the town quickly mobilized its people and resources. Since most had grown accustomed to the shriveled vineyards, considering them almost a part of Swanson Lake's identity, they regarded Doc's warning as simply a way to continue and reinforce that tradition. After a few weeks of excuses and dubious promises, Doc refused to let his frustration discourage him. He alone pursued his crusade for Swanson Lake's prominence. He interested a local beekeeper, Mr. Bayer, to concentrate on the more gourmet honeys of the raspberry and lavender flowers.

A DROWNING IN SWANSON LAKE   81

" . . . . We need to stand out in the market place if we are to compete . . . . We must create a niche . . . . "

I asked Dad about that.

"How come we needed an itch?"

"That's just high filutin words to impress us with . . . . "

I waited for his explanation.

" . . . . It's got something to do with selling, that's all."

Doc next bought a new *Philco* color television. He planned to raffle it off to help pay for the extra equipment Mr. Bayer would need. Doc's willingness to risk his own money on the venture impressed Dad.

" . . . I guess you really believe in this if you're shellin' out your own dough."

"Of course I believe in it. Haven't you figured that out? . . . . It's one smart investment . . . . and that's why I'm not worried one rat freckle about the money . . . . "

Doc then ordered jars and had labels printed. He flagged down Dad and me one afternoon to get our reaction.

" . . . . Except for the honey itself, the labels have to be right . . . . I had these designed by an art student at the community college . . . . saved a few bucks."

Doc took one out to show us. The shiny yellow and black foil was eye catching and very "beeish" looking. I leaned over to read what it said.

Swanson Lake's Angel Nectar, Gourmet Honey from the fragrant meadows in Swanson Lake, New York . . . . "The Purest We Can Bee" . . . . Gerhardt Bayer, Apiarist . . . . Honorable Henry Wyatt, Mayor.

Doc waited for our reaction. Just then I heard a flushing sound and in a few seconds, not time enough to wash his hands, Stan returned to the front.

"Showin' you his handiwork, huh? Funny how his name got on that."

"It shows we're genuine . . . not made up. A real town with a real mayor . . . "

Stan and Dad looked at each other and broke out laughing.

" . . . . Who cares what you think?! . . . . It's called marketing. I know what I'm doing."

"With your name attached to it, we'll all have to go through life with paper bags over our heads."

Stan hiccupped a laugh over his imagined cleverness. Dad became the peacemaker.

"No, no, Stan. Doc has a point. He did the work, so why not let him take some of the credit?"

This failed to satisfy Doc, who still felt a need to justify the importance of what he contributed. He spoke emphatically.

"Swanson Lake is gaining the prestige, the town is the beneficiary of all this effort . . . . and stands to become regarded as a mini Lourdes."

I turned to Dad for a translation, but he and Stan looked just as confused. When Doc took a deep breath, sat up, and rubbed his chin, Dad and I knew "the Dr. Blowhard show" would soon begin. He gave one last long look at the ceiling, almost seeming to draw his greatest inspiration from the fly strips that dangled precariously over our heads.

"The layman is often ignorant of the miracles that abound in nature . . . . "

Stan let out a loud yawn.

" . . . . There are curative properties in honey that have been known since the ancient Egyptians . . . . especially for rheumatism. Evidence now points to it as a remedy for headaches, high blood pressure—"

"It sounds like snake oil you're peddlin'."

Doc turned to Stan.

"To the ignorant, perhaps. That's why we'll need to educate . . . . "

Doc leaned back, relaxed.

" . . . . It's all part of my marketing plan."

He smiled and appeared satisfied with his explanation.

"Swanson Lake better get itself a new name. I ain't tellin' anyone I'm from here."

"Good. Go one better and move."

"I wouldn't assume too much."

"Exactly, Jack. I knew there was someone else here with brains."

Doc's comment didn't offend me. I knew I would stop being invisible when I became an adult. Dad cleared his throat.

"Actually, I was talking to you, Doc."

Stan was thrilled to have an ally.

"Ha! You see? I'm not the only one who sees the hocus pocus in your scheme."

"Is that what you think too, Jack?"

"No . . . . I just think people only care about whether your honey tastes good . . . . I don't know if they're gonna believe the medical stuff anyway."

"But they are facts . . . . Medical and historical facts."

Dad strained to be diplomatic. He measured each word.

"I'm sure there's truth to what you say . . . . but if you get people expectin' too much, they'll only be disappointed and-"

"-And they'll sue the pants off of us. We'll all be liable."

Doc turned to Stan.

"You've got nothing useful to say. Go busy yourself in the back and let two intelligent men have a discussion."

Stan brought his stool from behind the counter and sat within three feet of Doc, just out of harm's way.

"You spiteful s.o.b . . . . I'd punch your face if-"

"If you could pry your ass outa that chair."

Doc made an effort to stand when Dad put his hand on his shoulder.

"Sit down, Doc."

He fell back into his chair.

"Then tell him to get out of my face."

"Come on, Stan."

"All right, all right. I just don't like being talked to like that."

Stan took his stool and returned to his position behind the counter. Doc looked at Dad, pausing to recollect their conversation.

"Okay, so you think I should forget about the health benefits . . . . "

"I think you should take it slow. When the honey begins selling, you can use the money to help spread the word about the other benefits. But first let's get people liking our product for the way it tastes, because if they don't like that, they're not likely to wanna use it anyhow."

Doc looked at Dad and considered the advice too logical for him to dismiss. When Stan began to speak and threaten the peace, Dad quieted him with the wave of a finger. Doc no longer spoke with the authority he had a few minutes earlier.

"But one could help sell the other . . . . If it also helps what ails you . . . . "

"Eventually, yes. But you know as well as me too many businesses fail because they try and do too much . . . . I don't wanna see you go bust for something you coulda avoided."

Doc sat hunched, looking much smaller than when he first began speaking. He trusted Dad and agreed to take things slowly. He became animated when Dad spoke of the future sales.

" . . . . But after awhile we'll have to put the bees on second and third shifts just to keep up."

"You called it, Jack . . . . I have big plans for this. As soon as sales begin taking off, everyone's gonna want a piece of the action. I can see the entire town involved in the process, from gathering the honey to shipping out the jars to stores throughout the country."

"The only thing we'll ship out is you . . . to a loony bin."

Doc ignored Stan's remark.

"I can see people making detours to our town just because of our honey."

Stan tried again.

"They'll be detourin' to see you . . . . the yahoo who ended up in the loony bin."

This time Doc took the bait.

"Can't you ever shut up?!

Stan laughed.

" . . . . You won't be laughing when everyone else is making money, when everyone but you is involved in this communal effort to—"

"-Communal effort? . . . . Like in commune . . . communism. Ha! I want no part in anything that smacks of treason . . . "

Doc relished his chance for revenge.

"Yesiree . . . . one huge communal effort . . . . sharing the work . . . . sharing the profits . . . the food, the clothes . . . everything . . . . the Swanson Lake revolution. What a cover story. Huh, Jack?"

Dad smiled.

"A national one, at that."

"Then I'm movin'."

"Now there's a threat."

"And before I do, I'm destroying anything that can get into the hands of those Red sympathizers."

"Yessir . . . we'll put the honey in our store windows, a huge display case and all."

Stan moved closer to Doc.

"What are you deaf?"

"I heard you. When you make sense, I'll listen."

"When I make sense?! You wanna put that honey in this store, in the window . . . . Over my dead body."

"Better yet."

Doc didn't have to murder Stan to put up his display, although he did have to assure him any and all communal efforts would be restricted entirely to the town's honey venture. That was an easy concession for Doc, who never intended to go beyond that. He also had to promise Stan extra profits from any of the honey sold in the grocery. Convinced that capitalism still thrived in Swanson Lake, Stan agreed. But that evening Dad confided to me.

"The scheme's destined to fail . . . . He'd be better off leaving well enough alone . . . . "

Over the next few months, Dad's prediction proved accurate. Doc's hopes far exceeded the actual results. Even with all the newspaper and magazine advertising Doc did, and even with getting all of the merchants in Swanson Lake and most of the ones in Brewman to stock the honey, sales were embarrassingly low. Whether people didn't want to pay more for this gourmet honey, or simply distrusted the homegrown quality, the jars remained on the shelves gathering dust. Swanson Lake never became the tourist mecca Doc hoped for, and he never again tried to make us more than what we were.

7

I received my first tattoo when I was nine. I wore the suitably ferocious pirate's head proudly on my forearm, careful not to get it wet and see the black and red face disintegrate into an unrecognizable splotch of ink. From a battleship to a fire breathing dragon, these washable, interchangeable expressions of courage always made me feel a little tougher and braver. The girls had their hearts and rainbows, but Ollie and I never accepted them as genuine tattoos.

"Pukey . . . Huh, Dusty?"

I could not have said it better. Some of my finest displays of tact and restraint occurred when Opal showed off her latest tattoos. Extending her arm as though to reveal a new diamond bracelet, she always waited for the compliment I choked on before delivering.

"They're really . . . . pretty . . . . lots of colors."

She had flowers up and down her arm that reminded me of the wallpaper Dad sold, and the old people bought.

"Aren't they so real looking? Don't you just want to water them?"

I kept myself from shouting "yes". Suddenly, she pointed to my arm.

"Yucky . . . . that's creepy."

87

I felt hurt. I wore the tattoos to impress her. When the blood dripping corpse failed to do that, I pointed to the ones on my other arm. Unfortunately, perspiration had already distorted the faces of Davy Crockett and Wyatt Earp.

" . . . . They're not pretty, like the flowers."

I wasn't trying for "pretty", anyway. But if neither of us approved of the other's tattoos, Ollie expressed disgust for the practice in general.

"It's dumb to put marks that don't belong."

I thought the remark interesting from someone whose body catalogued his flings with danger and became an encyclopedia of scars. I wondered if he felt jealous, even contemptuous, of the badges of bravery he thought I had no right to wear. He could justify his marks, his scars, as trophies of his courage. And it would matter little that these trophies perhaps said more about a reckless foolhardiness, than about any act of courage. Oddly enough, however, Ollie's most prominent scar resulted from neither recklessness nor courage.

Ollie loved to imitate the cowboys. He watched all the westerns on television, from *Wanted Dead or Alive* to *Cheyenne*. He could mumble his words like Steve McQueen, or swagger like Clint Walker. But his favorite impersonation was of no one in particular, just the cowboy in general. He wore a black meshed straw cowboy hat and dangled a hard peppermint candy cigarette from his lips. Ollie would then cock his head and try to talk with the tip of the cigarette barely clinging to his lips. When he removed it from his mouth, every finger moved perfectly to maximize his tough image. He was convincing, too convincing, because Ollie's father suspected he had already begun smoking the real article, or would soon graduate to it. Mr. Magnusson warned Ollie about smoking, even prohibiting him from buying the candy cigarettes. Not one to shy away from challenges, he continued incorporating the cigarettes into his routine. One day Mr. Magnusson spotted Ollie leaning against the telephone pole and dangling his candy cigarette from his lips. Charging towards him, I tried to warn Ollie. However, by the time he left Dodge City to return to the here and now, his father had smacked the cigarette from his mouth. It lodged in Ollie's upper cheek, less than an inch below his right eye. He pulled it out with no more ceremony than he would give to plucking a dead insect from his skin. That left a hole almost perfectly round, as though someone pressed a tiny biscuit cutter to his face. It took a few seconds for blood to bubble out from the deep hole. Mr. Magnusson felt so grateful he didn't blind Ollie, and so guilt ridden over what he had done, he dropped his objection to the candy cigarettes. That took away most, if not all, the appeal for Ollie, and he soon began preparing himself for greater and more dangerous challenges.

At twelve years old Ollie climbed an electrical pole to rescue a cat. Unlike Ollie, the animal felt terrified, swinging its claws at every attempt to grab it. His movements became increasingly unsteady, and a fall to the ground would have meant certain death for him and the animal left stranded. But even if he managed to maintain his balance, Ollie would not be disappointed. Another opportunity for death still existed. He had begun approaching a transformer that could zap twelve thousand volts through his body and sizzle his insides like overcooked steak. Opal couldn't watch and began to cry. I screamed for him to come down.

"Forget the stupid cat, Ollie, before you get killed."

"I'm okay. I almost got her last time."

Opal screamed.

"Get down this instant, Oliver Magnusson! Or I'll get Dad."

"And I'll call the sheriff . . . . I mean it, Ollie."

Our threats only encouraged him. Then he paused and I thought they succeeded, after all. But he did not budge, seemingly intrigued with something in the distance.

"You can see lots from up here. Come up, Dusty. We'll be Injun scouts . . . . "

I could neither climb a pole nor had I the inclination to do so. I feared high places as much as I feared electrocution. Ever since I saw James Cagney die in the electric chair on *Million Dollar Movies*, his brain catching fire and smoke coming from his ears, I knew I wanted to die differently. Ollie called again.

" . . . . You comin' or what? It's really great. You can see Brewman from here."

"Get down, you fool!"

He began taunting me.

"Hal is a chicken. Cluck, cluck."

The remark would not have bothered me so much if Opal had not been there to hear it. I didn't want to appear cowardly and yet I also didn't aspire to become fried chicken. For a few brief moments I toyed with attempting to climb the pole and drag Ollie to safety. I would then become a hero to Opal, especially if I did not survive. I enjoyed imagining Opal's reaction, throwing herself to the ground in grief, screaming my name, and waiting for my body to stop convulsing and smoking so she could hug and kiss me. It would be worth it, I decided, and I would risk it all for her. Her voice startled me.

"Do something, Hal! . . . . Please."

I looked up again at Ollie and decided I had too quickly dismissed the power of persuasion.

"Ollie, get down! The cat will find its own way down . . . . That's what they're good at!"

He ignored me, still fascinated with his view. When I called to him again, I expected the same response. But as though snapping out of a hypnotic trance, Ollie remembered his purpose for being there and resumed his attempts to grab the cat. He began inching towards it, and to my and Opal's horror, his elbow rested no more than six inches from the transformer. I wanted to shout a warning, but didn't, afraid Ollie would jerk his arm into certain death. Opal became hysterical, her body shaking with sobs, and I felt unable to do more than I had already done. I hoped common sense or, far more likely, luck would get him to the ground safely. Suddenly Ollie lunged, nearly falling, and grabbed the cat by its neck. It began choking. Ollie tried to adjust his grip, but the animal jerked and fell towards me like a kickoff punt in football.

"Catch her, Hal! Catch her!"

Opal's scream sounded miles away. My knees began trembling as I struggled to move a few inches back and forth, my arms outstretched, and my heart pounding so hard it hurt. I pretended it was a football, not a living creature, and when it landed in my arms and then bounced safely to the ground as though off of a trampoline, I felt my body go faint. My knees began to buckle when Opal grabbed me.

"You caught him, Hal, you caught him!"

Ollie began making his way down and I assumed all danger had passed.

Then he called to me.

"Now catch this, Dusty."

As I looked up I saw him spit one of his trademark "loogies" at me. I dodged it easily and he laughed like a hyena. Opal became furious.

"You're disgusting, you know that?! Sometimes you're not worth caring about."

Ollie answered that with some more laughter. Opal turned to me.

"You're wonderful."

She kissed my cheek and hugged me. I didn't have to risk death, after all. I said nothing, wanting only to hear and hear again the words she spoke only a few moments before. I then began to smile, and I smiled long after I knew it looked stupid. In fact, I smiled even when I returned home and, I suspect, long after I fell asleep.

⁊ ⁊ ⁊

If Ollie's recklessness taunted death, daring it to smite him, then I was guilty of a different kind of imprudence. I simply ignored death, and in so doing, found myself unprepared for what happened one hot July fourth.

Dad and I had gone into Brewman to watch the annual Independence Day parade. It had become a ritual both of us felt compelled to honor, despite our absolute boredom with the event. Each year the same red, white, and blue adorned service trucks and civic organization floats crawled past throngs of fathers whose children sat high atop their shoulders, and mothers who attended to face wiping and drink dispensing. *Callum's Plumbing and Heating* and the *Daughters of the American Revolution* again won top honors with their natural flower busts of the American flag and Thomas Jefferson, respectively. The only surprise was which signer of the *Declaration Of Independence* would the *D.A.R* choose that year. But if I dreaded the boring predictability, I soon yearned for it. Just as the Shriners passed in their miniature go carts, Dad leaned into me, nearly knocking me over and into a group of people. I became annoyed at a joke I didn't find funny. However, when I looked at him, his face had become so pale it reminded me of a zombie. I anchored my legs, spreading them enough to distribute Dad's weight and allow me to keep him upright. I then stepped back gradually so that he could lay down without falling. His forehead dripping wet, his eyes glazed, and his hands clammy, he just stared ahead. I became terrified.

"Dad! Say something! Are you sick?"

Only later could I appreciate the stupidity of my question. But at that moment, my words focused less on logic and more on getting Dad to respond. He soon did so, propping himself up to where he could place his head between his knees. Dad struggled to whisper.

"Get help."

The people around us, although concerned, could offer us no more than sympathy. I ran to the fire truck that made its way down the street and shouted to the men on board.

"My dad needs help! Hurry!"

I can't remember if I said any more than that, but one of the men jumped off and we ran to Dad. As we approached, I could see him once again lying flat on the grass. I assumed he fainted, or worse. I refused to consider what worse meant. The fireman looked at Dad, felt his pulse, and then whistled to his buddies on the truck. He made the gesture of holding a phone, and within minutes an ambulance had come from the back of the parade down to where we were. More and more people began looking at us, pointing, and making us a part of the parade's festivities. My heart ran beyond my chest when I saw them take out a stretcher. I didn't know what I expected, perhaps believing a few pills would return him to his health, but I never considered the possibility he would need a stretcher. I watched as though immersed in water, the medic's words and the crowd's gestures becoming an incomprehensible mixture of garbled sounds and distorted, floating images. A sharp tug startled me.

"Let's go if you're going."

I followed the medic into the ambulance. Dad soon had a tube extending from his arm to a bottle of clear liquid hanging above him. His eyes remained closed the entire trip, and mine never looked away from the heaving in and out of his chest. I had always wanted to ride in a police car or on a fire truck with their deafening sirens, but now I could hear nothing beyond Dad's breathing and my heartbeat. I felt scared for him and for me. For the first time I confronted the possibility of Dad's death, and with it, the realization I had no place to go.

I had refused to accept the inevitable, or to even consider it. About a year before, after another fight with his father, Ollie talked about running away. The two were at odds over Ollie's purchase of three boxes, or one hundred and thirty two packets, of cowboy trading cards. He had hoped to win a *Roy Rogers* bicycle, although none of his packets contained the special card.

"Where will you go?"

"Anywhere I want . . . . maybe to my grands . . . . I don't know."

"You sure your grandparents can take you in?"

I almost substituted "will" or "would", more accurate choices than "can". I knew from Opal their grandparents could not be depended upon, although he didn't see it that way.

"Sure . . . . they like me."

I was considering a tactful way to ask if he had an alternate backup plan, when he asked a question I could not answer.

"Where would you go, Dusty?"

I just looked at him. He tried again.

" . . . . Where would you go if you got mad at your dad?"

"I don't get mad at him . . . . Not for long, anyway."

"Then what if he died?"

I thought the question vintage Ollie—that is, dumb.

"I'll be old when he dies."

"But suppose he—"

I didn't want to answer any more of his silly questions. I satisfied myself with the logic of my statement. Dad was as healthy as anyone I knew, and he would see me grow up and marry Opal. But as I looked at Dad in the ambulance, I realized I had been the stupid one. I began to cry. Then I prayed as I never did before, promising anything and everything. I understood my prayers for Dad had become prayers for me, and I might have felt more ashamed had I not felt so desperate. I had no place to go. After my mother died, Dad said her parents saw me when I was a year old. I must have made quite an impression because they never came to see me again. Aside from this clear message of their feelings, I had no idea where they lived, or even whether they lived. Dad's mother would have been someone I could rely on, if she were not an eighty year old invalid living in a nursing home. Dad took me to visit her right after doctors amputated her leg because of a diabetes induced infection. Since her stump inspired nightmares rivaling those of the concentration camps, I realized her age and circumstances really mattered little. I could never subject myself to years of sleeplessness.

We soon reached the emergency entrance where a doctor and nurse escorted Dad to an examining room. As I sat outside, I knew I was far more alone than I felt at that moment. Death was green, in the pea colored walls and linoleum, although I tried not to think about it. In fact, I tried to think of nothing at all. But the muffled voices from inside the room intruded, and I didn't know if I wanted the door to open and hear the news. After twenty minutes or a few hours, the door opened and the doctor approached. I couldn't look at his face, afraid of what his eyes might reveal. So I stared at his name tag, "Ohlenmeyer", and clenched my jaw in anticipation of what I might hear.

"He's going to be okay . . . . "

That's all I heard and all I cared about. I leaped from my seat and hugged him. I felt the doctor rub the back of my head and I didn't want to let go. But then I heard some more words, words that were not as reassuring.

" . . . . We need to keep him here a few days . . . . to run some tests . . . . "

"But you said he was okay."

"Just a precaution . . . . to check all the vitals."

I hated medical lingo. I also could see why Doc wavered from one moment to the next about someone's condition. A nurse now rolled Dad out of the room. He looked at me, smiled, and gave me the thumbs up. I smiled back, grateful he survived and grateful he recognized me. I wondered if he knew what I knew, that they still had to run tests before they could let him go home. I followed Dad to the third floor, where they put him in a room with three other men. Dr. Ohlenmeyer had arranged for me to sleep on an empty cot in a room down the hall. He must have sensed my fear in being separated from the person I needed most.

The doctors never did find the cause of Dad's illness. They guessed at heat stroke, but that constituted the extent to which they were willing to commit. The clean bill of health did nothing to ease his fears and he confided this to Doc.

"I got something ticking away in me and no one knows what to do about it."

Doc defended his profession.

"We can't know everything. We do our best . . . . I'm sure it's nothing to worry about."

Doc's certainties were cause for concern. Dad became worried.

"How sure are you?"

"I'm very sure."

Dad didn't realize he groaned. Doc looked at him.

" . . . . You okay?"

"That's what they tell me . . . . that I've got the strength of a horse. Only I fainted. You think that's nothing to worry about?"

"You could live another fifty years without that happening again. I've seen it."

Dad felt encouraged.

"Oh, yeah?"

"Sure, but even assuming the worst-"

"-I knew it."

"Quiet. Even assuming the worst, treatments are available for everything. Didn't Hank Babbage have the cancer ten years ago?"

"You're asking the right person. I keep checking to see if I put on my pants."

I giggled. Dad looked at me and smiled. Doc continued.

"And one day his cancer just disappeared. He'll tell you."

"He didn't even get treated for it?"

"Not from doctors . . . . in this case a nutrition gal put him on a regimen of rose petal tea and marzipan until one day, poof, gone! . . . So like I said, doctors can't know everything. But that still doesn't make something hopeless."

"If some witch's brew cured it, then he never had cancer to begin with . . . . obviously a misdiagnosis."

Dad stared at Doc. It took a few seconds for him to understand.

"Oh, there you go. As a matter of fact, I was not his doctor. He went to a specialist down in Newcastle . . . . what was his name?"

"It don't matter . . . . has nothing to do with me or my situation."

"You have your mind set on dying, that's your choice . . . . don't look like nothing I'll say will change that . . . . Might as well make the funeral arrangements and prepare the boy for the orphanage or whatever."

I could not believe he said that. Although Doc winked to show he was joking, he had not considered just how close to the truth it was. I waited for Dad to answer with a solution or plan to counter Doc's. However, none existed and we both knew it. Dad then attempted to reassure me with words that once did, but which now sounded hollow.

"Then I'll just have to live, God damn it . . . . If only for the boy's sake."

He and Doc laughed. I seemed to be the only one who understood the seriousness of the situation. I wanted to shout at them and say it wasn't funny, but I didn't need to. Dad's face soon became serious and I knew he worried about me at least as much as he worried about himself. Over the next few days I thought only about Dad dying and what that would mean to me. I thought I could protect him from death if I monitored his every cough and sneeze and made sure he never felt too cold or too hot. But I soon recognized the impossibility of that. I knew I needed a real plan. It occurred to me one day when Stan was looking at some photographs in the special magazine he kept under the counter.

"It makes life worth living . . . . yessir. Beautiful women make our miserable lives bearable . . . . "

He smiled as he looked at the magazine. I wasn't sure if he was actually talking to me or just mumbling aloud to himself. Then I heard my name.

" . . . . One day, Hal, you'll know what I mean."

I already did. Opal made me feel better than anyone else. And then it occurred to me. Dad needed the same thing. I would set about finding Dad a wife, and in the course of it, get me a mother.

8

"Slim pickin's" was the expression that immediately came to mind. Now, admittedly, you would never have mistaken Dad for James Dean, but the women were either Doc look-alikes or were married. That left only one real possibility, Lenora Tipton, whose relative good looks and ready availability made her perfect for Dad. As luck would have it, she had already begun her overtures towards him. She made three or four trips a week to Dad's store, buying a hammer one day, nails the next, and something to hammer a day or two after that. She only bought one item at a time, spending far more time than money. She always seemed too dressed up, as though she were on her way to church. At first I thought she wore her navy blue suits, matching shoes, and white frilled blouses to impress Dad. But even on days she didn't stop in, she still dressed up. It could be very intimidating if your eyes didn't zoom in on the gaudy concoctions she had pinned to her suit jacket or let hang from her ears. Pieces of shiny metal and bits of multi colored fabric were combined in a misguided attempt at fashion. Those regrettable lapses in good taste then made her as imperfect as anyone else. Dad looked forward to her visits, finger combing his hair with spit when he saw her approaching. There seemed to be very little matchmaking I needed to do. All that remained was to try and keep Dad from revealing too many disgusting personal habits, and to determine if Lenora would be a good mother. I began with the easier task and interviewed her one day when Dad had stepped out.

"Do you like pizza?"

She smiled.

"I love it . . . "

"With everything?"

"That's the only way."

I felt encouraged.

"Can you cook?"

"Can I cook?"

She laughed.

"I love to cook. And that includes pizza."

"You can cook pizza?!"

She nodded. The possibility of pizza breakfasts already had me drooling. I wiped my mouth and mentally framed a request that wouldn't appear too forward. But she anticipated it and spoke first.

"I'll bring you some next time."

I saw no need to interview her further. She was perfect. When I tasted the eight topping pizza she baked for me and Dad later that week, I began deciding what to get her for Mother's Day. But that was before she went out with Dad, and before she began wearing bizarre hats.

Lenora's parents had left her an arts and crafts store, *The Crafty Hobbyist,* when they died. Located in Brewman, I had only been in there once, with Opal, during one of Mr. Magnusson's Saturday trips. Ollie had not finished distributing his flyers, and Opal used the time to explore the shop. Instead of model plane kits and woodcarving sets, there were endless rolls of different colored yarns, an infinite number of small boxes containing everything from rhinestones to glass beads, and row after row of bottled glue. I did an about face thirty seconds after entering this toy store for grandmothers, but was yanked back when Opal wanted me to help her choose some lanyard to braid into a key chain.

""I'm gonna surprise Ollie . . . . he's always losing his key. Now he can attach it to his belt."

I later found out the kind elderly saleslady was Lenora's aunt, whom she hired to run the store while she created new fashion accessories from her inventory. It was just one of those fashions that startled me and Dad late one Saturday afternoon.

Lenora had stopped in, supposedly to buy a larger screwdriver than the one she purchased the previous week. Dad and I could not help staring at what rested on top of her head. Even as she spoke, our eyes focused on the object she later called a hat.

"Oh, do you like it? I made it myself."

We now looked at her. I let Dad speak for both of us.

"It's very . . . . unusual . . . . And interesting."

Faint praise, but more than it deserved. She had apparently taken a perfectly good blue straw hat and humiliated it with pieces of plastic fruit that went all around a pink satin band. She was seeking a stronger compliment than the one Dad gave her.

"I know men have trouble understanding what we women like in fancy hats . . . . I suppose you need to see it through a woman's eyes."

I suspected a blind man would have taken offense at what she wore. Dad made another effort.

"No, no . . . . it's very striking . . . . with the fruit salad and all."

"Oooo. I like that word. Good fashion is always striking."

I wanted to say she looked like Carmen Miranda, but I kept quiet when she referred to her creation as "one of a kind". When she left the store, Dad and I said nothing for a few moments. My curiosity broke the silence.

"Do you really like her hat?"

"Did I sound like I did?"

"Yeah, kinda."

"Good. Then you just learned something about talking to women."

I thought for a moment.

"You mean "lie"?

"I didn't lie. I never said I liked her hat. But you thought, and she did too, that I did like it . . . . and that's all that matters."

Dad seemed especially wise just then and I took advantage of his shrewdness.

"How come ladies wanna put those things on top of their head?"

But even his wisdom had limits.

"Women have their ways . . . . It's not for us to know."

Later that evening I lay in bed and began to worry. I could forgive Lenora for her hats, but I felt less confident about Dad. I feared he would never look at her again, not able to separate her face from the monstrosity that hovered over it. Apparently, he overcame that obstacle because the next day Dad told me he and Lenora were going to a movie. But that's when he discovered things he could not ignore.

If Lenora appeared delighted with her imagined stylishness, Dad prided himself in the number of years he could get from a particular shirt or pair of pants. His garments became associated with particular Presidents, even outliving the office holders themselves. That evening he wore clothes purchased during the Truman administration and which constituted his only dress attire. The shiny brown pants and frayed collar white shirt were Dad's concession to the social graces. Besides wearing them for his date with Lenora and for meeting with my teachers during Open School conferences, I could not remember any other time he had occasion to wear "the outfit". When Dad also brushed his hair and polished the brown loafers he rescued from under some boxes in the closet, I knew this date took on more importance than he would admit. I waited for the transformation to complete itself before I spoke.

"You look good, Dad."

"Thanks . . . . but I sure don't feel good."

"You sick?"

"Not yet . . . . I don't know, Hal. This dating stuff ain't for me . . . . "

He took one last glance in the mirror before looking at his watch and rushing past me.

" . . . . Remember. Homework before television . . . . Don't wait up for me . . . "And he bolted out the door before I could say anything else. I had to smile. Dad's nervousness reminded me of the first time Opal and I were alone, although I felt certain he would not resort to punching Lenora's arm as a means of relieving anxiety. I planned to wait up for Dad and hear all the details. In order to succeed, I knew I had to disobey his command. My strategy included watching *Maverick*, *The Texan*, and *Wanted Dead or Alive*, before starting my homework. Then, even if I fell asleep, Dad would return to find me lying amidst the scattered textbooks. Impressed with how much time I spent studying, he would answer all my questions. But my plan had its flaws, one of them being my failure to stay awake long enough to remove the books from my briefcase. I had never considered this a possibility, and when the *Star Spangled Banner* ended and the station shifted to loud static, I awakened to consider the possible repercussions of my poor planning. Everything from revoking my television privileges for a week, to restricting my after hour playtime, seemed likely and appropriate. I assumed Dad had felt too angry and tired to give me a tongue-lashing when he returned home, deciding instead to mete it out with the eggs and toast at breakfast. As I passed his door, I expected to hear the usual symphony of gasps, nose whistling, and phlegm scrapings. But I heard nothing. When I peeked in and saw his bed empty, I concluded Dad and Lenora were having a good time. I smiled at that and at my good luck in escaping punishment. Soon I heard the key turn in the downstairs door. I ran to my bed and waited as Dad's footsteps shuffled up the stairs. I waited for him to make a noise loud enough to wake me and give me the excuse to find out about his evening. However, when I heard his door close and the symphony begin, I knew I would have to postpone the interrogation.

The next morning Dad left earlier than usual. I suspected he did this to torment me, and he succeeded. I had no choice but to wait until later. That afternoon I jumped off the steps of the school bus and raced to Dad's store, only to find him and Lenora arguing. She wore her fruit hat, which undermined much of her argument.

"Respect yourself and others will do the same."

"I respect myself."

"Your dress says otherwise. You're a respected member of the community."

"I sell nails for a living."

"You see? You don't respect yourself. You're a businessman. And there's no reason why a new, clean white shirt, a tie, and a pair of decent pants should become the obstacle to your self-respect . . . . "

Apparently, Dad's dress clothes fell short of the mark. I wanted to tell her Dad never dressed better for anyone else, but I kept still. Lenora persisted.

" . . . You'll be amazed how much better you'll feel about yourself . . . . even here, while you're working . . . . "

Dad gave her a look similar to the one he once gave Stan after he claimed the communists spied on us through our television sets.

" . . . . It's true. And even your customers will like it more."

"So you think people wanna buy hammers and paint from a well dressed hardware store salesman?"

"Proprietor . . . . And why not? It also shows them respect . . . . "

Dad shook his head.

" . . . . I'll help you pick out some clothes. We can start small . . . . maybe with your flannel shirts."

She would have had more success suggesting he peel away the skin from his body. Dad regarded his three or four flannel shirts as a tiger would his stripes, crucial to who and what he was.

" . . . . a nice dress shirt would be far more-"

"-You know what, Lenora? Go out and buy yourself a doll and dress it anyway you damn please!"

Lenora just stared at him. It took her a few moments to recover.

"I didn't mean anything by it . . . . It was for your own good."

"You don't hear me telling you what to wear or not wear."

"Me?"

She snorted a short nervous laugh. I knew what was coming and I wanted to stop it. I signaled Dad by shaking my head, but he just ignored me and continued.

"I didn't say anything about your hat."

I lowered my head. I felt embarrassed for both of them.

"My hat? What about it?"

"Just forget it."

"No, no. I want to know what you don't like about my hat."

There was a pause. I knew Dad could be mean when angry, but he exceeded my expectations.

"It's silly looking . . . . like something you'd stick on a mule . . . . on a mule you hated."

Lenora began to shrink, finally crumbling at the cruelty of Dad's remark. She burst into tears and ran out. I looked at Dad, who seemed sorry for what he said. Although he went outside and called after her, it was too late. My chance for a mother and protection from an orphanage vanished with her footsteps. Maybe I would have been more disappointed if I really thought their relationship had a chance of succeeding. Or maybe I felt glad not to be rewarded for my selfishness. I wanted a mother more than I wanted a wife for Dad. I did not deserve having my wish granted, and I would have thought God a chump if He had done so.

Dad and Lenora eventually reconciled to the point where they exchanged pleasantries and nodded hellos, but they never dated again. I thought I learned the power of words in saying the unforgivable, and the futility in attempting to undo what could not be undone. But my knowledge would have to come firsthand, which it did a few years later, on the day I lost and won Opal Magnusson.

9

It was a June morning and the scent of the nearby pines and wild roses made me drunk with euphoria, and emboldened me to move closer to Opal as we walked. Soon it was Opal I began breathing, her fragrance clean and fresh as honeydew, and I became enamored with her scent as I did with her looks, as I did, ultimately, with her. On a dare I took her hand, and although she seemed somewhat surprised, she appeared stunned when I kissed her lips. For a few moments she remained paralyzed, shocked by a spontaneity usually foreign to me. But she soon recovered, her blank expression disappearing into eyes warm and wet with emotion. I felt invincible. I squeezed her hand and she smiled and I knew nothing could spoil this moment now and forever. Until I heard laughter. I had misjudged how long it would take Ollie to wreck his kite, and as he strolled back into our field of vision holding a few odd pieces of cloth, wood, and string, my jaw tightened at the price I would soon pay for my miscalculation. Ollie's laughter grew louder as he approached.

"Hal gives fish kisses. Dusty gives fish kisses."

He then proceeded to mimic a fish, sucking in his cheeks and moving his lips up and down. I felt grateful Opal didn't smile or laugh, Ollie succeeding in delighting no one but himself. But he did succeed in returning me abruptly to earth. I became angry, too angry for words, and I just glared at him. Opal articulated her annoyance.

"Go away, Ollie! You're a brat!"

I might have left it at that had Ollie not taken the reprimand as a challenge. He proceeded to continue the fish imitation, this time moving his elbows as though they were fins. He actually looked more like a chicken, although that mattered little. I flushed red and I wanted to charge him and punch his face. But the core of my anger held just enough reason to remind me of Ollie's strength. I also knew Opal would be angry with me for fighting. So I just stood there as my skin went hot and cold. I felt humiliated and I couldn't look at Opal. She squeezed my hand and told me to ignore him. I tried to, but something made me go on. I looked at Ollie.

"Why don't you just leave us alone? Who needs you around us all the time?"

And then I said the unforgivable.

" . . . . You're a retard, Ollie. That's what you are and what you'll always be."

No sooner did I say that than I regretted it. Opal pulled away from me as though burned. She turned quickly to face me, a stricken look in her eyes. Tears began to well, and in a voice that trembled with hurt and anger, she asked simply,

"How could you? . . . . Hal . . . . how could you?"

She ran off and I knew it was no use to go after her. Ollie looked in her direction and then at me. I had said the worst thing I could have said to him and yet he stayed with me. Confusion warped the muscles in his face, reminding me of a whipped dog still ready to lick the hand of the master who beat him. I wanted to say something, to apologize, but I couldn't say anything. When he finally ran off after Opal, I felt certain Ollie had already forgiven me even when he did not fully understand why I became so angry. He poked fun all the time, at me, at Opal, at everything that struck him as funny or made him uncomfortable. And we all could enjoy the joke. But the lines of joking blurred and the rules had changed suddenly, and he didn't know why. I suspected he did not have the feelings Opal and I had, the ones that would enable him to understand how serious that moment had become for us. I realized he had not intended cruelty, although I had. I meant to wound him. I also knew Opal and I would remember my words long after he no longer did.

As I lay in bed that night, Dad's bone rattling snoring grew increasingly less intrusive. My mind reconstructed the day's scene a hundred times, each time making the changes necessary to alter the outcome. One time I ignored Ollie's remark, another time I ignored it but continued to kiss Opal, and another I undermined Ollie's taunts by enjoying the joke. I knew any response would have been preferable to the one I gave. Even fighting, although earning me Opal's disapproval, would have soon merited her forgiveness. But no matter how much I rewrote, the script could not be rewritten nor the outcome undone-at least for awhile. I would explain to Opal the shame and humiliation I felt when the stakes were so high. I would tell her that, and she would understand, but not then, not that night. I completed my customary prayers with a footnote to the day's events, promising to forego swear words for the next year if He would only do this one favor for me and return Opal's love. I had already committed myself to missionary work in Africa for the Nels Nelgren episode, so this promise seemed much less difficult to keep. I closed my eyes to sleep, finally confident in His ability to succeed where I could not.

The next morning brought rain and a dampening of my spirits. I wanted to see Opal, talk with her in person, and I didn't want her to use the weather as an excuse for not seeing me. When I telephoned her, Ollie answered the phone. He was as cheerful as ever.

"Hi, Hal. You been outside yet? It's a good rain. I just got back myself."

Ollie loved walking in the rain, snow, or anything that brought him discomfort. My preference would have been to stay in my pajamas, catch up on my comic books, and eat food in bed. But I wanted to see Opal.

"Is she there?"

"Yeah. She's washing up or something."

"Would you ask her to call me?"

"Sure, but I think she's still mad at you."

"How do you know?"

"She told me."

"Well . . . . ask her to call."

"You wanna do something? We could go mud splashin'."

Ollie enjoyed stomping hard on the mud and splattering me and Opal. Over time we learned to schedule these romps, both to appease Ollie and to allow us the opportunity to wear our most grungy clothes.

"Maybe later, Ollie. Now don't forget."

"What?"

"To have Opal call me. Okay?"

"Okay."

I felt sure Ollie would forget to tell her, or he would tell her and she would not call back. I was ready to call her again when the phone rang. I could see my hand tremble as I lifted the receiver. My "hello", weak and breathy, soon became energized by her voice.

"Thanks, Ope, for calling back. I wasn't sure Ollie would remember . . . "

I stopped myself.

" . . . . I wasn't sure he would tell you."

"He remembered just fine. And he obviously told me."

Opal seemed determined not to make this easy for me. I became nervous again, afraid of saying another wrong thing. My voice quivered.

"I was hoping I could see you . . . . and talk . . . . Maybe we could meet at our headquarters."

Headquarters was the old shed that once stored Swanson Lake's wine bottles, until the collapse of the town's wine industry converted its use to a playhouse stockpiling *Monopoly*, *Clue*, and a dozen other board games. It became a meeting place whenever it rained. I closed my eyes hard and clenched my teeth as I waited for the rejection I felt sure would come. I was ready to plead with her when I heard her soft response.

"Okay."

That word became my lifesaver, my salvation, as she agreed to meet me an hour later. It seemed like days, and thinking about what I would say only made me more nervous. I decided instead to finish the latest *Superman* comic, drawing inspiration from his ability to overcome any obstacle. When I arrived at the shed, Opal stood inside, waiting. I took a deep breath.

"I'm glad you came. I was afraid you wouldn't . . . . I'm glad you did . . . . "

She did not respond. I stared at something cold and hard, a stone facade which had once been Opal's face. She waited for me to continue. I had nothing rehearsed and I stuttered and stopped, waiting to be introduced to my tongue. Finally, I just spoke what I felt and hoped for the best.

" . . . . I'm sorry . . . . for what I said. Ollie's my best friend, next to you. I didn't mean to hurt his feelings. Honest I didn't."

I stopped, pleased with my words, and more confident Opal would forgive me. Once again I miscalculated.

"Of course you meant it. How can you say you didn't? Everyone sees him as a fool, someone to laugh at or blame. But he's no fool, except for trusting you and expecting you, of all people, not to see him like the others see him and not to call him . . . that . . . that name."

Opal choked on her last words.

"You're right, Ope. It was dumb and mean . . . But if I really felt that way about him, I could never have called him that . . . . Hell, I know he's anything but . . . "

I knew Opal now believed me. Ollie's spontaneity, his bizarre insights, made him far too complex to categorize with one word, especially the one I chose. My next words came quickly, without thought, and without editing.

" . . . . He's like my brother . . . . I love him, too."

I felt embarrassed saying that, but I didn't regret it. I almost half expected Opal to laugh at the word, "love", a strange one for me to have used and especially with another boy. However, I believed I did love Ollie in the way I said, as I loved Opal in another way. But I would wait to tell her that. Opal now looked at me and smiled. She walked over and kissed me on my cheek, then on my lips. My face felt scalded.

"I know you do."

That's all she said. Opal then became relaxed and playful again, pushing me and then running out into the rain. I ran after her, catching her, and kissing her on the mouth, longer this time, much longer, and holding her shoulders tight to prevent any escape. We were soaked, but we stayed in the rain and laughed. *I'm so goddamn happy*, I thought, and then I remembered the promise I made to Him about using swear words. Fearing he would take all that away, I prayed a "sorry" to Him, unconsciously seconding it with my lips. Opal looked at me.

"I know you are . . . . I know you are."

And she kissed me again.

10

One hot, humid afternoon, just as Doc's eyelids began their pre-sleep flutters, the screen door burst open.

"No time to sleep now. I need help."

Dottie Ketchum stood before him, bleeding from her left shoulder. Doc blinked a few times, perhaps unsure if he had already fallen asleep and was dreaming, or unsure he actually saw what he thought he saw.

"So?! You're just gonna stare or what?"

After his third attempt, Doc rose from his chair.

"Sorry . . . half asleep."

You couldn't really fault Doc for not recognizing immediately the purpose of her visit. Dottie's injury, although obvious, was not the first thing one noticed about her. It was likely to take a back seat to . . . . well, her back seat. Her butt ignored the generous parameters set by her stretch pants, even extending beyond what seemed physically impossible. They struggled to contain the shifting pockets of flesh, and created the impression of two giant water blisters on the verge of bursting. Dottie further burdened these pants with a tool belt that slung a hammer from her side like a policeman's billy club. Everyone assumed she was a Miss Fix-it, but she quickly corrected the misconception.

"No, no . . . . For protection . . . . "

She would pat her hammer and repeat it.

" . . . . for protection."

That seemed unnecessary in a town where you were more likely to meet your Maker from one of Ronnie's luncheon specials than from any crime, but Dottie and her protector remained inseparable. However, when she stood before Doc and explained her injury, it became clear whom she feared.

" . . . damn too many squirrels . . . . Crazy things . . . . One chased itself in a circle for hours before my cat ate her. Then she died, too . . . . I ain't goin' the same way, no sir, I ain't . . . . "

Then she took out her hammer and related her most recent encounter with the enemy.

" . . . . So the critter is perched on a fence, not a foot from my face, hissing like a rattler. Rabies, for sure. I stepped back, took out my hammer, and swung at it with all my might . . . . except I missed."

I theorized her disproportionate physique gave her an unsteady center of gravity. When she finished swinging, the hammer found itself two inches into her left shoulder. Doc related the story to Dad a little later in the day.

"To get a gash like that . . . . she musta spun around like a top."

I no sooner thought of Dottie twirling like a top than I burst out laughing. Dad and Doc looked at me.

"Ain't right to enjoy someone's misfortune . . . . I've taught you that."

"I wasn't glad she got hurt . . . . "

I explained the twirling human top I pictured spinning around. Dad stared at me, saying nothing for a few moment. Then he continued with his moral instruction.

"Still, it's wrong . . . the poor woman is in pain. So like I said, you never want to be unfeeling like that."

I might have felt more cavalier about Dad's advice, dismissing its obviousness, had I not been guilty of insensitivity with Ollie. When Dad offered me a half dollar to buy a malt at Ronnie's, I assumed he wanted me to remember that despite moments such as these, when my behavior disappointed him, he still forgave me. But as I stepped outside to go and buy my malt, I heard their laughter and Doc's voice. I soon understood Dad's moral posturing had been for my benefit only.

"It's only fair, Jack. . . . I stitched her and now she's putting us in stitches."

The two hyenas screeched. When I returned about ten minutes later, they were still laughing. I waited for a pause before entering. Two faces as solemn as death itself greeted me. Dad now rose.

"Good. I see you got your malt . . . . I'll catch you tomorrow, Doc . . . . I'll think some more on what you said."

I looked at Doc to see if he could stay poker faced and not undermine Dad's act. He did, only nodding, and repeating the word "good". As Dad and I walked to the car, he suddenly let out a laugh that he quickly transformed into a cough. I knew Dad would enjoy privately the jokes he and Doc shared. I felt left out, but I knew one day soon Dad would include me, and he then wouldn't have to apologize for his laughter.

That day came sooner than I expected when Dad finally relinquished his role as the standard bearer for our family's morality. Unencumbered by the restraints of propriety, Dad could allow himself to be funny and disrespectful without mincing words for my benefit. He enjoyed his new freedom, poking fun at people and things he thought deserved ridicule. Ronnie Dawes became the inspiration for Dad's greatest irreverence, never missing an opportunity to take a swipe at her. Ronnie always seemed to work too hard at distinguishing herself in peculiar ways. Besides her cigar smoking and foul language, which Dad said neither threatened or enhanced her femininity since "she was more mule than either mare or stallion", Ronnie's annual European vacation provided the most fodder for his annoyance. When she returned from France after a ten day holiday, she donned a beret for the next eight months and sprinkled "s'il vous plaît"s and "merci"s into her conversation like salt on an egg. Dad referred to her as "Mademoiselle hoity-toity".

"She's ashamed of her roots, son . . . . gotten beyond herself. . . . And that's a sorry way to be."

After a trip to Italy, she played only opera music in her restaurant. What made that particularly unpleasant were her attempts to sing along in the broken Italian she learned for our benefit.

" . . . . She thinks its a freakin' hootenanny. She'll soon be clappin' her hands and stompin'" her feet . . . . "

As she strained to reach a note her husky voice never had a chance with, Dad's face pursed as though having bitten into a worm infested crabapple " . . . . Ah, put the poor animal to sleep. It's suffered enough . . . . "

I laughed at Dad's remarks and at the jokes he would later tell Stan and Doc.

Dad's attacks on Ronnie became his warm up act for the main show. It seemed only logical to follow personal vilification with the denigration of what she did. Dad never wanted for material, Ronnie always returning from her trips with an exotic new menu addition. She featured these under the "out of this world" heading, something most of her customers regarded as the closest thing to truth in advertising. Ronnie knew how to cook well, but the baked brie or veal kidney stews did not fit into the dietary habits of the town. French fries and pizza were as foreign as most of her customers cared to go.

" . . . . I'm not eating something that smells and looks like something my body already rejected."

Dad's view was typical, as was the one expressed by Doc.

"The internal organs were never meant to be eaten. It's savage, it's dangerous. And it's the reason the French are so short."

Doc would then discuss in detail the functions of the various organs so that if anyone had been inclined to try the veal kidneys, the sweetbreads, or the English tripe, his or her daring vanished immediately. But Ronnie persisted, partly because she believed she was bringing culture to the town, and partly because she had two steady customers.

Blue Armondsen was an itinerant laborer who lived in nearby

Kingston. A tall, handsome man in his thirties, he traveled the local area in search of any painting or carpentry jobs. He rarely spoke, except to Whitman, his yellow Labrador. He would ignore everyone else as though they could add nothing to what he and Whitman already discussed and concluded. He never let the dog out of his sight. When Blue ate at Ronnie's, he sat at a table facing the window and his truck. At the counter, he sat sideways so that Whitman stayed in his peripheral vision. Even when he worked, his dog lay next to him or secured nearby. Whitman was quick to make friends, but if anyone approached to pet him, Blue's body would stiffen and the hairs on his neck would stand up as though he were the watchdog for his master.

"There's one you don't wanna meet in a dark alley. Could be rabid for all we know."

I didn't agree with Dad.

"Whitman's a good dog."

"I was talkin' about Blue. Something unnatural about him. Just stay away from the both of them."

I didn't consider Blue any stranger than Stan. Dad laughed.

"Remind me to tell him that, son. That'll make his day."

I became angry.

"Don't tell him. He'll just get mad and not let me buy baseball cards."

"Trust me. There's no chance of Stan ever refusing your money or anyone else's."

"But just don't say anything. Okay?"

Dad saw I was serious.

"Okay, but that is funny . . . . No, no. Stan still has his senses about him. He'd never touch Ronnie's culinary landmines."

Stan had made that clear whenever the opportunity arose.

"She could throw in a life preserver with each of her meals and I still wouldn't go near them . . . . "

But despite what he, Doc, and Dad thought, Blue remained loyal to Ronnie. And not everyone believed Blue's dining choices were indicative of a disturbed mind. Doc had another theory.

"I'm telling you. No one puts himself through an ordeal like that for nothing. There's gotta be something else . . . . We know it can't be her looks, or her warm, feminine disposition. Let's face it. Marriage material she ain't . . . . "

He, Stan, and Dad laughed. I knew I had missed something, but kept quiet. I waited for Doc's conclusion.

"Therefore, it could be only one thing. Moola."

"How does he expect to get her money?"

"Not by charm, that's agreed. He neither has any, and she is not susceptible to any."

"We don't know that for sure."

Doc went over and put his arm around Stan.

"You're such a babe in the woods. Trust me. She is not susceptible to the charms of any man."

Doc made it all sound so mysterious, although I still couldn't be sure what he meant. Dad must have sensed that because he didn't ask me to leave or promise to keep quiet.

"So he's getting' on her good side just waitin' for a chance to grab the golden ring?"

"Deception . . . . flattery . . . . There are a thousand ways to dupe someone."

"Tell me about it. I made you my partner, didn't I?"

Doc appeared ready to answer the challenge when Dad stood up.

"And let the games begin. Let's go, Hal."

As we left we could hear their raised voices. I felt disappointed. Not that I wanted to hear another one of their arguments, but no conclusion had been reached about Blue. And despite the speculation about Ronnie and Blue, no one ever saw them together outside the cafe and no one ever heard anything about her losing money to anyone. The tribunal at Stan's grocery concluded finally that Blue ate her exotic specialties because he liked them, plain and simple. Once that avenue of speculation closed, Dad, Doc, and Stan pursued another. However, this one had far more importance since it involved Ronnie's other steady customer, Ollie, and the false assumptions that almost led to scandal.

At first, Ollie's preference for Ronnie's exotic experiments could

A DROWNING IN SWANSON LAKE   117

be explained away as just another one of his life threatening exploits. Doc spoke first.

"If the boy can't electrocute himself or die from a fall, then he'll guarantee his death that way . . . . But, mind you, that's a slow and painful way to go."

He laughed heartily and Dad and Stan raised their sodas to acknowledge Doc's wisdom. But in the days ahead, their talk became more serious.

"The boy spends way too much time there . . . . and then he's running errands and doing God knows what for her."

I welcomed the newfound privacy Opal and I had, and felt reluctant to look a gift horse in the mouth. The others saw it differently.

"There's something to what you say, Stan . . . . Makes no sense . . . . If it was someone else, but the nurturing kind she's not."

"I think you're both makin' somethin' outa nothin'. She's just taking him under her wing. He's a lost soul if there ever was one."

"I don't know, Jack . . . . if it was someone else."

"So maybe it's somewhat unnatural—"

Doc leaned closer to Dad.

"That's exactly my point."

Dad stared at him for a few seconds before realizing.

"Oh, no, Doc. You can't be serious. He's a boy, for God's sake . . . . And he's Ollie."

"Who better to take liberties with?"

Stan motioned with his chin to where I stood browsing, or pretended to browse, at the comic books.

"Hal, go and check on the store."

Whether I had been demoted or I presumed too much, my expulsion both surprised and humiliated me. Being privy to all conversation was something I felt entitled to, especially after Dad's willingness to share with me his irreverent remarks. I returned the comic book to its shelf and ran his bogus errand. He and I knew customers could be seen entering his store from where he sat. When I stepped outside, they resumed their conversation. I could hear bits and pieces of it as I stood outside Dad's store. "Immoral" and "disgusting" were repeated often. But then I heard something whose meaning I didn't know. It sounded like "bed of vile" and I tried to imagine what that had to do with anything. Only when I saw "pedophile" in a newspaper story a few months later, did I understand what they had been talking about. By then, Swanson Lake discovered the older woman in Ollie's life had actually been Victoria George, Stan's daughter.

If Stan knew about his daughter's feelings toward Ollie, he kept quiet and pretended not to know. And if he didn't know, it wouldn't have surprised him when he found out. She was born a flirt and a tease, and was the reason Stan insisted his ex-wife enroll her in a Catholic boarding school at an early age. Early one summer she decided to make a rare visit, apparently disgusted with the rules her mother set out for her, and anxious to test the will of her father. In the midst of "the worry years", as Dad called them, her behavior had become potentially more dangerous. Extremely pretty, her honeydew green eyes and auburn hair brought her a popularity she relished. Dad suspected she harbored some hidden resentment towards her parents because aside from the fact Ollie was nearly handsome, he seemed to have few qualities to recommend him. A conversation or even a quick exchange of words sufficiently marred the impression his good looks created.

"But you know what would be somethin', Hal? If it all didn't matter to her and somehow they went through with it . . . . Oh, boy. Let the fireworks begin with Ollie his son-in-law . . . . 'Stan and son-in-law-proprietors' . . . . "

Dad laughed at his improbable, if not impossible, scenario. However, their relationship did not have to go any further than it already had. Stan endured the ridicule, real and imagined, becoming distraught and angry each day, throughout the day. So Victoria pursued Ollie relentlessly, buying him ice cream cones and finding excuses to touch him or just get close to him.

"Oh, Oliver. There's a speckle of dirt just waitin' to jump into your eyes and blind you . . . . "

Then, with her face no more than two inches from his, Victoria would either blow or rub away the objectionable matter. A stranger in town might reasonably assume this was a couple beginning a courtship, the shy, good-looking boy being pursued by the forward girl. But what appeared innocent at first, seemed less so as the weeks passed. And it finally came to a boil one morning outside of Ronnie's cafe.

Opal and I had been sitting on the curb in front, waiting for Ollie to emerge with our sodas. Inside we heard a commotion that soon spilled into the street. Ronnie was screaming at Victoria, whose arm draped Ollie's waist.

"You no good tramp! Coming into my place of business and acting like some whore with this boy . . . . "

Victoria smirked and moved even closer to Ollie. I expected Ronnie to lunge at her throat and throttle her, but she didn't.

" . . . . You might not know what decent and respectable is, but he does. So take your arm off him before I do it for you!"

Victoria didn't budge. Instead, she smiled and let out a defiant "ha!" The small crowd moved back, expecting the battle to begin. But just then, as though dropping from the sky like *Superman*, Stan pulled his daughter away like a rag doll and took her inside his store. And despite closing the door, you could hear the slap, then her crying, before she ran from the store and disappeared. Ronnie waited a few moments to see if Victoria would return. When she didn't, Ronnie went back inside the cafe with the crowd following. Ollie looked at me and Opal.

"She was just foolin' with me. Victoria likes teasin' me like that."

Opal looked at me and I knew Victoria was only part of her worries.

"How come Ronnie cares so much about you?"

"I don't know. She likes me. She's my friend."

Opal looked at me again before turning to Ollie. She hesitated asking the next question.

"What kind of friend? . . . . "

Ollie seemed puzzled. She tried to clarify it.

" . . . . Like what kind of friend? Like Hal? . . . . "

Ollie shook his head. Opal's voice grew louder.

" . . . . What do you mean not like Hal?! Then like who?"

Ollie kept silent for a few moments before answering.

"A friend like mom used to be, before she got sick."

Opal's entire body relaxed. She smiled, but she looked sad.

"Well, that's okay, then. Sounds like Ronnie's a good friend."

She then pulled Ollie towards her and kissed him softly on the cheek. He rubbed it off.

"Don't germ me, Opal. You know I don't like no one kissing me."

Opal and I burst out laughing, understanding immediately that Ollie was never in any danger with either Victoria or Ronnie. Soon even Doc admitted he misjudged Ronnie.

"Never woulda figured it . . . . But the more I watch her with the boy . . . . She's a mamma hen, that's all. And he needs that kind of lookin' after."

The speculation and jokes about Ronnie virtually disappeared when Stan was present. The mention of her name rekindled the memory of the embarrassing incident with his daughter. Victoria did stay away from Ollie, his preoccupation with summer school leaving her time for most of the other boys. When one of her illnesses turned out to be a miscarriage, Stan shipped her back to her mother and the boarding school in Ohio.

Dad persisted in his jokes about Ronnie when he and I were alone. I soon began to suspect his motives, believing he might be jealous of her fierce independence and of the time and money she had to take exotic trips. He seemed to be addressing my suspicions one day while we watched her cross the street, oblivious to everything except the imaginary orchestra she conducted with her finger.

"I couldn't do what she does . . . . "

I thought he meant her conducting.

" . . . . She can't be happy . . . . doing what she does. Always flyin' in the face of what's normal and what others think. And you know what gives it away? . . . . "

I shook my head.

" . . . . It's those trips she takes. Sure they sound exciting and

A DROWNING IN SWANSON LAKE 121

all, but when it comes down to it, she takes them because she's not happy where she is, doing what she's doing. Ronnie's restless, always looking for something different from what she has and what she is. And that's a bad way to be, son. I'm tellin' you . . . . "

I thought back to *Around The World in Eighty Days* and the adventures David Niven had on the screen, and the ones I could only imagine as I sat with Opal in the apple basket. I wondered if they would ever happen, and if so, would they only lead to disappointment. For the time being I wanted to believe they would be better than I expected, despite what Dad said. So I ate the bread given to me and pretended it was steak, hoping one day I would no longer need to pretend.

11

When Mrs. Morrison went to Germany to stay with a dying friend, she left, unchecked, the rapid freefall into unabashed chaos. After a few weeks of tiptoeing around underwear grave sites and sidestepping dirty dishes and empty pretzel boxes, I realized Dad and I would become buried under debris long before Mrs. Morrison returned. Our chance of finding a temporary cleaning lady appeared futile, Dad guessing our reputation already well established. So early one Saturday morning, after Dad left for work, I decided to surprise him with a deluxe cleanup. As when I first leaped over a pile of broken bottles on a dare from Ollie, I did not allow hesitation to build my fear and deter me from the task at hand. I moved quickly through the litter, bagging empty soda cans, candy wrappers, and potato chip bags before scooping countless piles of dirty underwear. The pungent odor overpowered my hunger pangs and allowed me to work straight through without distraction. When I finished vacuuming the carpets and drapes, dusted and polished the furniture in the living and dining areas, I moved to the more ominous bedrooms. They seemed like mini funhouses, with the unknown ready to jump out at me from a closet or a dresser drawer. I rarely stepped into Dad's room, only entering when he was there. Extremely territorial, he only allowed Mrs.

Morrison to dust and vacuum after moving his personal articles to "safe havens". Now I needed to move his belongings, straighten his papers and books, and I felt naughty doing it. But I had no choice as I handled everything from a dirty sock stuck to a *Popsicle* stick, to his reading material. Dad did not read much, although the few books he had, *Lady Chatterly's Lover*, *Naked Lunch*, and *Candy*, he liked well enough to read over and over again. Whenever I asked him what they were about, he always said they dealt with relationships. Since he never let me borrow them, I knew he considered me too young to understand or appreciate what they had to say. Now I couldn't resist the opportunity to dust the covers and inside pages as my eyes zoomed in on words I heard before, such as "breasts" and "buttocks", and on ones I never heard, such as "clitoris" and "honey pot". A great deal of kissing and touching occurred, and I tried to understand why Dad had been so reluctant to lend me these books. I felt sure he knew Opal and I already kissed and held hands. I also realized Opal would get breasts in a few years. I returned the books to his night table. However, as I did, a bookmark fell out of one. Dad would soon know I leafed through his books. I became upset, and grew increasingly more so when I read the postcard Dad used for his bookmark.

Jack. You cannot make what can never be. I thought you would have understood this by now. I wish you the best but please do not contact me anymore.

It was signed, Harriet, and had been postmarked five years earlier. Harriet had also been my mother's name, although she had died eight years before. That's what Dad said. Suddenly I felt as though I had been branded, my skin and flesh burning with the realization of the lie I had been told. I looked again at the writing, the loops and curls that came from my mother's hand. There was no return address, nothing but her name and postmark to tell me she existed. I didn't know what to do first. I wanted to call Dad and confront him. I wanted to rifle through his chest drawers to see if he kept any more letters or cards from me. But my hands trembled, I felt furious and happy, excited and fearful, and I needed to lie down. Dad would return home in a few hours, and when he did, I wanted to be ready for him.

I had almost fallen asleep when I heard Dad throw down his car keys. For one brief moment I had forgotten about the card. But it lay next to me and I soon felt overwhelmed by the same flush of emotions I experienced earlier. Dad stopped at my bedroom, a huge grin on his face.

"Either Mrs. Morrison is back or you worked your tail off. . . . "

He expected a laugh or a few self-congratulatory words, but I remained silent. My somber look erased his grin.

" . . . What's up?"

He walked into my room and waited for my response. My anger choked out any response.

" . . . . Somethin's the matter. You might as well fess up."

I showed him the postcard. He looked at it, his face becoming ashen. He spoke barely above a whisper.

" . . . . I knew it would catch up with me . . . . I guess I kinda wanted you to find it."

I looked at him, not sure I understood.

"You wanted me to find it? Then why didn't you just tell me when I was little?"

"I wasn't sure you'd understand then . . . "

"But now . . . Why couldn't you tell me now?"

He started to speak, then stopped. A few seconds later he spoke again.

"I was planning to . . . . I was . . . . really . . . . "

We both knew he lied. Only my excitement in knowing my mother was alive could keep me from dwelling on how much I hated him at that moment.

"Where is she?!"

He pointed to the card.

"That's the last I heard of her . . . . Who knows where she is now?"

Something must have possessed me, because I started punching him and screaming.

"You're a liar! . . . . You're a fucking liar!"

A Drowning In Swanson Lake   125

He restrained my hands until I grew too tired to resist. I closed my eyes, expecting a smack across my face. But none came, and tears poured from my eyes. Dad pulled me towards him and hugged me.

"That's okay, son. I know you didn't mean it."

I did mean it and I wanted to tell him that. But I wanted something more, and I didn't want to jeopardize my chance of getting it.

"Tell me where she lives . . . . Please, Dad . . . . "

He walked away as though ignoring me, then turned around.

"I only know where she lived when she sent that card . . . . I'll have to dig it up."

Dad's sense of future was limitless.

"Do it now . . . . please."

He looked at me and sighed.

"Okay. I owe you that at least."

He went into his bedroom and emptied the bottom bureau drawer onto his bed. There were papers of all sizes, with various scribblings, and paper clips, old chewing gum, and an assortment of screws and nuts. He looked at twenty pieces of paper before staring at one in particular. He handed it to me.

" . . . . I can't stop you but . . . . "

I smiled when I saw the address.

"She's right here, Dad . . . . in New York."

"It's still a good seventy miles."

That seemed just around the corner.

"I wanna see her."

"I know you do . . . . but I'm not sure that's such a good idea right now."

"She's my mother! I can see her if I want!"

"I'm not sayin' you shouldn't see her . . . . one day. But there's a lot you won't understand . . . . "

"I will, too, and you can't keep me from her anymore."

"I know that . . . . "

I was prepared to hitchhike, sneak onto a train, or walk if I had to.

" . . . . I'll have to call first . . . . "

"No, don't. I wanna surprise her!"

"I don't know if she still lives there."

"Then ask the operator."

Dad paused before looking at me.

"She has a new life . . . "

I grew excited.

"Do I have brothers and sisters?"

He ignored my question, seeming to ponder something else. Then he looked at me again and spoke in a very soft voice.

"She left us, Hal . . . . and she wants to forget us."

"No, you're lying."

"You read the card . . . . "

I didn't care if I hurt him.

"She doesn't want *you*."

"She's never tried to contact you . . . . "

"You're just sayin' that to keep me from her . . . . if I didn't find that card . . .

"I wanted you to know one day . . . . I wanted you to find that card . . . . "

"I don't believe you."

"I know it hurts to hear this but it'll hurt a lot worse if you contact her."

"I don't care."

Nothing Dad said could have kept me from seeing my mother. His words would be suspect, not only because of his earlier lies, but because his anger and hurt over her departure likely colored everything he thought and said pertaining to her. Dad picked up the postcard and made one last appeal.

"For years after she left, I kept hoping she would change her mind, believing she would someday come to recognize all she left behind that was so good . . . . until I finally stopped waiting. This card finally woke me up . . . . And whenever I slip and begin to miss her, I just read and reread this card . . . . It's like smelling salts . . . . and I remember where I am . . . . "

Dad seemed embarrassed at his confession, staring down at

the floor. I felt confident I could do what he could not, and it would take only one visit to convince her to return. A few moments later he looked up at me.

" . . . . Maybe you are ready for that . . . . I don't know . . . I don't know."

I only heard the first part of what Dad said and accepted it as his blessing for the mission I would soon undertake. In fact, he helped me prepare for it, taking me to Brewman to shop for a present to bring her.

" . . . . She always had the sweet tooth, especially for those *Whitman Samplers* . . . . "

I worried she might be as huge as Dottie Ketchum. However, I drew comfort from an old photograph Dad found. She was thin and pretty, prettier than her name, although not quite as pretty as Macy Magnusson.

" . . . . Of course there's no tellin' what she looks like now. Women tend to balloon out after awhile."

Dad's words prepared me once again for a Dottie Ketchum. I tried erasing that image and anything else that might make my mother less than perfect. Soon I no longer had to try, convinced thoroughly of her perfection. I could now begin working on convincing her of mine.

In the next week I gathered my life's achievements to show my mother, just in case she asked. I packed all my A and A+ book reports, my *Red Cross* certificate for safe swimming, a picture of Opal, and my two best report cards. The operator had confirmed the address, and Dad purchased my *Greyhound* tickets. When that day arrived early one Saturday morning, I felt too nervous to speak. Dad understood my silence, asking or telling me things that only required a nod or shake of the head. The bus stood waiting when we finally arrived at Brewman's gas station/bus depot. Dad then kissed me on the cheek, something he had never done, before stuffing some money into my pocket. He whispered.

"There's thirty dollars . . . . just in case . . . . "

Dad always gave me "just in case" money, preparing me for emergencies that never occurred.

" . . . . And you have your ticket? . . . . "

I nodded. I knew that would not satisfy him, so I took it out.

" . . . . it's round trip so make sure he gives it back."

I nodded again. When the bus door hissed open, I hurried to take my seat behind the driver. I not only wanted to look out his massive window and see every tree, hill, and house on the way to my mother's town, I felt better knowing I sat right behind the person who would make sure I did not miss my stop. I gave Dad one final wave as we began to pull out, and he waited at his car until I could no longer see him.

During the nearly two hour ride, despite my intentions, I saw very little of the forests, mountains, and lakes of upstate New York. Instead, my sight turned inward as my mind played with all the possible reactions from my mother. They included everything from outright disappointment over the way I looked, to exhilaration over finally seeing me. I imagined all the questions we would ask each other in trying to catch up for the past eight years. I wondered whether Mom would like me well enough to forgive Dad, for whatever he did, and return home. I soon grew increasingly nervous speculating on the infinite possibilities arising from our reunion. I tried to calm myself by not getting too ahead in my plans, choosing instead to begin with the basics and take each step slowly and surely. I thought about the taxi I needed to take, the one Dad arranged to meet me, and I looked at the address Dad told me to give the driver. When I looked up, I saw a sign to Meadow Brook, a town of thirty thousand in the Adirondacks, and I knew I was less than twenty minutes from Mom's front door. I then began to panic over possibilities I had not considered. In my insistence on surprising her, I would not let Dad call her. Now I feared she might not be home, or worse yet, she might be away on vacation. The bus approached the Meadow Brook depot and I debated between taking the next bus back, or getting off and taking my chances at my mother's front door. I decided I would take the taxi and have him wait, just in case. But when I stepped off the bus, I heard my name. I turned to see a woman who looked older than in Dad's photograph, but who was unmistakably my mother.

A DROWNING IN SWANSON LAKE   129

If Dad infuriated me for ruining my surprise, that feeling evaporated almost immediately and gave way to relief and gratitude in seeing my mother.

"Let me get a good look at you . . . . "

She circled me as though I was a car she considered buying.

" . . . Handsome don't do you justice. You're a heartbreaker, yes you are."

I liked her lies. I also liked her reassuring smile and the kiss she gave me on my forehead. I searched her face for any irritation or disappointment in me being there, and finding none, I followed her cheerfully to her car. We did not say much along the way and I attributed that to our nervousness. She smelled of cinnamon and apricots and I took deep breaths to breathe in as much of her as I could. We rode up and down tree-lined streets and I stared at the white wooden homes with wrap around porches, trying to imagine the lives inside.

"I think you're going to be disappointed."

I looked at her and was about to ask what she meant, when we pulled into the driveway of a dilapidated white bungalow half the size of the house Dad and I had.

"It's bigger than our house."

"It is?"

She seemed pleased. Mom waited for me to grab my bag of belongings and we proceeded to the front door. But before either of us could turn the knob, the door appeared to open magically. Then a dark haired woman, a little taller than my mother, emerged from behind it.

"I heard you pull up."

Wearing a housedress imprinted with pink butterflies and fluffy blue flowers, her pink lips and blue eyelids continued a color scheme that even extended to her pink toenails. I couldn't imagine Mrs. Morrison cleaning our house in that dress or with that much makeup.

"Hal, this is Margie."

"Harriet. You didn't tell me he was such a looker."

Never having heard that expression, I assumed I had stared

too long at her. I felt obligated to apologize for my rudeness. I also welcomed an opportunity to impress Mom with my display of good manners.

"I'm sorry.... I didn't mean it."

Mom and Margie looked at each other, and then burst out laughing. I pretended to understand the joke, smiling feebly.

".... Oh, he's precious, Harriet."

"That can't surprise you."

Mom smiled at me.

".... Now you're probably wonderin' if I'm gonna make you stand in the doorway all day.... "

She then ushered me quickly into the living room, a neatly furnished area that continued still further the theme of Margie's dress. Although the fabric was not as shiny, butterflies and flowers suffocated the couch and chairs. The couch cushions were so soft that when I sat down, I expected to be swallowed and forever made part of that freak display of nature. Margie sat on one of the chairs while Mom continued standing.

".... Can I get you something? A *Coke*? A sandwich?"

I shook my head. I wanted both, but I didn't want her to leave the room. I couldn't understand why Margie sat there while Mom continued standing. I wanted and expected her to leave, and waited for her to do so. Then it occurred to me that Mom planned to take me somewhere, just the two of us. I looked at her and hoped my eager expression would speed her invitation.

"... Hal.... "

I stood up, ready to follow her.

"... No, no.... you sit and relax. I have to get going... "

Her words scalded.

"... Your daddy called too late for me to change my hours. The beauty parlor is a madhouse on Saturdays and they wouldn't let me off.... except to pick you up. But I'll come home early if it lets up. Promise. And with all the extra tip money I'll make today, I'll take us out to dinner.... "

I knew her "us" included Margie, especially when she made no attempt to leave after Mom picked up her car keys and pocketbook.

I did not need a babysitter, and I did not want Margie joining us for dinner. Although I soon realized she didn't work for Mom, I felt no obligation to entertain or be entertained by one of her neighbors-even if she was Mom's friend. I just wanted Margie to go home and leave Mom and me alone. My face must have said that and more.

" . . . . I know you're disappointed . . . . "

"I'm okay . . . . "

My emotions stepped aside long enough for an idea to emerge.

" . . . . Can I come with you?"

It seemed to be the perfect solution, although Mom appeared uncomfortable with it.

"Why would you wanna hang around a bunch of gossiping old ladies while I fuss with their hair? I won't be able to talk with you . . . . You'll just be bored silly."

"No I won't. I can watch you."

"Watch me? . . . "

She laughed.

" . . . . I'm a blur on Saturdays, moving so fast I don't even stop to . . . . take a coffee break . . . No, honey, you stay here. I want you and Margie to get to know each other . . . and I'll be back before you know it."

I looked at Margie, who smiled before speaking.

"We can play *Parcheesi* or watch football. I love football."

I was outnumbered. I resigned myself to an afternoon of Margie and football when I remembered the gift I brought Mom. If my words could not persuade her to take me with her, maybe the chocolates would. I pulled out the *Whitman Sampler* box and handed it to her.

"Aren't you a honey . . . . these are my favorites . . . . "

I stood there beaming, waiting for her to now invite me.

" . . . . Whaddya say we open this as soon as I get back? It'll give us something to live for . . . . "

Mom looked at her watch.

" . . . . I gotta get back. See you in a bit."

Even as I watched her leave, I still expected her to turn around and invite me. She didn't, and I spent the next five hours watching *Notre Dame* defeat *Penn State* in football, and Margie defeat me in *Parcheesi.*

I barely recall the few meaningless comments we exchanged. Not only was I reluctant to share anything Mom could not hear firsthand, I had no interest in anything Margie said. My monosyllabic responses left gaping periods of silence, allowing me to hear an imaginary clock ticking away and chipping away the moments until Mom returned. The sound of a closing car door made time real again, Mom entering the house at six o'clock.

"A good day?"

"Everyone took a shampoo . . . . lots of good tips . . . . "

Mom slapped her hands together.

" . . . . So . . . You two famished yet?"

I was. I had been eyeing the box of chocolates since she left.

"I'd guess you have a couple of customers . . . . "

"Whaddya say, Hal? Is Margie right?"

I nodded. My tongue had not yet shifted from the silence mode.

"Then what are we waiting for?"

I didn't know if that was the signal to open the chocolates or go eat. I mimicked Margie, standing up when she did, and then following her to the car. We soon arrived at the *Acropolis*, a diner serving everything from Greek food to hamburgers and fries. When Mom sat next to me, I began immediately to like everything about it. The menu reminded me of Ronnie's, the choices ranging from the exotic to the mundane. I never had Greek food and felt too embarrassed to ask what feta and baklava and a host of other dishes ending in "aki" were. I soon became distracted by a glass case rotating mile high cakes and pies. They made Mr. Maxwell's seem like cupcakes.

"You'll have to eat your dinner first."

Mom smiled. Her motherly words, the first ones I ever heard her say, saddened me. But I returned her smile.

"I already have one picked out."

The apple pie looked as though it contained an entire orchard.

"Everything here is wonderful. This is our favorite restaurant."

A Drowning In Swanson Lake

"Me, too."

She and Margie laughed at my comment, although I didn't know why. The desserts alone earned the restaurant my unquestioning loyalty. I looked again at the menu, hoping a second reading would make more sense. Even the appetizers were in hieroglyphics. Mom spoke.

"Do you like lamb? That's their specialty."

I had never tasted it.

"Yes."

"There's lots to choose from."

I ordered a lamb dish Mom suggested and we all waited for our food to be served. I looked around the diner, uncomfortable with the silence at the table. Then Mom spoke.

" . . . . I bet you have a girlfriend."

I suspected Dad told her. I nodded.

"Her name is Opal."

"What a pretty name . . . . But only one? . . . "

My confused look told her she needed to explain more.

" . . . . Only one girlfriend? I would think a handsome boy like you would have two or three at least."

She looked at Margie for confirmation, who nodded her agreement. I didn't want to disappoint her, but I also didn't want to lie about Opal.

"Only Opal . . . "

And then, as though to justify her as my sole choice, I blurted out something that turned my face red even as I said it.

" . . . . I'm going to marry her."

It seemed like a silly thing to say, although Mom and Margie smiled and took my words seriously.

"It's good to know your own mind and what you want . . . . that shows you're real grownup . . . . "

I liked Mom calling me that. She leaned back in her seat and I waited for her to ask me more about Opal. But she only looked at Margie, saying nothing. Believing she waited for me to tell her more about Opal, I debated what next to say. However, just as my lips molded the first word, Mom spoke.

" . . . Margie is an *Avon* lady . . . "

I waited for the punch line. I couldn't believe Mom thought I actually wanted to know about her. But apparently she did.

" . . . . the first time she came to my house and sold me, barely sold me, one lipstick. She spends an hour showing me her entire case of cosmetics and I buy one measly lipstick . . . "

She looked to me for a reaction. I said what I thought.

"You don't need makeup. You're pretty like you are."

"Aren't you the sweet talker? . . . "

And then she wrapped her arm around me and squeezed hard. I felt disappointed when she let go a few seconds later.

" . . . . But every woman needs a little help. It's just I didn't have any extra money to spend on more cosmetics . . . "

She gave a short laugh.

" . . . . I felt so bad for Margie . . . . spendin' all that time for one lipstick. And then one day I came here to eat, and there she was, right over there at the counter all by her lonesome. We started talking and . . . . and that was that."

The food now arrived. Famished, I ate so fast I could have eaten cardboard for all the attention I gave to its taste. Then I ordered a slice of apple pie that kept my mouth moving for ten minutes. No one said much as we ate, except to comment on the size and taste of the portions. I wanted to stay and talk more about Opal, tell her about Ollie, but Mom had already requested the check before I half finished my dessert. I ate hurriedly and listened as she spoke.

"Have you ever gone to a drive-in movie?"

I covered my mouth.

"Uh-uh. They don't have any near me."

"Then you're in for a treat . . . . And guess what they're showing? . . . "

I shrugged. Ever since *The Ambassador* went out of business, I had no interest in knowing about the latest movies. When she mentioned Rock Hudson and Jane Wymann, I prepared myself for the ordeal ahead. I couldn't hide my reaction.

" . . . . I thought with a girl friend and all, you wouldn't mind a romantic one . . . . "

With Opal next to me, the movie would be palatable, if not outright enjoyable. Mom realized and understood.

". . . Of course. What was I thinking? You should take Opal to see it, instead of going with a couple of old fogies like us . . . . "

I couldn't be sure Mom had prepared an alternate activity, and I feared she just might drive home and go to sleep. Determined not to let the evening end, I rescinded my objection.

"No, I wanna go. We don't have a movie near us anymore . . . . and I always wanted to see a drive-in."

"You could duck down during the luvvy duvvy scenes."

I ignored Margie's comment.

"Then we better hurry. It starts in twenty minutes."

We rushed off to the drive-in and found our place among the hundred or so other cars. The movie had not yet started and the screen enticed viewers to buy their popcorn or soft drinks. None of us felt hungry and we just leaned back against the seats and waited for the movie to begin. Mom suggested I take the back seat in case I grew tired of the movie and wanted to stretch out. I felt tired and welcomed the chance to sleep if the movie became too romantic. However, although the movie bored me, I became restless rather than sleepy. I squirmed and looked around at the other cars and the people inside. When this also bored me, I decided to give the movie another chance. I moved forward so my chin rested on the top of the front seat. Mom and Margie were engrossed in the kissing scene now on the screen. As I looked down to avoid seeing it, I saw something far more embarrassing. Mom and Margie were holding hands. I leaned back in my seat, not sure what to make of it. On *American Bandstand,* girls often held hands when they danced together. Dad considered that okay, although he never explained why. But this seemed different. I leaned back in my seat, afraid I saw something I shouldn't have, and soon fell asleep.

When we arrived back at Mom's, she had to lead me to the couch and my bed for the night. I felt so groggy I barely heard her wish me "pleasant dreams". Only when I awoke the next morning, did I begin to understand what had so confused me just a few hours before.

When the sunlight spilled across my face and I realized where I was, I became too excited to sleep any longer. Only six thirty, I hoped Mom was an early riser who awoke as hungry as I always did. I also hoped she liked going out to breakfast, something I enjoyed doing with Dad whenever we went into Brewman. I felt tempted to drop something accidentally, something that would wake her and get our day going. But I decided to remain patient. I turned down the volume and watched *Mighty Mouse* and *Heckle and Jekyl* cartoons. However, after a couple of hours my hunger pangs became intrusive. In the kitchen I found a package of chocolate *Mallomars* and a bag of potato chips, eating just enough to hold me until breakfast. When another hour passed and Mom's door still remained closed, I grew frustrated and increasingly annoyed. Not knowing what to do, I reviewed the papers I brought to impress Mom, organizing them for maximum impact. With that done, I returned to the couch and closed my eyes. I knew a short nap would help me endure the wait. However, when the smell of coffee awakened me, I saw it was almost noon. My bus would be leaving in three hours. Mom stood before me in her bathrobe, her face creased from sleep.

"I slept way too much . . . . Did you get yourself something to eat? . . . . "

Her question remained unanswered because just then Margie walked out from Mom's bedroom. I had only seen one bed. I thought back to the previous night when they held hands and I understood they were more than just friends. When Dad told Doc he heard Ronnie Dawes once had a girlfriend, he used the words "butch" and "dyke". I had guessed that to mean the female equivalent of "sissy". As I looked at Mom, I knew she too had become a "sissy". I wondered if that was what Dad meant when he said she had a new life. My thoughts continued spinning, and only Mom's voice brought them to a standstill.

" . . . . Would you like to eat?"

I nodded. When Mom and Margie went to their bedroom to dress, feelings of anger and disappointed began to overwhelm me. At first I assumed they had to do with Mom's relationship with

Margie, and the realization she would never return to Dad and me. However, I soon understood those feelings arose from something far more immediate. I felt more anger towards Mom for sleeping late, than I did for sleeping with Margie.

We went to eat at *The Palace Gardens* Chinese restaurant. Although starving, I resolved not to eat too much or enjoy what I did eat. I wanted to punish Mom. I expected her to become upset and concerned, not enjoying her meal until she pried and discovered the causes for my behavior. But even my one-word responses failed to elicit more than "aren't you the quiet one today?". Not getting much of a response from me, Margie and Mom chatted on about the previous night's movie, the local baseball team, and a host of other topics I couldn't care less about. I decided I would not show her my awards, even if she begged me. By the time we finished lunch, I was seething. It was also time to take me to the bus stop. When Mom and Margie hugged me, I stiffened like a wooden Indian.

"Tell your daddy he's done a fine job . . . . You're a real gentleman. Isn't he, Margie? Isn't he a gentleman?"

"He sure is."

They both seemed uncomfortable with their smiles. I cared little that nothing was said about another visit. When Mom tried to kiss me, I pulled away and took my seat on the bus. As we started to roll out from the depot, I refused to look at them. I didn't want to see them waving and I didn't want to wave. I reached into my shirt pocket and took out the photograph of me and Dad that I planned to give Mom. I put it with the rest of the papers I brought. I closed my eyes and tried not to think about anything, and I succeeded until the bus pulled into Brewman and I saw Dad's car. As I stepped off the bus, Dad approached me as though I had dynamite strapped to my chest. He tried to read my face.

"Did it go okay?"

I nodded. But as with the drive to the depot a day earlier, Dad sensed I didn't want to speak and asked me nothing else. The ride home seemed endless. I didn't know what I would tell him. I tried to piece it all together, the words, the gestures, and it all remained as pieces. What was not logical to my mind, became so to my heart. I knew Mom had chosen a life I would never understand. I also understood I would never be even a small part of it. I had become an intrusion, and the realization felt like a kick to my insides. I tried again to block it out, reading the advertising billboards that we passed. *Texaco's "Always trust your car to the man who wears the star", and Brylcream's "A little dab'll do ya",* echoed through my head and drove out all other thoughts. When we arrived home I walked quickly into the house, still not knowing what my first words to Dad would be. When he caught up with me in the kitchen, I wanted to run to my room. But when we looked at each other, I ran instead to him, hugging him with all my strength. His arms enveloped me. Although we said nothing, I could feel his body trembling and I knew he too was crying. I squeezed him and I wouldn't let go until my arms hurt and became numb, finally dropping to my side. Relief swept over me with the realization I was home now. We were too exhausted to speak, but Dad and I knew I would never leave again.

12

The crocuses, daffodils, and forsythia erupted in a yellow splendor that heralded the approach of spring. Those first few days always made me lightheaded as it transported me into another, more hopeful, time. With the lavenders and pinks and greens, the landscape began to slowly fill in like in some large pastel coloring book, and the world seemed no more complicated than whether one described the sun as lemon, or goldenrod, yellow.

Already late in meeting Opal, I ran until I became too breathless to swallow. I rested on my knees and grabbed for air, my mouth opening and closing like a frog attempting to catch an elusive fly. I felt dizzy, and I prepared myself to collapse or die. Neither possibility upset me. In fact, I took comfort in knowing Opal's grief over my death or near death would excuse my lateness and anything else I had done to offend her. But the spasms in my chest began to subside, my throat muscles relaxed, and my recovery left me without an excuse to give Opal.

I had stayed to hear Doc and Stan argue whether Casey Stengel was a better baseball manager than Leo Durocher. They resolved nothing, as usual, and instead of acquiring new insights into the game of baseball, I received another lesson in time wasting. Recognizing I lacked an acceptable excuse for my lateness, I would bring Opal a peace offering, of sorts. I surveyed the grass around me for anything of color, any flower that seemed worthy of her. But the explosions of color I passed a mile back disappeared as I approached the brown and brittle vines near the shed. The vineyard held no promise of finding anything but weeds. So I scooped up the most attractive bunch of dandelions, hoping Opal would accept them as roses. I then ran with my bouquet like a runner carrying the Olympic torch, both of us on a quest for recognition, admiration, and more.

When I reached the shed, I saw Opal pacing furiously. I didn't know whether to hand her the weeds or run. I took my chances.

"I'm sorry, Ope."

She looked at me and then away. I considered whether to repeat my apology or just keep quiet while she prepared to yell at me. But, to my relief, her anger was not directed at me.

"They make me so mad I could scream . . . . "

I didn't know whom she meant. I guessed Ollie and her father, but I guessed wrong.

" . . . . I don't know who's worse, gramps or nana . . . . "

Then I remembered that each year at this time, Ellis and Loretta Magnusson drove down from their home in Schenectady to spend a few days in New York City. On their way back they always visited their grandchildren. Opal hated their visits because they had little to say, especially to her mother.

" . . . . They still blame her for Ollie . . . . and now they resent what she's become . . . . It ain't Ma's fault she's like she is."

I spoke too quickly.

"Whose fault is it?"

Opal became angry.

"It's no one's fault! Things just happen sometimes."

I wanted to smack my head and knock out any other stupid remarks. I knew people just changed sometimes, and for no reason anyone could explain. Dad said my own mother changed suddenly and I knew that happened to Macy Magnusson. I understood her mother no longer spoke to anyone, only sitting and staring at nothing in particular. I tempered my curiosity with diplomacy in phrasing my sentence.

"Don't they even wanna tell her stuff or ask her anything?"

"Oh, sure. They'll ask her where she keeps a certain pan or tell her to go and rest when they begin feelin' uncomfortable around her. But that's all they say . . . . They treat her like a vegetable and she's not a vegetable. She can do lots of things . . . . It just takes her longer."

I knew Opal's love for her mother distorted the picture. Ollie often talked about his mother just "sitting at the window like she was waitin' for someone that never came". And I knew it was this love that now inspired the hate for her grandparents.

" . . . . I don't know why they even come . . . except to irritate Dad and make Ma even sadder . . . . they're so thoughtless . . . . I hate when they come."

I nodded or shook my head, not willing to say anything that might upset her. I realized I still held the weed bouquet, which I dropped as we walked. I didn't care that our afternoon would not be the serene, romantic one I expected. I just felt grateful Opal was not angry with me.

13

One place in town you avoided, if at all possible, was the toilet at the back of Stan's grocery.

"It's like taking a trip to the Third World, maybe the Fourth, if such a thing existed. Even the germs got germs in that stink hole."

If that wasn't enough to discourage me, Dad added,

" . . . . I'd rather they strap me into a diaper than risk getting my butt sucked down into that *Venus Flytrap*."

But although his descriptions aroused my curiosity, I resisted the temptation to enter a place "darker than hell . . . . and colder". I heard him complain to Stan.

" . . . . You can't even spring for a light bulb and a pane of glass?"

"It's a toilet, not a lounge."

Stan repeated this mantra each time someone criticized it. He only varied his response once, the time Doc became its prisoner.

Doc had always struggled to hoist himself up from a toilet unusually low to the ground, his weight contributing a large part to the difficulty. On one particular morning he became so absorbed in a magazine, his legs and feet grew too numb to move. After hearing Doc's cries for help, Stan, with the help of Dad, succeeded in raising him up long enough for him to regain the feeling in his legs. Once free, Doc vented his outrage with a steady stream of curses that left him breathless. Stan used the opportunity to respond.

". . . . It's a toilet, not a La-Z-Boy."

"A toilet bowl doesn't rest two inches off the floor!"

"Are we not exaggeratin' just a wee bit? . . . . Besides, whaddya expect when you sit over an hour?"

"You think I wanna sit on that thing any longer than I have to? I could have passed a baby sooner . . . "

"Do we really need to hear about your bowel problems?"

"You do if you say I stayed there by choice . . . . I'll never again use that foul, gurgling instrument of Satanic torture."

Stan shrugged.

"It's your plumbing."

Doc kept his word, periodically rushing off as though summoned to a medical emergency.

"I'm in motion! . . . Clear the gangway!"

Then he would race off to Ronnie Dawes's restroom, moving faster than I thought him capable. He sometimes reminded me of a participant in a roller derby, maneuvering skillfully around people, but always ready and willing to knock over anyone that slowed him down.

If I thought I could go through life without ever having to see, let alone confront, this black hole in Stan's bizarre universe, I was naively mistaken. I should have realized time and one of Dad's meat loaves would eventually catch up with me. It happened one bitterly cold January day on the school bus back to town. The insurrection in my digestive tract grew into a full-scale riot halfway into the trip. Richter scale size rumblings prompted my classmates to look around for the lion or elephant. I looked with them, hoping my participation would eliminate me as a suspect. But my body would have accepted a new liver sooner than Dad's meat loaf, an ever-changing blend of meat and leftovers according to his whim, and my classmates soon pinpointed the source of the roar. They scattered, expecting the human time bomb to explode any second.

Even Opal and Ollie abandoned me. I could not blame anyone nor could I provide any assurance. My face flushed hot and cold, pink and white, as the stomach pains came and went repeatedly. I knew God had become angry with me for reneging on my promise not to swear. However, with each painful thrust, I couldn't help but utter another "goddamn", thus perpetuating my torment. As the churning, rumblings, and roars continued and escalated, I realized I would never reach home in time. The realization terrified me. I could either use the toilet at Ronnie's, whose acoustics guaranteed an unappreciative audience for my performance, or Stan's house of horrors. Both provided enough indignity to make the experience memorable. Since Ronnie's had no back door from which to escape, I opted for the privacy and relative anonymity at Stan's. My shirt became soaked with sweat by the time the bus reached town. I ran from it, hearing applause and catcalls. I had not considered the toilet might be occupied, but my fears were unfounded as I shot past Doc and Stan and locked the door behind me.

The horror stories, and the reputation earned from them, did not do justice to the toilet I occupied that afternoon. Dad's descriptions almost seemed like endorsements compared to what he could have said. I felt both unprepared for, and intimidated by, the environment that assaulted my senses. Before I could loosen my pants, I felt weak from a choking mixture of urine and cesspool overflow. Even cold air coming through a broken vent window could do little to restrain a stench obviously more powerful than the forces of nature. I attempted to will my body back into a normalcy that would allow me to leave and go home. Suddenly, like the magician able to bend spoons with his mind, the indigestion disappeared. I waited to see if I had indeed performed a miracle, or I needed to stay and prepare for another attack. I stood, my scarf covering my nose, and looked around. My eyes now had adjusted somewhat to the darkness, and I could see a bit more of the devastation before me. Pieces of toilet paper soaked and drifted in small puddles of dirty stagnant water, reminding me of Ronnie Dawes's onion soup. Germ festering puddings of

A DROWNING IN SWANSON LAKE   145

gray green slime covered the blackened sink and the floor area
beneath it. An old rusted can of pine scented *Florient* lay in the
corner, having succumbed years ago to the hopeless mission assigned
to it. The more fortunate cockroaches had already contributed their
crushed carcasses to creating the wall's nauseating decoupage. I
looked down into the infamous toilet bowl and saw a blackness
seeming to go to the center of the earth. When jiggling the handle
failed to produce water, I became convinced the toilet bowl was a
clever disguise for something even more evil and dangerous than
the *Venus Flytrap* Dad referred to. I didn't want to sit on it. I feared
some terror from the deep would reach up, grab me, and pull me
through to its world. I felt scared being on the wrong side of this
locked door, and I hurried to leave. However, by the time I tiptoed
around the puddles and buckled my pants, the pains returned
with renewed vigor. I had no choice but to squat down, close my
eyes, and think of baseball and anything else that might calm me.
But a slow, steady drip from the faucet soon intruded, reminding
me of footsteps, and re-igniting my fears. Seeing no soap and
getting no more than a trickle of tap water, I moved quickly to
unlock the door and leave. I stepped on, what I believed to be, a
wad of toilet paper. Then I heard a loud pop that sounded like a
busted balloon. When I opened the door and light flooded the
room, I saw something that went light years beyond the revulsion
I had so far experienced. At my feet lay small clumps of brown and
gray strands that resembled the lo mein Dad once ate in a Chinese
restaurant. Some of it stuck to my shoes. When I stepped away, I
saw the charcoal gray casing of a mouse. The skin lay as flat as a
tanned pelt. It took me a few seconds to comprehend what had
occurred, and a few more for the disgust to fully seep in. One foot
had inadvertently caught the mouse's tail, pinning it, while I
stepped down with my full weight on its body. The mouse
exploded with the impact, making the popping sound I heard. I
carefully sidestepped its entrails, then ran out of the store, passing
Stan and Doc as before. Running to a toilet made sense, but running
from it had to confuse them. I feared Stan would go back there, see

the mess, and make me come back to clean it up. I was still running when Opal caught up to me. She had been waiting outside.

"You're as white as flour."

I resisted the temptation to tell her the gross details.

"Don't ever use that toilet. It's something out of a scary movie . . . "

She laughed.

" . . . . I mean it, Opal. I'll never go back, no matter what."

When I arrived home, I went straight to the refrigerator and the source of my misery. I stared at the meat loaf, trying to get a clue to its obvious destructive power. Just then Dad walked in and saw what I was studying.

"Not one of my finer efforts. Too much *Tabasco*. But it seems to have preserved it pretty good . . . . "

"Preserved" was not a word I wanted to hear. Dad then looked at me.

" . . . . You're not planning to eat that . . . . "

I felt too embarrassed and afraid to admit I already had. I waited for his reason.

" . . . Hell, I thought we threw that out two weeks ago . . . . "

I said nothing and began to scrape the meatloaf into the garbage. I half expected the plate itself to decompose.

" . . . Let's get that outa the house before it attacks. And you betta keep the lid tight on the trash bins. We don't wanna poison any nosy raccoons."

He laughed, but I couldn't be angry with him. Dad and I never looked beyond the first six inches of any shelf in the refrigerator. Once food went beyond that point, it just stayed there, untouched, until the odor caught our attention and the unrecognizable green, hairy lump was discarded. I should have known better than to risk eating anything from that wasteland, especially a meatloaf showered with enough spices to mask the critical warning signs.

Part of me wanted to tell Dad about my struggle for survival in Stan's abyss, although I knew what his reaction would be.

"Sure you heard enough about what to expect . . . . But you had to go and see for yourself . . . "

Then he would shake his head, frustrated at my failure to heed his advice.

I began to set the table for dinner. I soon heard snoring coming from the living room and knew there would be no rush to eat. I used the time to search the refrigerator. With renewed awareness, I moved and removed any suspicious food. The job went smoothly until I came upon a bowl of leftover spaghetti and meat sauce. My thoughts then returned to the toilet and the mess on the floor. I decided I would not return to the grocery until Dad had a chance to go there and hear if Stan made the discovery. When nothing out of the ordinary was said, I returned to the store as though nothing happened. Either no one used the toilet, or the darkness and filth concealed the evidence. But seven years later, that scene would haunt me as I watched television coverage of the Viet Nam War, and saw the explosions that blew bodies and body parts a hundred yards. I would have run away from that, too, had Dad not secured a position on the local draft board.

14

When Stan hired Ollie, at Doc's insistence, to work part-time in his store, most everyone deemed it an act of charity. As the details became known, all agreed the charitable one was Ollie. Since he had not yet reached the legal age to work, Stan paid him "off the books". Then he answered one illegality with another and paid him far less than the seventy-five cents an hour minimum wage. In fact, Stan ended up paying him nothing. Ollie's penchant for *Twinkies* and cream filled cupcakes bartered away the wages he earned. When his shift ended, he handed Stan his accumulated stack of sticky cellophane for him to tally. It became a win-win situation for Stan, since the harder Ollie worked, the more he ate. Occasionally, Ollie even incurred a debt he had to work off the following day. If some considered this arrangement a shameful exploitation of a pitiful adolescent, Ollie would be the first to defend it. I rarely saw him happier than when he worked there, or on his way to work there.

"Stan's store is messy. I like makin' it nice and clean."

Those words constituted the backbone of Ollie's mission, and the bone on which Stan often choked. Ollie's obsession with neatness and cleanliness was a natural irritant to a man who thought nothing of dispersing his bodily discharges over food and person alike. So it's little wonder that Ollie's attempt to sanitize the grocery caused Stan great anguish. He would concede the inside glass of the deli case had become nauseatingly dirty. But he couldn't understand why Ollie had to take out the meat when he sprayed and scrubbed it.

"A little glass cleaner ain't gonna hurt nothin'. He's making too big a production of it . . . . showin' off and all."

After Ollie finished cleaning every inch of glass, he then did something that further annoyed Stan. Ollie liked order. When he bought jellybeans, he separated them by size and color, discarding the black ones as "beetle bellies" and crushing them with his shoes. He organized similarly the stones and empty bottles he found. So it came as no surprise when he found the haphazard arrangement of meats, cheeses, and salads unacceptable. In fact, it drove him to distraction until he had every meat in its rightful place, and every salad leveled off perfectly. Ollie even positioned the serving spoons exactly the same in each tray, to the right and with the scoop side down in the salad. He saw meaning in all this exactness, even if no one else did. I once asked him about it.

"The stronger meats and cheeses go up front. They're the bullies and won't stay in back anyway."

I knew better than to ask for further clarification, but as I looked at his arrangement, it scared me a little to think I actually knew what he meant. Ollie attributed different personalities to the food, and deferred to them accordingly. Therefore, it only made sense for the bold and feisty Genoa salami to lead the row, with the less spicy corned beef following, and ending with the bland, and I guessed wimpy, bologna and chicken roll. The same logic applied to the cheeses, beginning with the overpowering blue cheese and ending with the weaker Swiss and muensters. For a few moments, I entered Ollie's head. It frightened me to consider what further exposure to his thinking could mean. I began to leave when Stan approached to look at the case. He just shook his head. Then he looked at Ollie.

"You cleaned it up nice but you spent over two hours doin' it. I don't understand why every pickle has to be standing at attention. . . . "

Then Ollie volunteered the explanation he gave me. It sounded even stranger the second time. Stan looked at him a few moments before responding.

" . . . . Ollie, you're givin' me the willies. These are cold cuts you're talking about, not your friends and neighbors . . . . "

Then he turned to me.

" . . . . Am I missing somethin' here?"

I had no intention of explaining the logic in Ollie's statement. I chose self-preservation and let my friend dangle in the wind. Ollie had nothing to lose anyway. They expected him to say those kinds of things. I left Ollie to his chores, satisfied I had jeopardized neither my reputation nor my friendship. But Ollie's days at the store were numbered, and it had nothing directly to do with the strange things he said or with his painstaking attention to details. Stan made some allowance for those. However, when Ollie's honesty, a quality foreign to Stan, became a two edged sword and threatened his profits, Stan found that intolerable.

The dirty glass in the deli case had always served Stan well, and his reluctance to clean it had some practical justification. He could keep secret the discoloration in the meats or the mold on the edges of the cheeses. Stan would trim off those pieces before selling the rest, the customer none the wiser.

"You'll see. You're foolin' around with people's health . . . . One day you're gonna poison someone."

Stan would then promise not to sell such food, but he did, and Doc knew he did. However, when he hired Ollie, the secrecy ended and the promises no longer mattered. Ollie not only warned customers of the approaching expiration date, he did not hesitate to throw out the partially spoiled food Stan would have surely sold. Stan bristled whenever he heard one of Ollie's caveats and he warned him about throwing anything away without his permission. Ollie obeyed for a day or two. Then he dumped food when Stan stepped out of the store, and he resumed whispering his warnings to the customers. Business actually picked up, people knowing they could trust Ollie to sell them only fresh food. But Stan saw his profits decrease, even as he ordered substantially more meat and cheese. Convinced the cause rested with Ollie, Stan knew exactly where to begin his investigation. In the dumpster behind the grocery, he found an iridescent olive loaf and a pinkish gray liverwurst. He brought the meat back into the store, screaming at Ollie before he even saw him.

"What the hell is this?!"

"Easy on the boy."

"Go back to sleep . . . . He was your idea."

"You're a mean s.o.b. Now ease up."

Stan ignored Doc and looked behind the deli counter.

" . . . Damn it! Where the hell are you?!"

Ollie had been crouching in order to stock some of the bottom shelves. He stood up and walked over to Stan, who now held up the two loaves of meat.

" . . . . So? . . . . What is this?"

Ollie assumed it was a legitimate question. He moved closer to get a better look.

"That one's olive loaf and that's the liverwurst."

Stan's face became as red as the pimento in the loaf.

"I know what they are! What are they doing in the dumpster?"

"I threw them there. They were too shiny. And they smelled."

Stan put them to his nose.

"I don't smell anything . . . . "

I found this difficult to believe, even coming from someone so oblivious to his own odors. I almost expected Stan to rinse the meat and return it to the case, although that would have been too much, even for him.

" . . . . You have been warned for the last time, Ollie. Next time you're out! You hear me?!!"

Old man Kensel could have heard him and he had been dead for years.

"Yes, sir."

Stan stormed out, almost tripping over Doc's legs. I smiled, believing he extended them purposely.

"Don't you mind him . . . . You're doing a great job."

Doc's words energized Ollie and he returned to work. Despite what Doc said, I felt badly for him. Ollie acted honorably, and his efforts earned him Stan's ingratitude. I wanted to cheer him up.

"Hey, Oll. Wanna flip cards later?"

"Sure. After I finish back here."

"How about I buy you fellas a pair of chocolate malts . . . . I'm getting one myself."

Doc knew it was a rhetorical question and he left for Ronnie's. I watched Ollie nervously, wanting him to move away from the deli case and the source of his troubles. But until he finished, satisfied with every detail, he would not budge from that spot. Then suddenly, to my dismay, Ollie dumped a tin of potato salad into the garbage.

"Are you nuts?! After what Stan just told you?"

"There was a fly in it."

Even I could concede this might be going too far. At barbecues, Dad often just scooped out the fly and we ate the rest of the cole slaw or potato salad.

"Chinese raisins", he would say, "a little too bitter for my taste."

Ollie had not finished scraping the salad into the garbage when Stan returned. He stopped and watched Ollie, not believing what he saw.

"Tell me I'm only imagining this . . . . or that you're playin' a joke on me."

"This potato salad is no good."

"Are you serious? I just made it yesterday!"

"There was a fly in it. He was dead."

I thought I had again hooked into Ollie's thought process. I volunteered an explanation.

"Maybe he thought the salad was spoiled because it killed the fly. He thought it would poison people."

This appeared to help, reminding Stan of the limitations in Ollie's reasoning. He spoke softly.

"Is that what you thought? That people might die from my potato salad?"

Stan laughed and I assumed the worst was over. Until Ollie answered.

"I don't think the fly died from the salad . . . . "

Then he paused before continuing.

" . . . . but he probably dweedled in it before he died."

I couldn't watch the massacre about to occur. I lowered my head. Stan's voice became angry again.

"It what?!"

"Dweedled."

"Get out, you gooney bird! You're fired! . . . . "

I looked up and saw Ollie remove his apron.

" . . . . One day, I swear it. I'm gonna sell that boy for body parts."

Ollie pulled me to follow him out. He stopped at the door, took some candy wrappers from his pocket, and showed them to Stan.

"I think I owe you money."

Stan made a face. His voice softened again.

"Forget it. We're all square."

After we left I remembered our malts.

"Doc's gonna be mad at us."

"Naw. It'll be okay . . . . when he finds out what happened and all."

I then expected Ollie to say something about it. But he said nothing, staying quiet for most of the walk home. Suddenly he became excited.

"Wanna flip? You said we could."

I smiled and nodded, and. envied him for the things he never seemed to feel.

15

Stanton George had moved to Swanson Lake from Ellison, Ohio soon after his discharge from the army in 1949. His good fortune in serving between two wars did not go unnoticed. Doc ribbed him mercilessly about it, often stepping over the line that separated good-natured kidding from outright obnoxiousness.

"Too young to fight in the big one, and discharged before Korea. His stars are blessed. Yes, sir. That young man has a future and I'm buyin' shares in it."

Stan's words, "I'm buyin' shares in it", overlapped Doc's.

"Don't you ever get tired of that story?"

Doc ignored him.

"And I still wanna believe your stars are blessed, despite mucho evidence to the contrary. Tell me, why aren't we millionaires yet?"

"Because you're a good for nothin' lazy lard ass who thinks his money entitles him to act like a slave owner."

Doc thought a moment.

"Besides that."

Stan threw up his hands and sighed.

"Okay, it's me. I was lucky before, unlucky now. I know piddle about running a grocery and I'm sorry for ruining your dream."

"There. That wasn't so hard . . . . "

Stan threw a loaf of *Wonder Bread* at Doc's head. He picked it up and showed Stan its crushed shape.

" . . . . I thought I had you better trained than that . . . . dribbling away profits . . . Shame on you."

Stan grabbed the bread and reshaped it, then returned it to the shelf.

"Spare me. We might actually make a profit if it was up to me . . . . Remember, you're the one who wants to toss out perfectly good food."

Doc let out a laugh.

"Perfectly good food?! That crap had microbes piggybacking on bacteria. It was a germ *Mardi Gras*."

"I told you. You wanna pull out, I'll buy your share . . . Or do the same. I don't need the grief."

"You don't have the money, and I don't need the extra headaches. Besides, where would I go every day?"

"I've got some ideas."

Doc went over to the apple basket, examining each one until finally making his selection. He then held it up, admiring it, before taking a bite.

"Mmmmm. I hate 'em mushy . . . Fine and crisp like this. That's the way nature intended . . . . Dee-lishius . . . . "

Stan ignored him.

" . . . . Did you hear the crunch it made when I bit into it? That's the sound of a gooood apple."

"Who are ya? Andy Griffith? What's with this 'goooood' crap?"

"I just wanted to emphasize how goooood it was."

"I got the point. I'm glad you like it. Especially since I'm payin' for half of it."

"Uh-uh. Watch it."

"Oh, sorry. How could I forget? . . . . Forty per cent. That's still part mine."

"I'll leave you the core and we'll be even."

Doc laughed, catapulting pieces of half chewed apple into the uncovered box of baked goods.

"Oh, brilliant . . . . You can clean this up . . . . I ain't throwin' them out, I don't care what you say!"

Doc watched Stan slam roll after roll of coins on the counter before spilling them into the cash register. I knew he saw Doc's face in that counter.

"Cool down . . . . I'm just baiting you . . . . Gives me something to do."

"Then do it to somebody else . . . . Ya know it does no good to piss me off."

Stan kicked over a display of canned tuna, and stormed out. Doc looked in his direction, shook his head, and mumbled "hot head" as he began to restack the cans. He also took seriously his own warnings about cleanliness and threw out the donuts. Doc then pulled two dollars from his pocket and put them into the cash register.

"That should satisfy the tightwad."

Later that afternoon, Stan and Doc joked with each other as though nothing had happened. However, their peace was a fragile one, and it ended a few days later, when Doc closed the grocery.

The morning had been a typical one. Stan's whining about the expenses lulled Doc to sleep. His head had just dropped to his chest when Mrs. Webster stormed in, awakening him. She shoved a package of bologna in Stan's face.

"Go ahead. Smell it. See how long you can stand it!"

He tried not to react to the smell, although he took a few steps back.

"It was fresh when you bought it."

"I bought it yesterday. How could it spoil in one day?"

"Maybe your *Frigidaire* needs adjusting . . . . "

Doc cleared his throat, not to speak, but to caution Stan.

" . . . . But when you bought it, you woulda seen if it looked bad."

"Who can see anything through that dirty glass. I trusted you to give me something that didn't smell and look like somethin' my septic system gurgled up."

I laughed at that, although no one else seemed amused. The situation had become far too serious. Ever since Ollie's departure, the deli display glass became increasingly opaque. Doc's continued warnings about this, and about selling food after their expiration date, went unheeded. Stan dismissed his concerns as "an old lady's worries over nothing." Now Mrs. Webster waited for justice, even as Stan defended the gray clump she pushed towards him. Doc stood up and walked over to her.

"I'm terribly sorry. Stan will be happy to refund your money, and throw in a couple packages of *Snowballs* for your boy. I know he likes them . . . . "

When Stan began to protest, Doc raised his cane to within an inch of his throat.

" . . . . You can stay put. I'll give Mrs. Webster her money . . . . "

Stan stayed like an obedient dog while Doc opened the register to get her money. She thanked him, then gave Stan a dirty look, and left. I knew I had a ringside seat to a championship fight and I waited for the bell. It took about three seconds for Doc to explode.

" . . . . What in hell's name is wrong with you, man?! Do you want us to go out of business?! I could smell that dog splat from where I was sitting, and you tell her it doesn't smell?! Even your nose hairs started bailing out!"

Doc shook his head.

" . . . . Just tell me what you were thinking? I want to get inside that tiny brain and try to understand why you act the way you do. Do you think you're smarter than other people? Or do you think maybe they're as stupid as you so it don't matter? Well, guess what? No one is as stupid as you! You are the stupidest, hands down! . . . . "

I had to agree with Doc.

"Fine. You made your point. You gave her the refund so be happy. Now let's sit back and wait for everyone else to march in and demand refunds."

Doc circled him like an animal in for the kill.

"You're so tightfisted your palms stay dry in a rain. You still don't get it. You think people are just trying to scam us? You don't think they have a right to maggot free food?"

Stan gave a short laugh.

"Don't you think you're exaggerating just a bit?"

"Am I? Well let's see."

Doc walked to the deli case, slid open the glass door, and jumped back.

" . . . Mother McCree! . . . . "

He cupped his nose.

" . . . . That stench'll blind ya . . . . "

Doc then proceeded to throw out everything. When Stan moved to stop him, Doc held up a carving knife.

" . . . . Stay back! I'm warning you! . . . . "

Stan froze. Doc's eyes grew large. I felt scared, too scared to even get Dad. When he finished dumping every meat and salad into the trash, he put down the knife. His eyeballs returned to their normal size, although he still breathed heavily.

" . . . . Now. I am only going to say this once. As of this moment, the deli case is closed-"

Stan began to protest.

" . . . . You've got nothing to say! I am closing this deli case, this grocery, until everything is scrubbed and disinfected. Then we are putting in new lighting so people can see what they are buying. And what they are buying is going to be fresh, as fresh as the spit in their own mouths . . . . Is that clear?"

"Okay, big shot. And who's going to pay for all that? I certainly ain't."

"You and I are paying for it."

"You can't force me. I'm an owner, too."

"I'm not forcing you as one partner to another. But as a doctor, I am declaring this store a health hazard and—"

Stan tried to speak.

"-and will go to the proper authorities to get it shut down . . . . "

Then Doc flashed a big grin.

" . . . . Hey, guess what? I am the proper authority."

He laughed a fun house laugh. Stan waited for him to finish.

"Sure. Go ahead. Play the part of mayor again. You were so successful last time . . . with your honey business and all."

Stan emphasized a buzzing 'z' sound in 'business' to irritate Doc, but to no avail.

"This store is now officially shut down until every inch of it is cleaned, and that includes the rodent infested back area."

"You're out of your head."

"Well, you do know you've got a choice. You could lose some money, or you could go to prison for knowingly selling contaminated meat that poisons someone . . . . Which is it, my friend?"

Stan said nothing. I don't think he ever thought through the consequences of his actions. Doc's mention of "prison" caught his attention, the possibility of which unnerved him. Stan sounded like a penitent schoolboy.

"I wasn't trying to poison anyone. You know that."

"Tell that to a jury after an autopsy uncovers a lethal chunk of bologna . . . . and we might not be talking about only one casualty."

Stan's forehead and upper lip bubbled with perspiration and he went to sit in Doc's chair. He looked at Doc for a few moments, hoping he would be told it was all a joke. But Doc remained serious and Stan's body and voice appeared to shrink.

"It'll take us weeks to clean up this place."

"Hire back Ollie. You shoulda never let him go in the first place."

Stan resisted his unconditional surrender one last time.

"Fine, but if I hear one pop in this store, he's outa here."

Stan referred to another of Ollie's peculiar habits. He loved to puncture the tightly wrapped cellophane around the *Twinkies* or other small cakes, relieving them of some imagined suffering. The pop allowed them to breathe again. These liberation pops drove Stan to distraction and he prohibited Ollie from doing this-even with the packages he bought. He thought he had the problem solved when he once gave Ollie a piece of bubble wrap. After his knuckles darted across the raised portions, pressed hard to create a rapid-fire succession of pops that sounded like a machine gun, Stan proclaimed himself a genius.

" . . . I've given him, what they call, a surrogate . . . . It's a basic psychological tool."

Doc and I said nothing as Stan continued with his self-congratulations. Soon the store became silent, just long enough for

Stan to flash one of his "I told you so" grins. Then we heard the familiar popping, only louder, as Ollie began working on the cellophane stretched tightly over boxed cakes. Stan had not understood what Doc and I always had. The cakes were like the deli meats. And Ollie would no more let them suffocate than he would let the meats wallow in chaos and filth. Doc now asked the impossible in wanting me to restrain Ollie. I promised I would try.

"That means you have to hire Hal also."

Stan nodded. He reminded me of a prisoner of war, having no choice but to yield to his captors. I thought about Doc's order to clean up everything, including the rat infested back area. Since I knew I could bribe Ollie to do it, I agreed.

"Sure. I could use the money."

I mentioned that so Stan understood I, unlike Ollie, would not work for a few packages of cupcakes.

So it came to pass that the store remained closed for five days, during which time a major facelift was undertaken. Dad poked his head in periodically to give the "thumbs up" sign, not wanting to visit and disrupt the momentum. Doc ordered the inspection and removal of every can, cereal box, candy bar—anything beyond its expiration date. He even replaced the refrigeration in the deli and dairy cases. Stan suffered it all without a word. One look from Doc with his fists close together as though in handcuffs, reminded Stan of the likely alternative if he resisted. Still, Stan couldn't stifle all of his frustration and periodically emitted a muffled whine that reminded me of a whimpering dog. But we all forged ahead, even Doc, who managed ten minutes of dusting before needing to sit, stretch his legs, and read the current *Life* magazine. Stan looked at him.

"How much more readin' you plannin' to do?"

"I just started the article. I'll catch up with you."

"I'm sure . . . . "

Doc folded the pages back.

" . . . . I told you not to do that. No one wants to buy a magazine that looks read."

"Go about your work and leave me be. This article on the widow Kennedy is a good one. You want me to read it to you?"

"Just finish and help me. I want this over with."

By the fifth day, everything had been polished to "a spit shine". The counters, the glass, the canned goods, the fixtures, and even that den of putrification in the back. Ollie scrubbed that for most of a day, and when he finished, we all approached it cautiously and respectfully, mindful of the terror we knew it capable of generating. But aside from the vent window and the rotten plumbing that Stan vehemently refused to fix, the void had once again become a toilet.

"Fine work, Ollie. A work of art to be sure."

Ollie sported a proud grin and waited for Stan and me to contribute our praise.

"You're a miracle worker, Ollie."

I patted him on the back a few times. Stan began to nod.

"If I didn't see it myself, I wouldn't believe it possible. A person could drop a sandwich on the floor and not think twice about scoopin' it up and chompin' on it straight away."

Stan's remark said far more about Stan than about Ollie's accomplishment. It also left us speechless. We continued with our inspection of the store. Ollie had aligned the canned goods so perfectly that when you looked at the first one, you could not see the others behind it. Stan smiled at the transformation and began wringing his hands in anticipation.

"I can smell money. Lots and lots of it. The *A&P* will soon know we're here to stay."

Doc remained more cautious.

"Now before your bristles start to rise, remember it'll take awhile for our old customers to return. We pissed off a hell of a lot of them . . . . What's so funny?"

I was giggling over Doc's bristle reference. Stan's flat top hairstyle always reminded me of a toilet brush. They all waited.

"I . . . . I thought how funny it would be . . . . to see this store crowded."

I couldn't believe I said something so feeble. They looked at me. Stan became annoyed.

"So what's so funny about that?"

Ollie started laughing.

"I think I get it, Hal . . . . Then we couldn't make enough change . . . That's a funny one."

Stan shook his head.

"Kids . . . . "

Doc went to the dairy case to get a gallon jug of chocolate milk. Then he picked up a box of *Oreos*. He brought them up front and held each up.

"I raise this milk and these cookies in a blessing . . . . "

I looked to see if anyone bowed his head. No one did.

" . . . . may we always have enough to eat and drink. And may we prosper in our honest dealings . . . . Amen."

After we all uttered an "amen", Ollie and I drank our chocolate milk and ate our cookies with the finesse of a couple of half starved wolves at a carcass.

" . . . . Boys, boys . . . . This isn't *Beat The Clock*. No one's taking it away from you . . . . "

I felt only a little embarrassed. I looked at Ollie's chocolate covered lips, nose, and chin, and knew my face had to be a close second. Doc had not fared too much better, black crumbs coating his chin and dropping to his shirt each time he moved his lips. Only Stan's face remained unblemished. I realized he had not eaten or drunk anything. Either our table manners nauseated him, which seemed rather unlikely considering his own indelicacies, or he didn't want to have to open another bag of cookies. When I saw him nervously pick his fingers nails as we continued eating, I knew my suspicions had been correct. Doc handed me and Ollie a few more napkins before speaking.

" . . . . I propose we have a grand reopening the day after tomorrow. Balloons, free punch and cookies . . . . Whaddya say, Stan? . . . . "

Apparently, Stan's ego had not recovered fully. He nodded obediently.

" . . . . Great. You men wanna come in tomorrow and help us out? . . . . "

Although Ollie agreed quickly, I said nothing. I did not like the sound of the phrase, "help us out". Before I could mention a fictitious chore I already committed to, Doc answered my concern.

" . . . . Of course you'll both be paid the same as today."

I agreed, ignoring once again the whimpering sound I heard earlier.

The next morning Ollie and I pretended it was Christmas, and the grocery a giant tree. We looped red crepe paper around the ceiling fixtures and draped blue, white, and green streamers over shelves. When we placed a huge "Grand Reopening" sign in the window, all that remained was for me and Ollie to distribute flyers announcing the event. Doc seemed nervous. Stan looked panic stricken. Within twenty-four hours they would know whether any of what we did mattered.

When I arrived in town just before eight o'clock the following morning, I half expected to see most of the town lined up, filled with the agitated curiosity of onlookers at a movie premiere hoping to catch a glimpse of their favorite movie star. But when I turned the corner onto the main street, I saw only Stan and Doc sitting on the front steps, each looking in opposite directions for the same crowd I expected. As I approached them, it became obvious Stan's subservience had ended.

"Yessir . . . . A great success . . . . And how much did this little undertaking cost us? I'll tell you. Almost eight hundred in expenses and lost revenue!"

Doc looked at him.

"Is that all?"

Stan appeared ready to burst.

"Is that all?! . . . . Is that all?!"

He sounded like a hysterical parrot.

"I thought it was more. Seems like a small price to pay for what we got."

"What we got?! And what do we got?!"

I wanted Doc to smack him out of his annoying repetition. Doc turned to me.

"You pass out all the flyers?"

I nodded.

"Ollie and me made sure every store got a few, and anyone we passed on the street."

Doc looked disappointed. I knew he wanted something to explain away the disastrous outcome. He paused before speaking again.

"Well . . . . I said it would take awhile to get back our customers. Word'll spread . . . . but it'll take awhile . . . "

He turned to Stan.

" . . . . At least we'll be able to sleep at night . . . . and not worry about poisoning anyone."

"I slept fine. And no one got poisoned. The only one who's ill now is me."

I saw Ollie inside the store. I should have known he would come early to do his final checking and straightening. He came outside to join us.

"Hi ya, Dusty. Sleep in?"

He laughed. He had chocolate cake stuck to his teeth that made him look like a jack o' lantern. Ollie took out another cupcake from his pocket and offered it to me. I shook my head. Stan watched him stuff it into his mouth.

"Damn it, Ollie! How many is that now?"

Ollie counted on his fingers.

"Five."

"Five! Five cupcakes?!"

"Five packages."

Stan stood up and pointed to the store.

"Does that look like your kitchen? Do you see your refrigerator and kitchen table in there? . . . . "

Ollie looked at me, not sure if there was a joke attached to this. Stan didn't wait for answer.

" . . . . Do I walk into your house and help myself to any food I see?"

Ollie laughed.

"That's funny, Stan."

Stan growled.

"Leave the boy alone. He worked his tail off for us."

"So? We paid him, didn't we? Does he get free snacks on top of that?"

"They're not free, Stan. I left the money on the counter."

Doc smiled at Stan, who sat down and stared at the ground.

"Well, hell . . . . he coulda said something."

Dad emerged from his store and walked toward us. He had come early to catch up on inventory, and to witness the huge reopening day turnout I told him to expect. When he saw just the four of us, I knew his mind toyed with a joke he thought might cheer up the somber faces before him. Dad's jokes were rarely funny, even when told to people in a good mood. Now they could very likely goad Stan to uncontrollable rage. I expected the worst, but Dad just took a few steps into the grocery, looked around, and came out saying nothing. Stan spoke instead.

"Go ahead. Say something humiliating. We deserve it."

Dad looked at him.

"What's the matter with you? You guys did a great job. The place looks fantastic . . . . You should be proud of yourselves."

I liked that he included me and Ollie. Stan repeated his previous song.

"Yeah, a lot of good it's doing. Cost us a fortune and for what?"

"Give it time. You can't expect to have a mob of customers after a few days. I mean, it took you years to drive them away . . . . "

Doc chuckled. I waited for Stan to rise, exchange words with Dad, and maybe more. But when he just sat there, mumbling to himself, I knew his depression was genuine. Dad showed compassion.

" . . . . Come on, Stan. You know this is only temporary. Why wouldn't people come back now that it's all clean and bright?"

"That's what I told him, Jack. They'll soon stop going to the A&P so much . . . . They've always wanted to shop close to home, and now they've got good reason to."

Doc's words didn't have any effect on Stan. He continued looking at the ground. Dad turned to me.

"Hey, son. How about a few donuts and some milk? We'll be Stan's first customers in his new store."

We heard Stan's frail voice.

"You're too late."

Dad looked at me for an explanation.

"Ollie beat us, Dad."

Ollie stepped forward proudly when he heard his name, his face sporting a chocolate goatee.

"I was the first. Right, Stan. I was the first."

"That's what I said."

Dad tried to be funny again.

"Stan, you snake. Crying about no customers and there are three right under your nose . . . . Come on, son. Let's make our purchases."

"You can help yourself. I don't care anymore. Take the whole damn store if you want to."

Doc lashed out.

"Fine. Feel sorry for yourself . . . . You're too much of a fool to realize the good that will come from all this. You're just a shortsighted blockhead who's pouting because he didn't get his way!"

When Doc finished, Stan neither said anything nor looked at anyone. He simply walked back to his grocery.

"Maybe you were too hard on him, Doc."

"Augh! He's just a big baby, Jack. You know that."

"Well, don't forget you're friends first and last."

"It's easy to forget with the likes of him."

Dad looked toward the store. I could see Stan sitting behind the counter, just staring ahead.

"You know what, son? Let's get our milk and donuts later."

That suited me since I had eaten before I left the house. Doc looked at Dad.

"You see? He's already begun losing customers again."

"Stop it . . . . I'll be back in an hour."

Doc didn't answer. Dad returned to his store and Ollie and I went to play kick the can. The following days and weeks saw only a slight increase in business, people apparently reluctant to trust the changes. Maybe it was Stan's personality, or their anger at having been victimized so many times, but the anticipated miracle never happened. Even Doc became discouraged, and when business still failed to improve after a month, he grabbed at anything that could benefit them. That's when he insisted new promotions be undertaken. Stan stared at him as though he had just transformed himself into a giant *Hostess Snowball*. His mouth hung open for a few seconds.

"Wha . . . . Ha! Sure . . . . Why not? Your last one was so successful. I can't even keep up with the new business? . . . . In fact, why don't we look at expanding? Let's see if Jack's willing to sell us his store."

"Are you finished?"

He wasn't.

"That cleanup was the best investment we ever made . . . . "

He paused.

" . . . . Now I'm finished."

"Good . . . . I'm not talking about anything so major. I'm just referring to the next step."

"In case you haven't figured it out, the next step is bankruptcy."

"There you go again. Mister gloom and doom."

"Then say something to make me smile . . . . like this grocery rests on a bedrock of gold ore."

Doc sighed before continuing.

"I'm talking special promotions, "come ons", to get people back into the store. We lower the price of our milk, make it cheaper than the *A&P's*, sell two for one on the donuts, and maybe throw in free chips and a soda with each sandwich."

Stan laughed.

"And that's gonna bring in customers?"

"It might. It's worth trying."

"It always comes down to givin' away somethin' or reducing the price. Don't you ever have ideas to make money?"

"This is the kind of thing all the successful stores do. Let's try it for a month and see what happens."

"A month?! . . . . No way, no how."

"Then two weeks."

Stan thought a moment.

"Fine . . . . but I'm giving less meat in the sandwiches. I won't give away the store."

"Then don't make it obvious . . . . maybe a little more lettuce and an extra slice of tomato."

They both accepted the compromise and waited with renewed anticipation for the increased business.

Activity did pick up somewhat during the following week, but people bought mostly the milk and donuts, and little else. They still stayed away from the sandwiches, their reputation a horrible lingering aftertaste. Stan looked out his window like an abandoned puppy, searching for customers to rescue him.

I had just stopped in for a soda and a snack when Stan and Doc were engaged in another of their heated discussions about insignificant things. On this day their argument focused on toe flossing to alleviate itching. Doc used his medical knowledge to bolster his conviction.

"You always have to find some foreign object to do your dirty work. Did you ever hear of fingers and a wash cloth?"

"The pulley method works much better . . . . like a toe shoeshine."

"It's bad for your toes and bad for your hand and arm . . . . It's not natural . . . . too much strain. The muscles aren't made for it."

Stan laughed.

"Is that what they taught you in medical school?"

"That, and how to dissect a human being."

Doc leered at him, baring his teeth.

"I'm shaking."

I chose my soda and was about to grab some potato chips, when I heard my name.

"Hi, Dusty . . . . "

Ollie had just returned from breaking cardboard boxes in the back alley. At first I wondered why Stan would hire him with business so poor. However, when I saw Ollie munching a *Snickers*, I realized he had been rehired under the former compensation arrangement. Stan also did not have to worry about Ollie's obsession with the deli case. New lighting and refrigeration, and Doc's regular inspections, minimized the likelihood it would become a source of irritation to Stan, and an obstacle to employment for Ollie.

" . . . . Can't talk . . . . There's lots to do."

"That's okay. I'll see you later."

I took my soda and chips to the counter. Stan and Doc had concluded their toe itching discussion and moved on to an equally weighty topic.

"Olive loaf, liverwurst, head cheese, and hot dogs are your most maligned meats. They're the Richard Nixons of cold cuts."

I looked to see if Ollie had any inkling of his influence on their thinking. But the cult leader had just returned from another trip to the alley and seemed oblivious to everything else.

"Come on, Doc. You know what goes into them, especially the head cheese and hot dogs."

I liked hot dogs and wanted to hear what did go into them. But the corner of my eye caught some frantic movement, and when I turned to look, Ollie flailed about like a demented orchestra conductor. Stan and Doc also looked at the frenzy behind the deli case.

"What the hell is that boy up to? Ollie! Cut it out!"

Ollie stopped, looking cautiously around him. Then he began swinging again and ignored Stan's shouts to stop. Moving closer to him, I could see a yellow jacket circling his head. Ollie feared nothing, except yellow jackets and other flying, stinging insects. I could see the wasp move away, a safe distance from his much larger adversary. Ollie looked at it and neither one knew how next to proceed. Smart money backed the yellow jacket, which only seemed intent in getting some of the salami Ollie had begun slicing. My friend, however, his instincts for survival less developed, determined to make it a fight to the finish. Ollie stared at his opponent, waiting for it to let down its guard so he could smash it with the large serving spoon a few inches away. But before he could launch his attack, we heard a scream that seemed to echo across generations. It was Ollie who let down his guard, forgetting the electric slicer he left running. He held up his bloody hand.

"It got my thumb, Stan."

"For cryin' out loud! Get away from the meat!"

Ollie came out from around the counter where blood spurted like a small geyser. His injury had also sprayed blood on the wall behind the deli, droplets that hung like giant pomegranate seeds, before dripping onto the green and white linoleum floor. Doc stood up.

"Get it over here. Quick! . . . "

Ollie walked over to Doc, looking at his thumb as though fascinated it could bleed so much. Doc took his hand.

" . . . . You sliced the tip off . . . . Press here . . . . "

Ollie pressed the spot to slow down the bleeding. I felt relieved. I expected him to hand Doc a severed thumb. He now grabbed his black medical bag from under the counter.

" . . . . We gotta go upstairs."

I had always feared those words, not only because they meant a serious injury or sickness required immediate attention, they meant Doc's medical limitations could be stretched beyond their capabilities. However, I had always been curious about Doc's office. I vowed only to see it as a healthy spectator. Now I envied Ollie for getting to encounter the mysteries in that rarely seen room. I waited for him to return and tell me all about it. But no sooner did Ollie reach the stairs, than he turned to me.

"How come you're not comin'?"

I turned quickly to look at Doc.

"Is it okay, Doc?"

"Sure. We might need you for a transfusion . . . . "

I hated needles. I considered the high price of admission.

" . . . . Come on, come on. I'm only foolin' . . . . "

With that assurance, I ran to catch up to them and proceed up the dark and narrow stairs to Doc's office. As he turned the key, I expected the door to open into a world of flasks bubbling with exotic elixirs, their curative powers needing only to be inhaled. Large, overgrown plants and flowers, and a few animal parts such as bat wings and rat tails, would provide a steady source of natural ingredients for these medicinal brews. But when Doc pulled the light bulb chain, I knew immediately how the travelers to the *Land of Oz* must have felt when they realized the great and powerful *Wizard* was just a scared, little man. My disappointment equaled theirs as I looked at a large, mostly empty, room that reminded me of the cheap motel Dad and I once stayed in when we visited his mother. A torn plaid couch leaned against a wall, a scratched and faded coffee table in front of it. Stacks of old *Life* and *Look* magazines covered the table, and a *Philco* console television stood a few feet away. The floor had gray and pink linoleum that aspired to be tiles, and had no better chance of succeeding in that than the wood grained contact paper had in convincing anyone it was real paneling. A small kitchen area with a dirty coffee pot and a yellowed box of corn flakes completed the room's decor. The only indications this might be a doctor's office were the eye chart on the wall, a blood pressure machine, a glass cabinet with some vials and medical instruments, and a long, narrow examining table which Ollie now sat on as Doc attended to his thumb.

" . . . . Well, you haven't killed yourself yet, although it's not for lack of trying . . . . and at least you're bleeding real blood, so I know you're not one of those Martians . . . . "

Ollie laughed at the mention of Martians.

" . . . . I am right on that, aren't I? Or maybe you are some outer space creature in disguise."

Ollie became serious.

"Tell him, Hal. Tell him I ain't a Martian."

"He's okay, Doc. He's not one of them."

"Well, if Hal vouches for you, that's good enough for me . . . . "

Ollie smiled and returned to watching Doc. I couldn't watch as he prepared an injection.

" . . . . Just a tetanus shot . . . . Won't hurt a bit."

After a few seconds I heard Ollie.

"That didn't hurt like my thumb."

"Well, it's gonna burn now . . . . I gotta clean out any of Stan's salami still stuck inside your thumb. He might decide to ask for it back after I sew it up . . . . "

I walked away. I couldn't bear to watch Ollie getting stitched, even if his pain threshold rivaled *Hercules'*. It impressed Doc.

" . . . . My Lord. You didn't even flinch. You're a real soldier."

I knew Ollie liked hearing that and I wanted to see the expression on his face. I assumed Doc's words meant he had finished. However, when I turned to look, Doc had just pulled his needle and thread through a piece of flesh. Ollie sat there as though getting a manicure. He looked at me.

"Hi, Dusty."

"Hi, Ollie. How is it going?"

"Doc's sewing me back together."

Then he laughed.

"Now quit moving on me or I might end up sewing your thumb to your nose."

Now Ollie burst out laughing. I smiled as Doc winked at me. In about half an hour, Doc proclaimed Ollie "good as new" and "ready for some new calamity". We all went downstairs where Stan was still wiping up blood with paper towels. He stopped when he saw us.

"So what's the verdict?"

"He's gonna be with us a little while longer . . . . as long as he stays away from that machine."

"No arguments there. I spent all this time wiping blood from off the case . . . . I scooped out what fell into the salads . . . . although I never did find the tip of the thumb."

"I told you not to tell me these things . . . . I don't want to hear them."

"Suit yourself."

Stan either thought Ollie and I had suddenly become deaf, or he trusted us. However, he never considered any of his indiscretions worrisome, and there seemed no reason for him to begin then.

"What do you want me to do next, Stan?"

Ollie stood ready to return to work.

"Forget it, son. You'll need to rest that thumb for at least a few weeks . . . And keep it clean."

"But I can be careful. I promise."

"You heard what Doc said. Go home, Ollie. The sooner you heal, the sooner you can come back."

Ollie looked to me.

"He's right, Oll. Let's go."

I pulled him gently and we left to go home. I knew the healing would be slow. Ollie wouldn't let a bandaged thumb hinder him from picking up and tossing rocks, catching empty bottles and soda cans he threw into the air, and breaking fallen tree branches. When he left me to go to his home, his bandage had already become charcoal gray and a little bloody. Ollie always pushed the limits, and I wondered when they would finally push back.

16

I sat on the steps waiting for Dad to finish helping Miss Heggelhoffer, the two of us having a date to get some ice cream at Ronnie's. Miss Heggelhoffer had just walked in as we headed out, and now Dad began showing her various toasters. I watched her nod and smile, before pointing to the one she wanted. I tried to say her name, Helga Heggelhofer, five times without fumbling, but I couldn't. The name made me think of chalk dust under fingernails. I tried repeatedly to say this tongue twister correctly, getting it right only twice before saying Hoofa Feggelhoofer or some other comparable distortion. I imagined her marrying one day.

"Do you, Hoofa Feggelhoofer, uh, Holga Hoffenfegel, uh . . . . "

I began laughing at my own silliness when I heard a voice.

"Having a good time, are we?"

Mr. Magnusson came around from behind me, getting into his truck. He looked at me without smiling, and left. I wanted to bury myself. I felt sure he would tell Opal, who would then decide not to associate with someone no saner than her mother. I considered calling, and prepare her for what her dad might say. I hated Miss Heggelhoffer for the trouble her name caused between me and Opal. But soon I thought more about Opal's father, and I quieted

174

my concerns with the realization Mr. Magnusson was himself a strange fellow. Not as strange as his wife, but an impressive runner up. One day he would joke with you as though you and he were best buddies. The next day he would mumble a greeting and barely acknowledge he knew you. No bond ever seemed to get built, and each time your friendship with him began and ended. This behavior earned him a place in the same category as Blue Armondsen, someone most people stayed away from. If I felt relief in knowing his own quirky behavior called into question any judgments he might have about my unusual conduct, I felt badly for what it all meant to Opal. I hated seeing her drowning in a sea of strangeness, with no one in her family seemingly sane enough to rescue her.

I began once again to roll Helga Heggelhoffers on my tongue like so many butterscotch candies. After ten more minutes of this, I became bored and wanted a new toy. I looked again into Dad's store. Helga stood at the counter, holding a wrapped toaster. I saw her begin to move toward the door, stop to say a few words, then move toward the door again. But as I watched her, the corner of my vision caught something moving above Stan's store. When I looked, gray smoke began rising and swelling from the back. I ran inside where Doc sat fast asleep, his snoring a deafening clamor of respiratory clatter, oblivious to the impending catastrophe. I knew all the wood framed stores could ignite like a stack of kindling. Dad had always worried about this since neither he nor the other shopkeepers could afford the necessary insurance. Vigilance became their solution and now I would be the one to sound the alarm. I shook Doc, who only smiled and licked his lips. I then pushed him so hard, he nearly fell to the floor. He awoke just in time to catch himself.

"What in blazes name is—?"

I thought his choice of words fitting. I screamed at him.

"There's a fire in the back!"

I could see he had not regained total consciousness. He looked at me as though trying to figure out who I was, and what I was saying. I exchanged gestures for words, and pointed to the back of the store. Smoke moved toward us, black wisps ballooning like a giant genie exiting from its lamp.

"Get your dad and anyone else! Hurry!"

Doc then grabbed a bucket and ran to the back. I reached Dad just as he locked his door.

"Thought you gave up on-"

"Stan's is on fire!"

"What? Stan is on fire?"

With Doc and Dad unable to understand me, I wondered if my excitement had rendered my speech unintelligible. So I relied on what worked before and pulled Dad into the street to show him what I meant. Telling me to wait outside, he ran into the store. But I followed a few steps behind, concerned for his safety. The smoke prevented us from seeing beyond six or seven feet, and I imagined only the worst for Doc and the store. Just then Stan rushed in, only to become immobilized from the horror before him. His mouth remained wide open, seemingly unable to utter even a groan. Dad slapped him on the arm.

"Get a grip. Doc's back there. Let's go . . . . "

Dad looked at me.

" . . . . I told you to wait outside."

I ignored him. Dad and Stan struggled to see into the smoke, covering their faces with napkins as they took a few steps toward Doc. Stan yelled Doc's name repeatedly, each one becoming increasingly more strident. I knew they arose not so much from concern, as from wanting to reach and strangle the person responsible for the fire. Before Stan and Dad could move any further, they heard Doc's calm muffled voice.

"Yeah, what is it?"

He soon emerged like an emissary from the depths of hell, walking through the smoke, his face and clothes covered with soot. Doc then removed the handkerchief covering his mouth. He began coughing.

"You all right?"

Dad waited for an answer.

"It's out. A grease fire. No real danger . . . . "

He coughed some more.

" . . . . good we had the water from the toilet."

I wondered if he meant that literally. But I remembered only a trickle came from the one working faucet, so I knew he really did mean the toilet. Stan approached him.

"Didn't you hear me call you?!"

"I told you . . . I was in the toilet . . . . had that vent fan going."

That fan had long become an imposter, its clanging convincing no one of its effectiveness. But the broken vent window and open back door were more than adequate to suck out the smoke.

"You damn fool! You could've turned this place into charcoal!"

Doc stared at him.

"Thank you for your concern."

"You could've killed someone! I told you to turn it off at three . . . . Didn't you say you'd turn it off at three?"

"I fell asleep . . . . "

"It's almost four o'clock!"

"Well, if you didn't load so much fat into your damn meatloaves, they wouldn't ignite like flares . . . . they're a few fat grams short of lethal."

With a meatloaf nearly poisoning me, and another almost burning down the town, I guessed Swanson Lake would have no choice but to ban the dangerous concoction. Doc seemed ready to issue an executive decree. However, Stan had more immediate concerns, his concentration totally absorbed with the devastation surrounding him.

"Just look at all this . . . . After everything we've done . . . . just look at it . . . . "

He appeared to be talking aloud to himself. His face tightened and I expected him to burst into tears. He looked at Doc.

" . . . . How am I supposed to sell anything that stinks of smoke? . . . . You old stupid fool!"

Now Doc snapped back.

"Save your name calling . . . . It does neither of us any good . . . . As far as your question, you can sell the goddamn meat as smoked and charge extra for it . . . . I don't care anymore."

Doc wiped away the remaining soot from his face and hands. For a few minutes no one said anything, thoughts and emotions suspended in air like the smoke still drifting along the ceiling lights. Then Stan spoke quietly.

"We'll have to reduce prices on everything."

"Reduce prices . . . . give it away for free . . . . I'll leave it up to you."

"Well that's real big of you. If you woulda left it up to me in the first place, we wouldn't be where we are now. We squandered all this money . . . . and we're no better off than we were two months ago."

"The fire was an accident. So I-"

"I'm not even talking about that. I mean the entire cleanup, everything you wanted . . . . And what did it get us?"

"I kept you from poisoning-"

"Enough! Enough!"

Dad startled all of us.

" . . . . Both of you got a lot of nerve . . . . I've never seen such ingratitude . . . . How about takin' a few moments out of arguin' and thank my boy for savin' all our hides. Without him waking Doc or getting me, none of us would have a business to argue over . . . . "

Stan and Doc looked at me. I felt embarrassed, although I liked having Dad proud of me. Stan went to the register, hesitated, then opened it and handed me a ten dollar bill.

"You buy yourself a new baseball glove or football . . . . "

He appeared genuinely grateful. He patted me on the back and grinned, exposing his gold tooth.

" . . . . And I'm givin' you lifetime readin' privileges . . . . just so long as you don't eat while doin' it, and the magazines don't look so read I can't sell 'em."

This reward surpassed the other. Stan rarely let anyone look at the magazines more than a few minutes before shouting, "ain't a library . . . buy it or leave". Now I could actually finish the articles in *Sports Illustrated* and *Baseball Digest*. I smiled at my good fortune. Doc also shook my hand.

"Thanks, Hal. Your next injury is on the house."

Dad reminded me of our appointment.

"How about we do the malts after we go to Brewman for a . . . .
I don't know. You care for a kamikaze pizza?"

The question was an obvious tease. I began tasting the dozen
or so toppings before we left Stan's. Only a few steps outside, we
heard their argument resume.

"Well, maybe that meatloaf caught fire because it was trying
to commit suicide . . . . like those Buddhist monks over in Viet
Nam."

I heard more and more about that country, although I couldn't
believe anyone would burn himself alive. But I also never believed
people would put other people into ovens. Dad put his arm around
me and I thought again about the immediate and pleasurable, the
pizza and ice cream we would soon eat. The fire renewed Stan's
campaign for martyrdom, portraying himself once again as a victim.
And he did have reason to complain. The smoke had damaged
much of the store's inventory, and the stench had become
unbearable.

"Of course this couldn't happen before we cleaned up. No, God
needed a good joke . . . . Yessir . . . . Let's stick it to ol' Stan boy once
again . . . . Just look at this mess . . . . just look at it . . . "

He droned on like this for hours at a stretch, expending more
energy on his complaints than on actually doing something about
it. He satisfied himself with an occasional hour of cleaning, deciding
that the remaining ash and odor would somehow disappear without
any encouragement from him.

" . . . . We'll just leave the door open. The broke toilet window
and back door will give us enough of an good airing out."

The odor did eventually become tolerable, although nothing
short of a tornado would have blown away the black dust from the
shelves. Soon the store returned to its former glory, before the
massive cleanup, only now with soot replacing dirt as the decorative
theme.

Stan made a token effort to throw away any damaged goods. I
watched him examine a package of sugar wafers, its contents barely

indistinguishable under the blackened cellophane. After sniffing it, he decided he could return it to the shelf and sell the wafers "as is" at a reduced price, rather than blame himself later for recklessly throwing it away. Each toss into the trash bin evoked a sigh and a lament.

" . . . . It's the poorhouse for sure . . . . serves me right . . . . I asked for it. Right from the beginning I shoulda known . . . . I shouldn'ta listened . . . . "

Stan intended the last part for Doc's benefit, whose head rested on his chest with his eyes closed. I could not tell whether Doc chose to ignore the remark or had begun falling asleep, until I saw him reach under a display stand for a crushed chocolate mint patty. Still in its foil wrapper, Doc examined it, deemed it saleable, and tossed it in with the others on the counter. I expected that from Stan, although I attributed Doc's unusual behavior to the stress from recent events. He seemed especially preoccupied, ignoring Stan's barbs, saying little or nothing. I felt sorry for him. He wanted to bring respectability to the grocery, yet he jeopardized its existence with a nap.

Without a major cleanup, the grocery languished with an ever-present ash residue that reminded Dad of a crematorium.

"It's too eerie . . . . I even hate goin' in for a coffee."

So I became his coffee boy and had the unpleasant task of making excuses for him. But Dad was not alone. Although a few customers still stopped in for the odd item they forgot to buy at the *A&P*, their trips were fewer and their purchases smaller in the weeks following the fire. Stan understood he would soon be out of business unless he made a far more aggressive effort to clean his grocery. I assumed he would not hire me because of his finances, and he would not hire Ollie because he couldn't trust him with the perishables. Stan had no choice but to do what he hated most, and he had to do it without the pleasure he derived from complaining to, and irritating, Doc.

These same few weeks also brought a marked change in Dad's behavior. He hardly spoke, and when he did, his words were often short and garbled. He also rarely smiled, except an occasional forced one to assure me he felt okay. Soon Dad became short tempered, often storming out of the room after I inquired about his health. I felt hurt when he called me "an annoyance, a major thorn in my butt", but those words only motivated me to find and eradicate the source of his anger and depression. I knew the fire unnerved him, sobering him to the financial disaster he narrowly escaped. I had to assume he had become obsessed with worry and fear over another possible catastrophe. But when he began suffering from migraine headaches almost daily, I became convinced the doctors hid something from me the time Dad fainted. I risked his fury one morning at breakfast.

"Are you sure you're okay? I mean really okay?"

"I told you, didn't I?"

I didn't want to say he might be lying.

"I thought you might be afraid to tell me everything."

"No, son. I'm not holding back on you. You heard the doctors. Wouldn't I be dead by now if they were wrong?"

It made a certain amount of sense.

"Then how come you don't feel good? . . . . and you're so different?"

"I don't owe-"

Dad stopped. I suspected he caught himself before he said something mean. He then glared at me, sighed, and left. That afternoon, after Stan left on an errand, I decided to ask Doc about it.

"He's made himself scarce . . . . hardly see him."

"I don't think he's feeling so good, Doc."

"Is that right? How so?"

I began explaining Dad's behavior.

" . . . . You say his answers are short and garbled?

"Sometimes. Sometimes they're okay."

"Hmmm . . . . But he was checked out that time at the hospital . . . . of course that was a few years ago . . . . "

I regretted immediately my decision to confide in him.

"You think he's got something new?!"

"Certainly possible. The human body is constantly evolving—"

"You think he's sick worse than last time?!"

"Anything is possible . . . . Garbled, you say? . . . "

I nodded.

" . . . . Like mumbled?"

I nodded again, wondering how Doc could come up with a diagnosis when he struggled to understand the simple word I mentioned. He looked serious.

"What does it mean? You look worried."

"Now, now. It could mean, and I'm emphasizing the word "could", a possible minor cerebral hemorrhage."

"But isn't the ceree . . . . cerebum, the head?"

"The brain, yes."

He smiled, satisfied with his ability to answer my question correctly. I resented his cavalier attitude, seemingly more concerned with proving he really studied medicine, than with proposing remedies that could reassure me. I asked the question I feared most.

"Is . . . is he going to die then?"

"No, no. A minor stroke is not necessarily a threat to one's life. It's amazing how the rest of the brain can rally to the cause . . . . "

Doc's words only convinced me Dad's death was imminent. Knowing his father died from a stroke and hearing Doc's qualification that "it's not *necessarily* a threat to one's life", I prepared myself mentally for the funeral. I tried to stop them, but the first tears had already begun rolling down my cheeks.

" . . . . Now, now. I didn't say it was a stroke or anything of the sort. These are only possibilities, very remote . . . . almost non existent. But you say he has no trouble walking, no dizzy spells, and he talks normal most of the time? . . . "

I shook my head and nodded to each of his questions. He slapped his knees and sat up.

" . . . . Well, then. It doesn't sound serious at all . . . . Could be he's just a little under the weather."

"Under the weather?" Once again Doc's diagnosis hovered around extremes. I realized I had repeated his last three words out loud.

" . . . . Sure. Maybe he's down about something. A little depressed.

That could account for the symptoms you described . . . . "

I should have felt relieved, but I, like most people in town who sought Doc's advice, left feeling more worried and confused. I didn't know what to think. As I moved to leave, Doc grabbed my arm.

" . . . . Have him come in. I'll check him out."

"Don't tell him I saw you."

"I won't say a word."

"But why would he come in for an exam?"

"He won't know it's an exam . . . . I have my ways of finding out things. Don't worry."

He smiled. I liked his plan. The two could just chat and Doc could find out what he needed. It all seemed so simple until I approached Dad one evening after dinner.

"Doc says he hasn't seen you."

"True enough . . . . been busy."

"He was hoping you might stop in and say hello."

"Got no time. Probably won't have time for quite awhile."

I watched Dad continue reading his newspaper. I guessed he still harbored ill feelings over Doc's negligence.

"Stan says hi. He also misses not seeing you."

"I'm not invisible."

I pulled out my ace.

"Could we get sodas tomorrow?"

"Of course."

"What time you wanna meet?"

"Anytime after her lunch rush."

"I didn't mean ice cream sodas."

"It don't matter. We'll still go to Ronnie's."

I hesitated before proceeding.

"But I want to go to Stan's."

Dad slammed down his newspaper.

"Then you go yourself!"

I never knew Dad to stay angry with either Stan or Doc. I tried to be the peacemaker.

"Doc didn't mean it, Dad . . . . It was just an accident."

He stood up and pointed upstairs.

"Get outa here! Now!"

I ran upstairs to my room. I didn't understand what I said to infuriate him, but I vowed not to inquire anymore about what bothered him. As it turned out, I didn't have to. A few days after Dad's outburst, I found out what I wanted to know.

I anchored myself at the comic book rack, enjoying my newly acquired privilege. Stan stared at me and I thought he had either forgotten his promise, or planned to renege on it. When he cleared his throat, I braced myself for one of his yells. I had inadvertently creased the front cover and I felt sure he noticed it. But he spoke his words softly, and they had nothing to do with any wrongdoing on my part.

"He musta said something about me or Doc . . . . "

I shook my head.

" . . . . You mean he don't even talk about us?"

I didn't know what to say. Doc now chimed in.

"I wave for him to come in, he waves back, and then continues on his way. There's something wrong there. And when I ask him, he tells me he's busy. All of a sudden he's too busy for me and Stan . . . . You must know something, Hal."

"I don't . . . . honest."

I grew uncomfortable with their interrogation. I had neither the answers to their questions, nor the desire to speculate on what those answers might be. I closed my comic book and walked quickly to the door. But before I even reached the counter, Dad charged in like a rodeo bull released from its pen. He shook his fist at Doc.

"You better have answers, mister!"

Then he told me to leave. Doc protested.

"Let him stay. You won't pummel me in front of your son . . . . I hope."

"Don't count on it!"

Dad's breathing became labored. Doc rose from his chair.

"You better sit down, Jack. You don't sound good."

Dad sat in Doc's chair and took deep breaths. I felt scared and looked at Doc's face for any indications of alarm. But he remained calm and in a few minutes Dad regained both his breath and his fury.

"Your concern ain't worth a damn! . . . It's all lip service and I'm wise to you!"

"What's that supposed to mean?"

Stan came from behind the counter.

"Yeah, what's going on?"

"Stay out of it, Stan . . . . I don't think you had anything to do with it so this is just between the two of us."

I had never seen Dad so angry. Suddenly, he pushed me to the door.

"I told you to leave! . . . . Now get on home!"

I knew better than to protest his treatment or his decision. However, after walking about twenty yards, I backtracked until I stopped five feet from the entrance. I stood flat against the building as I heard Dad's voice penetrate the closed door and carry into the street.

" . . . . All these years . . . . and this . . . You're a miserable old bastard! . . . . Do ya really think I wasn't gonna find out?"

"Find out what?"

"Stan, I told you to stay out of it . . . . "

I heard Dad take another deep breath to calm himself. He lowered his voice, making it difficult for me to hear. I moved another two feet closer.

" . . . . You know what gave you away, Doc?"

"I still don't know what you're talking about?"

"What gave you away was how little you cared about it. If I just nearly burned down my store and everyone else's, I wouldn't treat it like just another day at the office . . . . And you walked through that smoke as nonchalant as Willie Mays under a fly ball."

"So what are you saying? That I actually expected Stan's meatloaf to become a torch? . . . . Overcooked meat just dries up . . . . becomes charcoal . . . . it's not supposed to light up an airport runway . . . . "

"You can kiss my support goodbye . . . . Go ahead, Jack."

"Who do you think you're talking to? A moron? . . . . Anything catches fire if it burns long enough."

"Okay, but it wasn't on the stove that long."

I heard Stan's voice.

"What are you nuts? It stayed on over an hour longer than it should."

"I overslept! I'm guilty of oversleeping and that's all!"

"That was all part of the scheme, wasn't it? . . . except Hal ruined it for you . . . . "

When I heard my name, I feared it might prompt Dad to peek outside and see if I had obeyed his orders. However, I gambled successfully his anger would keep him focused on the argument.

" . . . . Business is dead . . . . you need the money . . . . and whether people die or not is not your concern."

"How dare you?! You're a damn fool! . . . And a slanderous one at that!"

"Wait a minute, Jack. What money?"

"You wanna tell him Doc?"

I heard nothing and concluded they had decided to whisper something this important. I moved to the point where the window met the frame and still I heard nothing. Doc's voice then startled me.

"I took out insurance . . . "

"Let me get this straight. You're sayin' we have insurance on this place . . . . Well, that's ridiculous."

"That's what I'm saying."

"Don't you think I would know if I had or didn't have insurance on my own place?"

"Not if Doc insured it without telling you."

"Okay, so what? So I insured this place. I have that right, you know."

"How come you never told me?"

"Because you're like an old woman, Stan. You'd go on and on about the premiums and so I just paid them myself."

"Very generous, Doc . . . . and very convenient."

"Go to hell, Jack! You're just shootin' from the hip."

"I got no proof about the fire. That's right. But just know that

I know. Just in case something else happens."

I couldn't believe what I heard. Either Dad had gone crazy, or Doc was the meanest person in the world. I didn't want to hear anymore. Dad and Doc had been friends for almost twenty years, and now that evaporated in the time it takes to drink a soda. I peered through a peephole into the future, seeing an adulthood at least as fragile and unpredictable as anything I had known so far.

If Dad regarded Doc's actions, or supposed actions, as a betrayal of their friendship, Doc considered Dad's harsh accusations an affront to his reputation. Neither appeared willing to make the first move, and again I toyed with the possible role of peacemaker. I considered faking a life threatening illness, only to have Dad grateful to Doc for saving me. But I worried this might backfire. Doc would misdiagnose me, give me some medicine or procedure that would either kill me or transform my head into a puff pastry, and Dad would go to prison for then shooting him. I decided not to interfere and let time decide when or if they would resume their friendship. Finally he broached the subject.

"So you like going to Stan's every day?"

I considered it a trick question.

"Well yeah . . . . sorta . . . . but only for the comic books and magazines . . . . but I don't have to if you don't want me to."

"No, no. Go. I want you to . . . . "

Then he paused and I thought he might be considering a face saving way to ask about Doc. I was wrong.

" . . . . You keep going . . . . keep an eye on him . . . . Let me know if he's up to anything . . . . strange."

Dad gave me a lot of latitude with that word. Everything from discovering Doc with a blowtorch, to hearing him mention insurance related words, became the focus of my mission.

" . . . . And even if you don't know what something means, just remember it so you can tell me later. Okay?"

I nodded reluctantly. I resented Dad recruiting me as a spy and I decided to do what I always did at Stan's store—reading my comics and only listening when I wanted.

Doc acted no better. If Stan asked me about Dad or if I

mentioned Dad's name, Doc picked up a magazine and pretended to read. If he didn't have a magazine handy, he would pick up a box of donuts and read the ingredients to himself. Occasionally he would go outside until the conversation shifted. He and Dad sidestepped each other on the street, only looking at each other long enough to pass safely.

"Those big babies. Someone should lock them in the freezer until they're willing to be civil to each other . . . . Of course you can't make what ain't there no more."

Stan's words echoed those my mother had written to Dad. I learned their truth and recognized the friendship between Dad and Doc seemed over, no matter what anyone else wanted or did.

After a month I became thoroughly sick of their feud. Each day Dad grilled me about his enemy's behavior. And each day I told him basically the same thing. Doc ate, he slept, he broke wind, and he ate some more. The only departure from that routine came on Wednesdays, when he used the afternoon to "bet on the ponies" at the Saratoga racetrack. I knew he made that his opportunity to get away from Stan, Dad, and everything else he considered unpleasant in town.

"Nothing besides that? . . . . Nothing different about him?"

I shook my head.

" . . . . Oh, he's good all right. Clever like a fox."

I never thought of Doc in that way. He always seemed grateful just to get through a day without falling out of his chair. Dad waited for me to ask a question or make a comment about what he had said. But I refused to encourage his paranoia. I said nothing as I rushed through my dinner, anxious to leave Dad alone with his silly questions.

Almost a week passed when I witnessed the impossible, or what I had considered the impossible. The first thawing between Dad and Doc occurred, and it began showing itself in small and significant ways.

I noticed Doc and Dad exchange an occasional nod, then a more frequent one. They soon added something that resembled a smile, although neither would commit fully to it. But I knew they were both ready for friendship again. Dad grew tired of moping and of missing the daily squabbles between Doc and Stan. I also believe he felt guilty for making accusations he could neither substantiate nor even believe totally. Dad had always considered Doc his source for truth. Similarly, Doc also missed Dad's visits, and whatever insult or hurt he absorbed as a result of the fire, he appeared willing to erase the whole incident and move on from there. Dad had been standing outside his store when Doc walked up to him.

"Stan got some day olds . . . . the kind you like . . . . I saved a few for you."

Dad loved the raspberry filled *Bismarcks* Stan bought from Vitale's bakery in Brewman, especially when they became chewy.

"No . . . . thanks anyway. I ate a big lunch."

"It musta been a really big lunch then. Never knew you to refuse a *Bismarck* . . . . "

Dad didn't answer. Then Doc uttered words of magic.

" . . . . For what it's worth, I cancelled my insurance . . . . I figure if we burn, we all burn together . . . . and suffer the same. Until you and the others can afford insurance, I won't have any . . . . And that's a promise . . . . "

He extended his hand. Dad looked at it and then at Doc, before shaking it.

" . . . . You call Mike Stevens anytime and ask him. He didn't lie to you before and he won't now."

The Mike Stevens insurance agency held a monopoly in an area too small to justify competition. Dad apparently called him after the fire. He now took a deep breath and smiled.

"I'd be lying if I said I didn't miss your comebacks to Stan and our state of the world discussions."

"Atta boy! . . . "

Doc slapped him on the back.

" . . . . Now come inside and keep that lunatic off my back. He's driving me nutso."

Dad laughed.

"For a few *Bismarcks*? Sure."

"It's a done deal."

They shook hands again and went into the store. When I heard their laughter, I had to smile at how smoothly their friendship seemed to fall back into place. But I also wondered how much distrust and resentment remained, and would the friendship disintegrate as quickly and easily as it did before. I then began to wonder about Opal and Ollie, and whether our friendship would ever be tested in that way. I couldn't know, and for the time being, I didn't want to think too much about it.

17

I had just finished helping Dad stock a new shipment of paintbrushes when I stepped outside for some fresh air. The mustiness in Dad's store, "the scent of a good hardware store", he insisted, could be so overwhelming as to render my nose more decorative than functional. The cool October air gradually restored my breathing while I stood and daydreamed. But my radar soon zoomed in on Opal entering Maggie Crabtree's dress shop. It always seemed strange to see anyone enter or leave that shop, and especially Opal, who often joked about it.

"The only ones findin' clothes there are mummies and zombies . . . . Even the moths have died from old age."

The rest of the town referred to it as "the museum" or the "house of oddities". I had only been there twice, the first time when it also served as the post office. Buying Dad his stamps gave me the opportunity to satisfy my curiosity about the strange menagerie it contained, although the shop's choking mustiness and disconcerting shadowiness and darkness were obstacles I managed to overcome quickly. With my senses restored, I could appreciate the shop's well earned reputation. Women's dresses, looking as though they might have been costumes from a stage play performed fifty years earlier, hung from racks and wall hooks.

Most appeared well preserved, their colors still vibrant. Ladies' hats with huge feathers, along with scarves, lay scattered about the store like so many ornaments. Tray after tray of colored bead necklaces rested under the dirty glass of a display case. An area marked "antiques" contained some gaudy lamps resting on scratched and faded end tables. The furniture and lamps seemed more old than antique, although their age eventually qualified them as such. I wrote my initials in the dust that covered the counters, and only the emergence of the frail and petite Mrs. Crabtree assured me this place had not been totally abandoned. I heard Doc tell Dad this had been a boarding house in the town's heyday, its two upstairs bedrooms reserved for husbands too drunk to return home. When Brewman eventually absorbed the post office, Mrs. Crabtree volunteered to house the town's library. I became excited with the prospect of having resources nearby that I could use to research reports. When Mrs. Crabtree's put a sign in her window announcing the library officially open, I visited her shop for the second time.

I walked up the dull and splintered steps to reach the area designated for the library. If I anticipated row after row of books, and a well stocked reference section with an encyclopedia and a globe, I found something both pathetic and laughable. The reference section drew its entire identity from a dictionary missing its cover and half of the "A" pages, and from an atlas whose nations and cities disappeared decades before through name and border changes. The thirty or so leather bound books in general circulation dealt with the town's history, birds native to the area, and collections of verse whose rhymes and rhythms reminded me of the perfumes grandmothers wore to church. I half expected their yellow, brittle pages to crumble into dust at any moment. Seeing no reason to stay, I began moving to the stairs. I thought I had been alone until I saw an old man sitting with his back to me. He sat motionless in his wheelchair, staring at the bare white wall before him. I remembered Dad had once mentioned him. He said Mr. Crabtree had been a painter with some reputation, until "diabetic blindness", as Doc called it, reduced him to one of his wife's museum pieces. I imagined him sitting like that for most of his day, painting mentally what he once immortalized in watercolor. When

Mr. Crabtree summoned his wife, I tiptoed quickly down the stairs to leave. I opened the door, the harsh sunlight slapping me back into the present day.

As I now stood in front of Dad's store, I watched that same door open and an older gray haired woman emerge. When the door opened again a few moments later, Opal stepped outside, carrying a package. She appeared somber. My wave drew no response, except to have her look away and pretend not to see me. I felt tempted to go over and discover what, if anything, I had done to offend her. But I stopped when I saw her take the woman's arm. At first I did not make the connection between her and Opal, even as she helped the woman maneuver around a car to cross the street. However, when they reached Mr. Magnusson's truck, waves of shock, dismay, and sadness overtook me. Time and illness had ravished Mrs. Magnusson's beauty and reduced her to a cruel parody of her former self. She walked slowly, almost in a sleep, and when Mr. Magnusson finally helped her into the truck, I knew embarrassment kept Opal from acknowledging me or anyone else who remembered how her mother used to be.

Macy Shelton was born in Harlan, Mississippi, where the red Delta earth made brick making the best and sole industry. But the post World War II building boom never materialized in Mississippi, and when less expensive construction shifted away from brick to wood, aluminum, and concrete, her family "upped and left", as she said. Having read about the prosperity in New York State with the construction of Levittown and other mammoth housing projects, Lemuel Shelton moved his family there in the summer of 1946. They brought some clothes, a few pieces of furniture, and a host of Southern ways that never left them. Even when Macy left her family to marry Erik Magnusson, a native New Yorker and an apprentice carpenter to her father, I knew the air in her new home would always hang heavy with the scent of magnolia and the aroma of her Southern cooking. She often talked about those years.

"Imagin' hearin' my daddy come home one day and announce you're movin' clear across the country. When I heard him say New York, I thought Lord o' mighty, he coulda said the North Pole for that mattuh."

She laughed. With long and smooth licorice black hair, and eyes that blinked blue neon, I considered Mrs. Magnusson the prettiest mother, perhaps even the prettiest woman, I ever saw. Opal's beauty approached her mother's, although one day I knew she would even surpass it.

" . . . The last thing a high school girl wants is to leave huh friends . . . . and 'specially when you're goin' to a place wheah everyone talks so funny."

Opal and I looked at each other and smiled. " . . . . But daddy spoke and that was that . . . . Well, it was hard adjustin' but I'd say it turned out just fine. I met your fathuh and you and Ollie come along. So it was a happy ending, sure enough . . . . "

Her smile didn't look real. She seemed sad as she returned to her cooking. Opal now went to wash for dinner, leaving me to fend for myself. I had no thoughts in my head, at least none that I could share without sounding stupid. I wanted Ollie or Mr. Magnusson to barge through the door, but they went to Brewman for groceries and were not expected back for another hour. I felt relieved when Mrs. Magnusson spoke again.

" . . . . I don't need to tell you how gifted my children are . . . . "

Her remark seemed to originate in a vacuum until I connected it to the last words she spoke. I looked at her, not sure if she expected a response. She didn't look at me, and I said nothing. "Gifted" captured Opal perfectly, but "different" and "unusual" were the words that best defined Ollie. I never considered him gifted. Then I thought back to what Dad once said, how people used words that sounded better than the ones they really wanted to use.

" . . . . Ollie's won all kinds of awards and Opal is smarter than a *Saks Fifth Avenue* suit."

I had to agree. She answered the questions no one else could. But again I tried to understand how this applied to Ollie. Getting promoted had always been the goal set for him, and an achievement worth celebrating. But I never knew Ollie to win any awards. Mrs. Magnusson must have read the skepticism in my face because she pointed to a wall on the far side of the living room.

A DROWNING IN SWANSON LAKE   195

"Go ahead . . . . see for yourself . . . . I can't havin' you think I'm jest boastin' for nothin' . . . "

I walked over and saw Ollie's awards for "Attendance" and "Most Improved". At first it all seemed so silly. Everyone received these certificates at one time or another during the school year. I wanted to tell her about my awards in math and science, the most difficult ones to earn. Even if Dad joked about them being "unbankable" and my mother never saw them, I could appreciate their importance. I wanted to snicker at Ollie's awards, but I didn't. Instead, I continued looking at them. When I became too jealous and upset to look anymore, I returned to the kitchen.

With her focus now on the meal she was preparing, Mrs. Magnusson said nothing more about Ollie. In fact, she said nothing more. That left a void I felt obligated to fill, and I struggled to think of something to say. As I watched her work magic with the spices and utensils that surrounded her, I solved my dilemma. In a voice loud enough to compete with the boiling oil, I shrieked,

"You sure like to cook."

What had seemed so brilliant inside my head, became dim-witted when exposed to the air. I wanted to look around and find the moron whose comment was distinguished only by its obviousness. I pinched my knee hard, hoping the physical pain would help me forget my mental distress. I had wanted Mrs. Magnusson to regard me as Opal's potential suitor, although now I would be grateful if she just let me remain her friend. But I found no hint of judgment in her response.

"I'll tell you somethin', Hal. I don't know what I would do without my cookin' . . . . It's my one link to civilization . . . ."

This time I felt no shame in saying the obvious.

"And you're a great cook, the best in the world even."

"And you're a deah for sayin' it."

I smiled. I had always wanted to tell her that, although I suspected she knew how much I enjoyed her meals. Her etoufees and jambalayas became exotic adventures as I experienced tastes and smells I had never encountered, or would likely encounter again outside her home. But whereas Ronnie, whose specialties dared more than tempted, Mrs. Magnusson refrained from using the animal parts I found so repulsive. At least, when I visited.

" .... So you hate the innards .... Well I'm glad you warned me. Then I won't serve you chitlins .... And you can unfurrow your brow cause you're gonna be likin' this real well."

I had not realized I reacted.

" .... Catfish Acadian .... You won't find this anywhere but in the South. It's Opal's favorite. She's got her mother's Southern taste, sure enough .... "

Opal considered cheeseburgers her favorite food. I told Mrs. Magnusson that.

" .... Is that what she told you? Now don't you go believin' it. She just said that to please you."

I believed her because I wanted to. I also knew I would love the dish Opal loved, even though I hated fish. When I told Dad about it, he roared. "You ate what?"

"A catfish in the arcade .... it's Southern."

"A catfish? That alone 'll get me to a screeching stop .... I don't care what the rest of it means."

But he dismissed all the foods Mrs. Magnusson served. He especially couldn't understand my enthusiasm for chicken fried steak.

"It ain't natural for a steak to be breaded like chicken. A steak stands on its own just fine .... It's like adding water to good whiskey .... "

Dad hardly drank, so his comment surprised me. I didn't agree with his analysis and always hoped he would accept Mrs. Magnusson's invitation to dinner, if not for the fried steak or catfish, then for the fried chicken or barbecue. But he never did.

" .... I'm glad you've made some good friends there, but I'm not much for visiting or eating with strangers."

As I continued to stare at the dress shop where Mrs. Magnusson had just been, I understood how the dresses from another era, a happier time, suited her better. In Maggie Crabtree's dress shop, Mrs. Magnusson went to retrieve some dignity in a world gotten away from her.

18

Ollie's junior high and high school years included annual stints in summer school. The bus didn't operate then and Mr. Magnusson became his transportation. Often I would see them pass, Ollie staring out the window like a cow en route to the slaughterhouse. Without Opal and me, and the opportunity the school bus afforded us to engage in impromptu silliness, the closely supervised trips with his father had to be a torment. Opal's summers were accounted for at a Girl Scout Camp in Vermont, first as a camper, then as a counselor. Although she always hated leaving her mother, even sainthood had its limits. Exhaustion provided no other option but to get away. Whereas years earlier I worried about the "commies", my concerns now focused exclusively on Opal and what would become of us. I tried to fill my days with enough distractions to keep me from dwelling on her. I helped Dad out at his store, and read the comics and magazines at Stan's until Ollie returned from school. But even our time together became limited. When Mr. Magnusson decided that Ollie had to complete and understand every piece of homework before seeing me, he imposed a hardship on all three of us. With the tutoring chore now left to him, the enormity of Opal's contribution became obvious as it kept him and his son occupied until late afternoon and sometimes into early evening. That gave Ollie and me barely enough time to skim stones and talk baseball before dark. The occasional movie and pizza with Dad could not redeem the boredom of these days or relieve a torment I felt sure rivaled *Job's*. I hated the summers, and counted the moments to early September when school, the school bus, and Opal returned.

One Saturday in late September, as I sat on the steps in front of Dad's store, I spotted Opal about to enter Mrs. Crabtree's dress shop. Wary of the effect that shop produced on her last time, I feared my wave might result in another snub. But I became heartened when Opal walked towards me, grinning.

"You'll never guess what happened today . . . . "

She continued before I could answer.

" . . . . Ma asked for a dress . . . . a dress for dancing in."

"Oh . . . . that's great . . . . really great."

"What's wrong?"

I had tried to conceal my disappointment in hearing I played no part in her happiness.

"Nothing . . . . I was wondering what a dance dress looked like."

She became exasperated.

"That's not what's important . . . . She's wanting to get out and do things . . . . and that means she's getting better."

"That is great, Ope . . . . Then she's talking again . . . . like before?"

Opal's demeanor changed and I thought I might have said something wrong. Then she looked down.

"Not like before . . . . "

Her face brightened again.

" . . . . but now with this dress, I think she's turned the corner."

"That's great."

I gritted my teeth, self-conscious about the only response I seemed capable of making.

"And when she cooks again, I'll know she's cured . . . . "

She paused a moment, then placed her hand on mine.

" . . . . Ya know, Hal. Ma would love to see you . . . . "

She caught me off guard. My mind rummaged quickly through a host of possible excuses while she spoke.

" . . . . Last week she mentioned, of all things, the way you watched her cook . . . . "

Opal laughed.

" . . . . She said you hated chitlins . . . . I don't remember her ever serving that to you."

I smiled when I recalled that conversation.

"I told her I didn't like eating the insides of animals and she promised to never serve me chitlins."

"I musta been somewheres else. I don't remember that."

"You were probably stuck on the john . . . . "

She slapped my arm and it felt good. I missed her slaps. Now she stared at me and I knew why.

" . . . . I'll try and stop by soon. I promise."

"You'll *try?* I didn't realize it required so much effort."

"I'll call on her one day . . . . when I can spend some time . . . . "

"One day soon."

"Yes . . . . soon. I promise."

Opal squeezed my arm.

"Thanks, Hal. I'll tell her . . . . "

I forced a smile.

" . . . . Maybe that'll get her cooking again."

I nodded, then watched Opal practically skip into Mrs. Crabtree's shop as though she were six years old. I sat again on the steps and wondered what excuse I would give next time.

When Stan and Doc exhausted their wisdom on political and social events, and themselves from the years they spent with each other, they sat in sullen silence for hours at a time. They had nothing else to focus on except the weariness of the other's company. When a murder-suicide appeared imminent, they agreed one should leave and give both of them a much needed vacation. However, neither hurried to do it. Doc's weekly horse racing betting sprees constituted all the recreational energy he cared to expend. And Stan, aside from an occasional day or two, had not taken a vacation in fourteen years. His distrust of everyone and everything superseded his need for relaxation. But he recently hinted at getting away, and a conversation with Doc convinced me it would finally happen. I was about to stop in for a can of soda when I heard their bickering evolve into arguing. I stepped back and listened.

"You don't know what's it's like to look at your ugly face all day."

"Splurge on a mirror then . . . . I think you'll be astonished at what I get to see."

"There you go . . . . All you think about is wastin' money."

"And I'm ready to waste more of my money on a *Putz* like you . . . . for a relaxing little trip."

"No, no, no. You're makin' it too easy . . . . What's up?"

"What's up? Fine. The the trip is for me . . . . I'm sick of you . . . . You're an aggravating bastard and I want you to get the hell away from here. If I have to buy some peace, so be it."

"Don't you think I wanna do nothin' but fish . . . . but how can I put this place in the hands of a nincompoop? I'd sooner close it down than have you try and run it."

"I think I can handle this vast empire for a week. Look at the idiot running it now."

When I heard nothing more, I suspected the two armies began regrouping in preparation for another attack. But I no longer expected to hear any important revelations, so I opened the door and entered. Stan and Doc looked at me and stared. For a moment I thought my eavesdropping had been detected. But their faces soon formed wicked smiles that made me equally uncomfortable. I felt as though I had stumbled upon two cannibals.

"Come in, come in, my friend. I got one your favorites in this morning . . . . the *Hershey's* with the roasted almonds . . . . good and fresh."

I kept my foot in the doorway, ready to run if either of them approached.

" . . . . I always like pleasing my special customers . . . . and friend."

Stan's phoniness and saccharine tone made me queasy.

"I just wanted a soda."

Doc chuckled.

A DROWNING IN SWANSON LAKE   201

"You took away his appetite with that puke of yours. The boy's not stupid."

"I want Hal to have a few candy bars . . . on the house. There's nothin' wrong with that. Right?"

He looked at me, waiting for an answer. I didn't know who would laugh first at his joke, he or I. But he remained serious.

"Thanks . . . some other time."

I rushed to get my soda and leave when his words stopped me.

"How would you like to make some money?"

I welcomed the opportunity to earn money not originating in Dad's wallet. I contained my enthusiasm to strengthen my negotiating position.

"It depends . . . . "

"On what?"

"On how much it pays."

"Pay him what he wants, Stan . . . . within reason, of course."

I knew the desperation they felt, and only Stan, among the three of us, did not grasp this and believed he could negotiate. His attempt at bluffing only amused me.

"I don't need no money grubbers running this store."

Doc laughed.

"You mean besides yourself?"

Stan ignored him. He glared at me, and waited. When I said nothing, he became frustrated.

"Damnit! You want the job or don't you? It pays a buck twenty . . . . "

"That's what my dad pays."

"Off the books?"

"Yup."

Stan looked at Doc.

"Say something."

"I'm not getting involved . . . . "

"You picked a good time . . . . okay, then one fifty . . . . take it or leave it."

I relished the financial opportunity before me and used my negotiating advantage to propose the absurd.

"Two dollars."

"Two dollars an hour?! Get outa my sight . . . . "

I shrugged and began to leave, counting silently the seconds before Stan would call me back. His only other option, besides not taking a vacation or leaving Doc in charge, had to be far more painful. His doubts about Ollie never diminished, and even though Ollie or Doc or any other four legged creature could have run his store at least as well as himself, Stan refused to consider it. I factored that into the wage demands I expected him to accept. However, when I opened the door and heard nothing, I feared I had overplayed my hand. I almost turned around to renegotiate when Stan shot back.

" . . . . one seventy five."

This time I turned around and smiled.

"When do you want me?"

Doc slapped his knee.

"A done deal! . . . . Jumpin' Jehosaphat!"

"More like a swindle."

"Stop complaining . . . . It's letting you take your trip . . . . your free trip."

That seemed to pacify Stan.

"We'll work it out tomorrow."

I savored my newfound worth and debated whether to try my negotiating skills on Dad. I decided against it, Dad's situation not desperate, and his ability to retaliate far greater.

If I thought I negotiated the better deal, it didn't take me long to realize I might have been the one swindled. The first inkling of this came when I returned the following day to receive my instructional training. Diagrams of the store's layout, including the location of the heating and cooling systems, the fuse box, and fire extinguisher, lists of phone numbers and people to contact in case any of these failed, inventory sheets of products and suppliers, and a half dozen ways to reach him in an emergency, all bombarded me within five minutes of entering his grocery. That might impress someone who never met Stan or entered his store. But I knew better, and selling a faded box of corn flakes and making change for a dollar required only that I be present and conscious. However, he insisted I memorize and repeat every one of his instructions, quizzing me on how I would respond to a half dozen possible, but improbable, emergencies. I wanted to tell him I had just one response plan, to run from the grocery and not look back, although I just nodded and stayed quiet. Even when he gave me a "to do" list five pages long, with everything from dusting boxes and shelves to rotating the fruit and dairy products, I nodded some more and paid lip service to his requests. I knew that once Stan left, I would honor his practice of sitting on the stool and staring out the window. I felt confident I could uphold that tradition, and do no better or worse than Stan had done for twenty-five years.

On Monday morning I arrived exactly at seven o'clock to open the store for business. I imagined Stan tucked away in a cabin fifty miles north, frustrated he could do nothing more to try and erode the confidence I felt in my first management position. I jingled the keys loudly, hoping to alert everyone to the person Stan entrusted with his life's work. Unfortunately, my audience consisted of only Ronnie Dawes, whose preoccupation with rolling down her new crimson and beige awning made her oblivious to the excessive jingling coming from my direction. Undeterred, I forged ahead in what should have been my easiest task. But the half rusted lock required the finesse of a locksmith. I then heard the phone ring and I knew fifty miles would not insulate me from Stan's scrutiny. The phone's ringing seemed to grow louder as I hurriedly twisted the key, forcefully at first, then more subtly. When I finally unlocked the door, I ran to a phone I half expected to explode in my hand. I swore I heard Stan's voice before I even reached it. The loud, strident voice grated on me and made my skin crawl as though under a hair shirt. I placed the receiver on the counter and waited for his expletives and shrieking to cease. When I eventually heard nothing, I hoped his rage either satisfied or exhausted himself, and he hung up. But I could hear the heavy breathing and I felt obligated to respond. I thought my cheeriness might disarm him.

"Hi, Stan. Havin' a good time fishin' and-"

My plan failed and I spent the next ten minutes on the defensive.

"I'm not late .... crummy locks are half rusted .... It was seven .... because of the locks, I told you .... So what's the big deal? The lines haven't formed yet .... Okay, okay .... fine .... "

After promising to come earlier the next day to guarantee the doors opened at seven, I heard a click. I wanted to believe my assurances would appease him for at least a day, but I knew Stan too well. The next call would probably come in a few hours. This time, however, I would be prepared. Even if I had to dive to reach it, I intended to answer the phone on its first ring with an enthusiastic "Stan's grocery, may I help you?". I thought that might prove my capability, relieving him of the need to worry, and relieving me of his bothersome phone calls. Until that time, I would relax and conserve the energy I needed to pass his test. I carved a likeness of Stan's face into an apple, picked a few magazines from the rack, and readied myself for the day's customers.

The first customer arrived at seven thirty, choosing his *Bismarck* and grinning all the while.

"You must be the new owner .... "

He extended his hand.

" .... I hear you're a lot smarter than the other one .... "

I slapped Dad's hand playfully, saying nothing. The verdict was still out on my performance.

" .... How's it goin'?"

"Fine. Great."

"No problems?"

"Nope. None."

"Good .... "

With fixed smiles, we nodded like bobble head toys on automobile dashboards. I did not want Dad hovering over me, and I hoped my reluctance to talk would make that obvious. He soon picked up on my discomfort.

" ... You know where to find me .... if you need me ... "

I would obsess on those words a few hours later, when the expected phone call did not come, and two *Yoo-Hoo*s and a beef jerky began assaulting my stomach. A trip to the toilet became too risky to attempt. I grew angry with Doc for not showing up. I suspected he did not want his naps disturbed by any questions I might have, even though I never intended to ask someone so clueless about the day to day operations. I felt sure if Dad watched the grocery, Stan would choose that time to call. I could not decide which would be worse, having Dad answer the phone or having the phone go unanswered. I considered taking the phone off the hook. But I knew that would precipitate a panic attack, Stan interpreting the busy signal as an emergency Sheriff MacCauley should investigate. When my discomfort graduated to painful spasms, only one option remained. And when I emerged from the toilet a few minutes later, I felt confident I set a new world record. Then I heard the phone begin to ring. However, I soon realized the flush had kept me from hearing the other rings. I now walked the slow steps to my doom. I struggled to fabricate a story Stan might believe. When I considered telling him some customers kept me too busy to answer the phone, even I laughed. I decided to just confess. Even though I answered his next call exactly as I had planned, it failed to impress him or divert his attacks.

"I know . . . . but I had to make . . . . "

When he went on about not paying me for sitting in the toilet all morning, and paying me too much to begin with, I had enough.

" . . . . Actually, I didn't want to tell you . . . . but that switch in the back . . . . "

His frantic voice began shrieking "switch, what switch?" until I interrupted him.

" . . . . the one next to the freezer door . . . . the one I thought was a light . . . . "

I didn't need a phone to hear his next words.

"YOU SHUT DOWN THE FREEZER?! YOU SHUT THE GODDAMN FREEZER?!"

I tried to continue my story but couldn't, as I broke into laughter. Stan started and stopped his sentences a few times before realizing I had been joking. He then unleashed a barrage of curses Dad and Doc would envy. Unlike last time, he hung up after completing his volley. Doc entered and caught me chuckling.

"Laughing at the donuts? Don't tell me this job's getting to you already."

"I just spoke to Stan."

"There's a lot to laugh at there."

"He says 'hi'".

"Yeah, right . . . . "

Doc retrieved the current issue of *Life* and flopped down in his chair. I did not feel insulted when he began immediately to read, understanding how he might relish the peace and quiet Stan's absence brought. I straightened out some of the mess under the counter, contorting myself to reach into spots I knew had not been touched since the last cleanup five years before. I discarded the yellowed candy wrappers, stale, rock hard chewing gum, and the roll of dust that accumulated When I finished, I stared out the window and waited for anyone to come and relieve the monotony. Soon someone did. Oblivious to everyone and everything around him, Ollie marched toward us. His singing drew Doc's attention.

"Here's trouble . . . "

He returned to his reading. Ollie entered.

"What're you doin' behind there? Stan don't like that."

"I'm the boss now."

He turned to Doc, who now sensed a pair of eyes staring at him. He put down his magazine.

"It's true. So mind yourself."

"Yeah, Ollie. No foolin' around."

He began looking for Stan, and grew impatient at not finding him.

" . . . . He's not here . . . . That's why I'm in charge."

"So how come Doc ain't in charge?"

"Ask him."

"Doc, how come-"

"I want Hal running the operations."

I smiled at his gross overstatement. Ollie became quiet, then suddenly excited.

"Then let me be in charge, too . . . . with Dusty. We'll both be in charge."

A DROWNING IN SWANSON LAKE   207

Doc thought a moment.

"I tell you what. Next time Stan takes a vacation, you both can run the store."

Ollie smiled, although Doc and I knew the earth would reverse its rotation before Stan took another vacation. I recognized my contribution to that decision.

"Stan's on a vacation?"

Knowing Ollie's love of animals, I avoided mentioning something sure to upset him. If ants drew his respect and concern, fish would fare no worse. I spared all three of us from grief when I avoided any details and stated simply that Stan went visiting. Ollie accepted it at face value, asking nothing more about it. Doc smiled at my wisdom, then returned to his reading. In what seemed only a few minutes, time for me to wrap a stack of quarters, a sudden and rapid volley of popping sounds resonated through the grocery like a miniature *Tommy gun*. Doc dropped his magazine, I spilled the quarters, the unexpected noise startling us. When we saw Ollie standing at the packaged cakes display, we both became furious. Doc picked up his magazine just so he could slam it on his knee.

"Damn it, Ollie! Get away from there!"

I used my authority.

"Get out, Ollie! . . . "

He strolled to the counter, satisfied he had left no cellophane "unpopped", and freeing whatever he imagined lay trapped underneath. With his rescue efforts successful, Ollie could relax. He appeared unfazed by what Doc and I said. He showed me a package of *Twinkies* and handed me his money.

" . . . . You're gonna get me in trouble, Ollie."

That caught his attention and his face became serious.

"I'm sorry . . . . I won't do-"

Just then Mrs. Crabtree entered, and seeing my attention diverted to her, Ollie left. When she paid for her milk and eggs and left, Doc put down his magazine.

"I'll buy those boxes he busted . . . Stan doesn't have to know . . . . "

I nodded, and a half hour later Doc departed with a half dozen boxes of chocolate iced cup cakes and pecan coffee rings. I helped him carry them to his car.

" . . . . That boy'll send me into a diabetic coma yet."

Then he drove off, leaving me to ponder the seriousness of his remark.

My career in retail management came to an abrupt end later that day when Stan called and announced he planned to return that evening. Even answering the phone again on the first ring could not impact his decision, declaring himself the only one capable of running his store. My disappointment soon grew into relief. I knew no one could have pleased him, and the longer I stayed, the more opportunity he had to blame me for his own failures. When I stopped in the next morning, I only half expected to be paid. I never got to the "to do" list and would have settled for no pay on condition he refrain from any verbal attacks. But when he saw me, he said nothing about the list or anything else. He merely went to the register and retrieved a twenty-dollar bill, my full pay for the eleven hour day. I almost expected him to pull it back when I reached for it. But he handed me the money as though the mistake had been his in hiring someone in the first place, a mistake he would never repeat.

"I see we had a run on cakes . . . . Did you order more?"

I shook my head and he shrugged, seemingly not surprised. I took little comfort in knowing I did not disappoint him, and only slightly more in the twenty dollars I soon stuffed into my pocket.

19

When our school announced the date of its annual spring dance, I asked the only person for whom I would gladly make a spectacle of myself. Opal said yes and I proceeded immediately to watch *Shindig* and *Hullabaloo* and learn everything I could in the few short weeks remaining until the event. If I had expected Dad to help me with some dance steps, his words quashed my hopes.

"Except for the 'how do you do my darling' do-se-do I danced in Kindergarten, I never took a step that wasn't part of a normal walk or run . . . . "

Despite recognizing I would not approach any proficiency with the faster dances, I felt reasonably sure I could fake many of the steps. But I knew my forte would be the less demanding, yet far more exhilarating, slow dances. My excitement, however, became tempered with a concern about Opal's response. I mentally rehashed her "yes" over and over, each time becoming more convinced of her indifference. I knew Opal could be moody and I finally accepted that as the reason behind her lukewarm response. I assured myself that in the weeks ahead, her excitement would catch up to mine.

If I considered dancing my only liability in the upcoming date, it was because my eyes had adjusted to the clothes Dad and the other men wore. Their flannel shirts and dark colored slacks became a blur. From a distance, only the body type distinguished one person from another. But my refinement would leap a giant step forward when, on a trip into Brewman with Dad, I discovered the *Gentlemen's Quarterly* magazine and a way of dress I had never seen before. Surely television and the movies had their high society clothes and manners, but I never saw or heard of fancy body talc and exotic herbal shampoos intended exclusively for men. I found the revelation startling, and my initial reaction was to dismiss the magazine as one catering to "the swishers", as Dad referred to them. But it featured Kirk Douglas on the cover, an actor both of us admired for his machismo. I said nothing to Dad, afraid he would consider those new products and clothes a threat to the odors and appearance he cultivated over a lifetime, and which constituted his identity. So during another visit to Brewman, I secretly raided Emerson's drugstore to buy the colognes and shampoos required to enhance my desirability. However, I strove for irresistibility. And nothing less than a tuxedo would do.

"Thirty dollars?! . . . . to buy a tuxedo?"

"To rent one."

"Are you nuts?"

"That's what it costs . . . "

"For how long?"

"A weekend."

"Yikes! For that price you should get it for a year."

"It includes a shirt, tie, pants, and shoes."

"You got all those things. Just rent the jacket."

Dad's response did not surprise me.

"Please, Dad. It's real important."

"It shouldn't be. Don't let anyone tell ya clothes make the man. That's just bunk . . . . "

I thought back to the argument Dad had with Lenora Tipton over his refusal to wear dressier clothes. I could now accept the wisdom in what she said, the *GQ* substantiating the importance of one's dress. I began to mentally piece together another outfit to wear. Without Dad's loan, my old navy sport jacket, dingy white shirt, and gray sharkskin pants with frayed cuffs would have to suffice. I did not try to hide my glumness.

" . . . . Do you practice that hangdog look? . . . Because it's really good . . . "

I neither smiled nor spoke.

" . . . . Okay . . . . if it means that much to you . . . . "

I hugged him with all my strength.

" . . . . If you suffocate me, you won't get the money."

I let go.

Dad took out his wallet, removed the money, and held onto it.

" . . . . It's a loan. You'll have to work it off at the store."

When I agreed, he gave me the money and I reserved my tuxedo. The night before the dance, Dad drove me to pick it up. The huge box contained all the materials needed to transform me into a debonair and sophisticated gentleman. I now understood the excitement girls had for a new dress. I became almost giddy as Dad opened the trunk for me. He just shook his head, saying nothing more about it. The next day I telephoned Opal to finalize our meeting time.

"I can't go."

I thought she was kidding.

"Right . . . . Good one, Ope."

"I'm serious . . . . I'm sorry, Hal."

"Sorry?! I rented a tux . . . . cost me thirty bucks!"

Her voice became cold.

"Then I'll pay you back."

The money was the least of it and I regretted mentioning it.

"I'm sorry. You know it's not the money. I'm just . . . . disappointed, that's all . . . . "

I almost said "crushed", but I kept my dignity. Her silence began to irritate me.

" . . . . Well, you're obviously not disappointed."

"If you want to fight, I'll hang up."

"Then tell me why . . . . just do that."

"I have my reasons."

Just the answer I did not want. The possible causes ranged from me, to nothing whatever to do with me. I also suspected money had something to do with it, and I concluded Opal felt too ashamed to admit she could not afford a new dress.

"I don't have to wear a tux . . . . It's really not me, anyway."

"Don't be silly. You go . . . . Take someone else."

The hesitation in her command suggested this might be a ploy to test my loyalty.

"I don't want to take anyone else. Only you. And if you don't go, neither will I."

I considered my response noble. However, I soon understood Opal meant what she said, seeming almost anxious to pawn me off on someone else.

"That makes no sense. You have a tux. Just ask someone else."

This time I could not care less about my dignity or pride.

"Come on, Ope . . . . Please . . . . We'll have fun . . . . Please say you'll go."

"You haven't been listening."

"Then tell me why. I deserve that, at least."

"I told you I have my reasons."

"At least let me know what I did."

"Ma is havin' an episode. She needs me home . . . That's all you need to know."

"I thought she was okay."

"Well she's not okay! And even if she didn't need me, I'd think twice about going with you."

"But what did I say?"

"Never mind. You won't understand."

I felt reluctant to pursue something sure to increase Opal's antagonism towards me. I didn't know what else to say and paused to consider what else to ask. However, that became unnecessary when Opal hung up without saying another word. For the next hour I remained paralyzed in my chair. When I recovered, I kicked, screamed, and cursed before telephoning the tuxedo shop. I tried, unsuccessfully, to get a refund. That weekend I wore my tuxedo all day, and slept in it all night, prompting Dad to say I looked like a mix between a frumpy maitre'd and a down and out tycoon. I didn't care. I wanted to spend every moment in clothes that had promised so much, hoping somehow to recapture the optimism I felt two days before. When I saw Opal a few days later, she acted as though our conversation never occurred. I no longer expected her to apologize for breaking a promise, and any anger I still felt disappeared once I saw her. We went for a soda at Ronnie's and talked about a lot of things and nothing at all. Her words evaporated as they were spoken, my concentration devoted entirely to a face that grew increasingly more beautiful each day. Suddenly she stood up, looking disappointed, and I feared she had expected a response to something I did not hear. But when she excused herself to check on her mother, and did not criticize me, I flattered myself with the belief her disappointment stemmed from having to leave me.

20

If my high school days seemed as infinite as my elementary ones, that all ended abruptly on Career Day. The end of my junior year presaged the beginning of my realization that one day I would graduate and have to earn a living. I had only given passing thought to the job I might choose, often letting a flashy uniform dictate my choice. But baseball and firefighting no longer captivated me, and as I looked at the program, nothing else did either. The topics ranged from dairy farming, which Ollie could not wait to attend, to nursing, which Opal said she would "check out". I read and reread a program that seemed more like a bad menu, not finding anything I wanted to attend. That is, until I saw who would lead one of the discussions.

I arrived a few minutes late, sneaking in unseen at the back of a packed classroom. I assumed from the large turnout many, if not all, saw medicine as their ticket to wealth and prestige. And yet, before them stood a man who had very little of either. But if they came to hear about a doctor's daily lifesaving rescues, there existed no one more willing to tell them than Doc. His audience sat silent and motionless as he mesmerized them with his awe-inspiring anecdotes. Familiarity, however, provided me with a different perspective. As I watched the enthralled expressions, I could not help but think of a kindergarten class before a perverse storyteller, or naive tourists accepting unquestioningly information from a fraudulent tour guide. Doc's voice boomed as he related tales of horror and heroism to the smiling and adoring students before him. I felt certain he did not see me, his eyes focused on those closest to him. I suspect he really did not want to know who was in the audience, afraid that someone he knew might distract him from the fabrications he told.

"Many a time I was called on to do the impossible. But you can't pick and choose the situation like you were picking and choosing . . . . "

His mind drew a blank. I wanted to shout "*Twinkies* or *Ho-Hos*". Doc soon recovered.

" . . . . like picking and choosing which clothes to wear. An emergency is an emergency . . . . "

He stopped, and I thought he might be waiting for applause. But none came. Instead, his audience nodded their heads with such fervor, they reminded me of a television documentary I had seen about Jews praying at the Wailing Wall. Doc then licked his lips, and I assumed from either the juicy story he planned to tell or, more likely, from the juicy hero he would later eat.

" . . . . A doctor must be a detective, and a country doctor must be like . . . . a squad of detectives. A patient presents a complex set of symptoms, or clues, that a doctor must analyze and piece together like a puzzle in order to make the most precise diagnosis . . . . "

I thought of his "cancer or nothing" diagnoses. Doc raised his voice, along with his forefinger, to impart dramatic flair to his next point.

" . . . . But what if . . . . But what if . . . . you do not have the luxury of time?! Take this case as typical . . . . "

He sighed.

" . . . . I no sooner return to my office, exhausted from a day of house calls, when a young boy is rushed to me, his leg hemorrhaging from an apparent severed artery. The blood was pouring onto the floor like the Red Sea in the *Ten Commandments* . . . . "

At this, two of the three girls emitted an "ooooo" and a "yucky" that drew laughter from the boys. Doc ignored it.

" . . . . and I'm not Moses or Charleton Heston who can simply will it to stop flowing . . . . "

Doc waited, expecting laughter, but the response was quieter than the Dead Sea. He now leaned forward and spoke more softly.

" . . . A normal childhood activity, a simple game of tug o' war gone awry, and a new crisis . . . . and to complicate it even further, the lad is my best friend's son . . . . talk about the challenge to keep a cool head . . . . "

He stopped. I realized he had been talking about me. What I remembered as a cut, a few drops of blood, and an interruption of his lunch, Doc transformed into a Cecil B. DeMille epic. I wondered if he had seen me, and would he expect me to come up and confirm his skeleton of truth cloaked in robes of deceit. I crouched down, hoping that if he had not seen me, I could remain undetected. When he continued with his story, I relaxed.

" . . . . Massive blood loss could mean amputation or worse. Seconds are hours. The poor child is crying, screaming from the pain. But you must, absolutely must, stay calm when everyone and everything around you appears out of control . . . "

Doc leaned back in his chair, and said nothing more. I knew Doc employed this tactic to wring every last ounce of dramatic juice from his story. He spoke softly.

" . . . . Yes, the boy was saved. And do you know why? . . . . "

He didn't wait for an answer.

" . . . . It wasn't the medicine or the stitches or the tourniquet or anything in my little black bag. It wasn't anything you could touch . . . . No, it was something in here . . . . "

Doc pointed to his stomach. I became nauseated when I considered the extensive range of "somethings" in there. His next words seemed to justify his own inadequacies.

" . . . . The medical knowledge and training will only get you so far . . . . then it's the intuition-what's in your gut. That is what is essential for you to become a miracle worker . . . . Do you want to become miracle workers? . . . . "

A DROWNING IN SWANSON LAKE   217

We all assumed it was just another rhetorical question. Then Doc stood up and banged his cane hard on the floor.

" . . . . Well, do you?! . . . "

Everyone nodded. Not satisfied with that response and probably relishing another opportunity to exercise his dramatic flair, he backed up a few steps, and struck the blackboard with the heel of hand. He only reached the word "hear", in "I can't hear . . . " when the framed glass photograph of President Johnson fell off the wall, narrowly missing Doc's head. Seeing no one hurt in the audience, he looked at the spot above the blackboard where the photograph once rested, and at the floor where the pieces of glass surrounded him. I expected the incident to unnerve him and render him speechless. But true to his own advice about keeping a "cool head", Doc calmly and brilliantly incorporated the event into his speech.

" . . . . There. Two minutes ago everything is hunky dory. Then an accident. Glass shatters. But for the grace of God, an eye could have been cut, an artery severed. It happens every day and if you're the country doctor, you have to be prepared . . . . always prepared."

When he stopped speaking, I could have heard their eyes blink. Except none did. They had not yet recovered from their trance. Then someone clapped and soon everyone, including myself, applauded. The applause grew louder, and when Doc bowed to acknowledge their response, it grew louder still. He smiled and I could see he felt genuinely moved. I slipped out before he could scan the room for any questioners. I walked outside and waited for Ollie and Opal. The school buses were lined up, and I enjoyed a few quiet moments before the three o'clock bell created bedlam. The day had become overcast, a stinging late March chill refusing to be tamed. I soon heard applause coming from the other classrooms, although not as sustained as that given Doc. I thought again about his speech and the way he looked after the applause began. If I felt glad for the reception he received, I felt sad for him. I knew he described the career he once hoped it would be, and not the one it actually became. His glorious fantasies about his own self importance and capabilities had to crash against the sobering realization of his own limitations. And I knew that after he bragged to Stan and Dad about his performance, he would be left with himself and with the sadness that was his life.

The bell sounded and I stepped aside to avoid being trampled. Soon I heard my name. I looked to see Ollie coming towards me with a huge grin.

"Guess what I'm gonna be, Dusty?"

He had forgotten he already told me. I pretended to think.

"I'm not sure . . . . but I bet you'll make a great dairy farmer."

His eyes widened, his jaw hung open.

"Ha! That's right. That's what I'm gonna be! . . . . How did you know?"

"I just figured."

It seemed the perfect job for him. Animals, no people, and lots of hard work.

"I hope you like cheese. Because you can have all the cheese and milk you want . . . forever."

I smiled and patted him gently on the back.

"Thanks, buddy."

Ollie appeared pleased, as much for the kindness he could show me as for the new career he found. Opal soon joined us.

"Dusty guessed what I'm gonna be."

I jumped in quickly.

"I guessed dairy farmer because I thought Ollie would be perfect at it. Don't you agree?"

For a moment she seemed puzzled, then realized.

"Yes, I do . . . . You see, Ollie, what a good choice you made?"

Ollie beamed and skipped every third or fourth step on the way to the bus. On the way home, Opal seemed especially quiet.

"What's wrong, Ope?"

"Nothing . . . . just thinking."

"About what?"

"Today . . . . and the nurse that spoke."

"You didn't like her?"

"She was great . . . . what she said sounded terrific but . . . . I just never thought of that before . . . . of going to school so far away."

I looked at her. Sommerville Junior College was only twenty miles away.

"Sommerville isn't that far. You—"

"It doesn't have a nursing program. Nurse Fulton said the nearest accredited one was ninety miles away in Schenectady . . . . "

It took me a few moments to realize what that meant. She looked down at her lap.

" . . . . I guess I never thought about leaving."

Neither did I. If I expected our school days to last forever, I felt the same about our lives together. On the ride home, Opal and I sat silently while Ollie leaned his head against the window and stared out at the passing farms. However, except for an occasional cow or hog, those farms were devoted exclusively to growing corn, soybean, or wheat. I knew Ollie, too, would have to leave Swanson Lake to pursue his career. I reminded myself that a great deal could happen in the year until graduation, and I drew comfort from the belief they would eventually change their minds. But like Doc, who could delude himself for only so long, I knew the three of us had reached a crossroads. That day Ollie and Opal found their life's work, and they would have dreams and plans to carry them forward to graduation and beyond. It was only a matter of time before they would have to leave me behind.

As I expected, the summer never slowed down life long enough for me to catch up to Ollie and Opal. The gap only widened as they moved forward with their career plans, while I remained motionless and uncertain. I envied them for finding a "calling", as my school's guidance counselor, Mr. Hockney, referred to it, and I felt abandoned as they went off to pursue their dreams. Mr. Hockney arranged for Ollie to work on a dairy farm about forty miles northeast of Swanson Lake, near the Vermont border. Opal accepted a nurse's aid position at the local hospital. Neither could contain the excitement they felt. I contained my disappointment.

"I'm going farming, Dusty!"

"I heard. And you promised to send me cheese."

"I will . . . . and sour cream and buttermilk and—"

"You keep the buttermilk. It tastes like upchuck."

I felt a slap on my arm.

"Harold Moffat!"

"Well, it does."

"That's beside the point."

"Dusty, what kind of cheese should I send?"

"I like them all."

I pictured Ollie organizing them according to color variations and odor. Opal gently tugged at my arm.

"I already met the other nurses. I know—"

Ollie interrupted.

"I'm not sure I could send you sour cream. It's too runny."

"You hush, Ollie. I was talking."

I felt like a father whose two children vied for his attention. Ollie rarely challenged his sister, and he didn't now. He merely switched his attention to an empty corn flakes box a few yards ahead and began kicking it. Opal continued her story.

" . . . . They're payin' me next to nothin', but I'll learn so much . . . . And I'll be better able to care for ma . . . . to talk to people like her . . . . "

I nodded, although I didn't quite understand what she meant. We walked briefly before she spoke again.

" . . . . I'm really excited . . . And I'm glad I get to come home each day."

I knew she intended that for my benefit, but her smile could not reassure me. Our time together was ending. In another year, I feared it would be over. I smiled at everything she felt excited about, and said everything she needed to hear. When I returned home and lay in bed, I became convinced I would die from the ache pressing hard against my chest.

With Ollie gone and Opal working, the days seemed endless. I spent much of the day helping Dad at his store, home renovations and exterior painting making summers his busiest time. I could rarely pull him away to get a soda at Ronnie's. He feared he might miss a customer, or anger one.

"And with my luck, it'll be someone with a once in a lifetime order . . . . maybe for a thousand dollars."

A Drowning In Swanson Lake 221

I could not convince him to change his mind, even when I suggested Stan or Doc as his lookouts. He laughed.

" . . . . Yeah, right . . . . just tell me to go out of business, why don't ya."

I didn't know if that was a reference to the fire eight years before, but it didn't matter. I stopped asking and either went to Ronnie's myself, or stepped next door to Stan's.

If a record mid July heat wave brought Dad more business, his sale of air conditioners and fans almost double his previous summer's total, it brought Doc more misery. Already barely able to walk a block without wheezing, the near one hundred degree temperatures only intensified his difficulty. He struggled to breathe after only a few steps, his furrowed forehead acting as tributaries for the perspiration they washed into his eyes. Doc had neither the energy to read or argue with Stan. He mostly just slept in his chair, his chin burrowed deep into his chest, oblivious to the flies crawling on him and the wasps hovering over his head. I knew Dad had once sold him an air conditioner and I wondered why he just didn't stay home. I had to assume he needed company more than he needed comfort, although he received neither. Only awake for short periods, he barely said anything to Stan or me. We all expected him to return to his usual feisty self once cooler weather returned.

When I became listless and began to mope, Dad assumed I too had become a casualty of the heat. However, when the weather became much cooler a few weeks later, and my brooding only worsened, he realized the cause of my distress. Dad took me aside after we closed.

"Listen, gloomy Gus. Your friends didn't drop off the earth."

"They might as well have."

"Sure. Feel sorry for yourself . . . "

I made a face.

" . . . . Be glad you can see Opal in the evening."

I didn't answer.

" . . . . What's wrong?"

"She's usually too tired . . . . or she'd rather spend the time with her mom."

"She's quite the girl, Hal . . . . I hope you'll do the same for me one day."

I became annoyed. I didn't want to talk about "one day". I wanted sympathy and solutions for my dilemma that day. He seemed to hear my thoughts.

" . . . . I have an idea . . . . "

I felt a bit guilty underestimating him.

" . . . . it seems if Opal has decided to help her mom, there's no point beating yourself to get her to change her mind . . . . This is obviously something she needs to do."

"So that's it? . . . . Just give up?"

Dad gave a half laugh.

"Well for God's sake, Hal, what are you gonna do?"

He waited for my answer. I gave him the only one I had.

"I don't know."

Then I remembered.

" . . . but you said you had an idea."

"You didn't let me finish . . . . I think you've got too much time on your hands and so-

"I'm not helping you out at the store?"

"You are, and you do a very good job when you're there."

"I'm there-"

"Don't interrupt . . . . Since you admit Opal is too tired or busy to see you now, why don't you do the same? It'll not only keep you from dwelling on her, it'll prepare you for the future."

It took me a moment to realize.

"You want me to run a hardware store?"

I didn't care that I hurt him.

"Thoughtless me . . . . But do you know how much really goes into owning a business like mine? It's not just stocking shelves and ringing up purchases. There's bookkeeping-you see the accounting I do at home . . . there's deciding what merchandise to order, how much to order and when, and you can't make many mistakes or you find yourself out of business . . . . That's a lot you gotta know and it takes smarts to do it . . . . So instead of feeling insulted, you should feel flattered I think you can do it . . . . "

A DROWNING IN SWANSON LAKE

When Dad stopped talking, he went outside. I did not follow him. I tried to think of an alternative to his proposal, something that would excuse me from the career he planned for me. But I could think of nothing specific or concrete, and I soon joined Dad outside.

"Do you want me to open and close?"

"What make you think I want you at all?"

"I didn't mean to hurt your feelings . . . . I guess Stan-"

"Stan? What's he got to do with it?"

I gambled on the lie.

"I was worried I'd become another Stan and run the store into ground."

"You gotta be kidding . . . . "

I looked to see if he expected my confession, but he continued.

" . . . . You won't run my store into the ground, I promise you that. First of all, you're not the yahoo Stan is. You've got too many smarts to screw things up. And with me trainin' ya and the business the way it is, you can't fail. I guarantee it . . . . By the way, who says I'm giving you control of the store?"

"I thought you wanted me to run it."

"Yeah, I want you to learn how to run things and be ready to take over when I retire or keel over . . . . until then, we're partners."

Stan and Doc had made "partners" a dirty word. Dad went on.

" . . . . Tell me how many high school kids become an instant partner in a thriving business? . . . . "

I smiled to acknowledge the truth in what he said, but said nothing else. It seemed like hours before I could answer. My silence only put him on the defensive.

" . . . That's okay. I didn't like it at first either."

I could barely get out the next words, afraid of how he might react.

"But . . . . maybe I'll wanna do something else."

"Like . . . . ?"

"I don't know . . . . I'm checking out the community college and-"

Dad laughed.

"Since when?"

"Well, I'm thinking about it .... "

"Well maybe you're doin' more thinkin' than doin'."

"But once I'm working the store full time .... How am I gonna have time to consider anything else?"

Dad chuckled.

"You're not being pushed into slavery .... I'll give you time .... I'm just sayin' to give it a try."

Since I had nothing to lose, I accepted Dad's offer. The next day I began my work as a junior partner. Dad paid me for my time and displayed a good deal of patience in explaining everything about the business. After a few weeks I became proficient in accounting procedures, in ordering, deciding what and how much to stock, and in planning special merchandise promotions. I waited on customers with the tolerance of a saint, and organized his inventory so that logic replaced randomness. Dad expressed his pleasure in no uncertain terms.

"I'm proud of you, son .... You're a natural at this."

I tried not to read any more into the word, "natural". I accepted it as Dad's affirmation for the work I did at the time, ignoring any of its long-term implications. I continued impressing Dad with my long hours and hard work, and the job did manage to keep me from dwelling too much on Opal. But she made more time for me, mostly on the weekends, and we talked often about the futures that awaited us.

"But if you don't like it ... "

"Sometimes I'm not so sure .... I'm good at it .... "

"C'mon, Hal. I know you too well."

"It's not like I've found something better .... "

"You will .... I know you will."

"But for now, it's okay .... really ... "

I was eager to change the subject.

" .... Maybe I should go into dairy farming with Ollie."

"He'd like that."

"He's still rabid about it?"

"To say the least."

If I wanted to convince Opal of my desire to find something better, I first had to convince myself. I began by priming myself for any possible opportunities, even praying for the revelation that would send me in a new direction. But God had no answers. In the weeks and months ahead my mind generated no solutions and I drew no inspiration from anything around me. Instead, I continued helping Dad with the store, even after school started. If I felt no urgency in changing anything, it was because I ignored what had fast intruded on my life. With the escalation of the war in Viet Nam, my future grew more uncertain each day.

21

Ollie kept his promise about sending me cheese, which didn't surprise me. He might exaggerate something, saying "his stone skipped a hundred times across the pond" or "a snowstorm left fifty feet at least", but I never knew him to lie intentionally about anything. Even when lying was called for, as in the "hide and seek" we played as children, Ollie chose truthfulness over innocent deception. A simple question always brought the purely unadulterated response.

"Ollie, are you there? . . . Under the car?"

A loud whisper would soon emanate from that spot.

"Yeah, Hal . . . I'm here."

Needless to say, Ollie spent most of the game as "it". He couldn't understand why Opal and I didn't extend the same courtesies. Now I missed my friend more than I had realized. I became genuinely excited when Opal called one evening to say Ollie would be returning in another week.

"I can't wait to see him! We have lots to catch up on."

I had not spoken with him since he left, and my letters only generated a wheel of cheese and a note saying, "I really like it here. I hope you like the cheese". I enjoyed the excellent cheese, but his five word reply did not satisfy all my inquiries about his job and life.

"There'll be no gettin' a word in when you two get goin'."

"Maybe one or two . . . . We'll see."

Opal smiled.

"I was wonderin' if you wanted to take a ride Saturday to Brewman to—"

I heard enough. I had not seen her in over a week.

"Yes."

She laughed.

"I'm glad . . . . I thought we might pick up a welcome home present for Ollie . . . . "

"Great idea."

Opal agreed to pick me up at the store that Saturday, Dad giving me the afternoon off. Just before half past eleven, I began making strategic adjustments to my appearance. I had only thirty minutes to mute a recent eruption of pimples, neutralize the aftertaste and breath odor from three hours of soda and cheese snacks, and comb my hair in a way to make it look uncombed and wind blown. With a tube of *Clearasil* skin cream, two packages of wintergreen *Lifesavers*, and a bottle of *Lilac Vegetal* I kept hidden in the back, I transformed myself into a more "desirable commodity", as Dad would say, or irresistibility, as I preferred to call it. But I had not yet finalized the placement of my hairs when a customer entered.

"Dad, could you get that?"

In the middle of stocking shelves, he looked at me.

"Yes, Mr. Moffat. At your service."

As he returned to the front, I heard him giggle. When I finally became convinced I had maximized my full physical potential, I said a quick goodbye to Dad and waited outside. A sudden gust of wind imposed a far more natural look to my hair than I ever intended. Opal soon pulled up in a very used peacock blue '62 *Chevy Bel-Air*, her petite figure dwarfed by the enormous car Mr. Magnusson bought her for commuting to work. Her smile hypnotized me and I could not stop staring at her face as I entered the car. I kissed her and leaned back, relaxed and peaceful in her presence. We had only driven a couple blocks in silence when suddenly hands reached from behind my seat and grabbed my throat. I let out a scream that loosened concrete, jumping from my seat and hitting my head on the roof. Then I heard laughter, some of it Opal's, but most of it a tortured hyena laugh I heard a thousand times before. I turned around and saw Ollie, doubled over with hysteria. I felt torn between killing him and hugging him.

"I'm gonna grind you into lunch meat. I swear I will."

My threat only increased the shrillness of his laugh.

"He wanted to surprise you."

"That's not the word I'd use."

My heart found its way back into my chest.

"He's been waiting since yesterday to do that."

"Sooo, you and Ollie conspired against me?"

"Yup."

"And you don't feel a bit guilty . . . . "

"Not one intsy bit."

I smiled. It seemed we were children again. Ollie soon recovered enough to speak.

"Did ya think it was *The Thing* around your throat?"

"I'm not sure what I thought, except that I felt done in for sure."

I knew that would bring Ollie to a new boil, but I enjoyed seeing him laugh. In Brewman we spent much of the day doing what we had always enjoyed. We made the rounds of the candy store and ice cream parlor, and just walked. I didn't want anything to change. Not the shops, not the candies, and certainly not our lives. But consignment shops occupied the space where *The Ambassador* movie theater once stood, *The Crafty Hobbyist* had become a dry cleaners, Lenora Tipton marrying and moving away, the penny candies now cost a quarter, and our lives were exploding apart like rockets in a fireworks display.

The next morning I invited Opal for a walk near the pond. The chrysanthemums trumpeted the first colors of autumn and I enticed her with a promise of their beauty. She agreed to meet me early that afternoon at what had always been one of our favorite meeting spots. We would sit sometimes for hours, saying very little,

A DROWNING IN SWANSON LAKE   229

our shoulders pressed against each other as we stared at the splashes
of color shimmering on the pond. As I waited for Opal, I thought
about my disappointment in not having her to myself the day
before. Our times together had become increasingly infrequent. I
felt as though I was losing her, and the opportunities to win her
back were diminishing rapidly. I wanted her to hear what remained
unsaid over the years—that I loved her from the time I first shoved
the rock into her ear. My hands began trembling and my tongue
became hard and dry. I popped a half dozen *Lifesavers* into my
mouth and waited, before the trembling in my knees forced me to
sit on one of the large mossy boulders. Soon I heard her voice and
jumped up. But she had directed her words to Ollie, who now
followed her a good six lengths back.

"Sorry I'm so late. Ollie insisted on coming the last minute."

"Hi ya, Dusty."

I stared at Opal in disbelief. My emotions became a carnival
game wheel, and I waited for it to stop spinning before I knew
what to feel. Anger, disappointment, and hurt overwhelmed me as
they did years earlier, when I visited my mother. But this time I
would not cry. I just stood there staring into Opal's face and seeing
nothing in particular.

"Are you mad . . . . that I'm so late?"

My first attempt to answer ended in a sigh. When I recovered
enough to speak, I uttered, uncensored, the words still reverberating
in my brain.

"What is he doing here? . . . "

Opal's eyes widened from astonishment over the insensitivity
of my remark. She then turned to Ollie, who seemed unsure
whether to stay or leave. I had no intention of retracting my
statement, although I softened my protest.

" . . . . You always come alone, Ope, when we meet here . . . . "

If I secretly and naively hoped Opal would consider me the
victim, I soon discovered otherwise. Her eyes narrowed and I
steadied myself for the assault.

"What is he doing here?!. . . . . What is he doing here?!"

Her repetition of the question only reinforced Ollie's insecurity, convincing him his sister had seconded my statement. He began to leave when Opal called him back.

" . . . . Stay, Ollie! Hal wants to know why you're here . . . . "

Ollie looked down at the ground and then up again at Opal.

" . . . Tell him, Ollie."

He spoke barely above a whisper, as though afraid he might not give the correct answer.

"I wanted to see Dusty . . . . He's my friend . . . "

"And what else did you tell me?"

Ollie thought for a moment before remembering.

"I missed him."

"That's right. You hadn't seen him all summer and you missed him."

Ollie smiled, pleased he had passed the test. I tried a defense.

"Come on, Ope. Ollie and I just saw each other yesterday . . . . "

"The first time in ten weeks. So what if he wants to see you again. You should feel flattered."

"I do . . . it's just I wanted to be with you . . . . just the two of us . . . . We hardly see each other anymore."

"It's very difficult now . . . "

I wanted her to say more, that she wanted to be with me also, but she didn't. When I took her hand, she pulled away. Opal's coldness became her revenge for my remark about Ollie. I decided to make amends to both of them.

"Hey, Ollie. How about us havin' lunch tomorrow? Two cattle rustlers sharin' some grub . . . . "

"Yeah!"

The word burst from him. I knew Opal would not join us. With barely two weeks remaining before we all returned to school, she worked both ends of the day at her nursing job.

"Ronnie's . . . . eleven tomorrow . . . . Okay?"

He nodded so hard I thought his head would fall off.

"What're you goin' to have?"

I thought a moment.

"A cheeseburger with extra pickles . . . . or a b.l.t."

"Me, too."

A Drowning In Swanson Lake   231

We shook on it, Opal now smiling. As we all walked to the far
side of the pond to find the driest piece of ground to lie on, I took
her hand once again. This time she did not pull away.

Late Monday morning I set out to keep my lunch appointment
with Ollie. When I approached Stan's on my way to Ronnie's, I
saw Doc and Sheriff MacCauley leaving. Although it seemed strange
to see the sheriff carrying Doc's black medical bag, I figured his
age and health earned him the assistance. Both appeared somber
and I assumed they were responding to an emergency.

"Hi, Doc . . . . Sheriff."

Only MacCauley answered, mumbling a "hello" before going
to his car. Doc glanced at me, said nothing, as he went to sit in the
passenger seat of the patrol car. I speculated it might be another
suicide, thinking back to Ben Maxwell and the time Doc and the
sheriff worked together, or perhaps a homicide, where a challenging
forensic medical examination would enable Doc to experience the
excitement and self-importance he talked about on Career Day.
My mind entertained numerous possibilities, from a suspicious
heart attack to a grisly mutilation. But when the sheriff drove off
without lights or siren, I resigned myself to a routine post mortem
or a relatively minor driving accident. I thought no more about it
and soon arrived at Ronnie's, where I took a booth in the back,
across from the air conditioner. While I waited for Ollie, I looked
around at the drawings of *The Leaning Tower of Pisa* next to the
advertised featured selection, "calamari marinara". I had never heard
of a calamari, although I suspected it came from the most
undesirable part of a creature. Ronnie plastered the walls with the
tricolor Italian flags and alternated her hi-fi music selections
between Perry Como or Dean Martin, and Italian Operas. In case
someone still doubted the authenticity of her Roman trattoria,
the hanging garlic cloves and Genoa salamis, and the red and white
checkered tablecloths were meant to sway. When Ronnie crashed
through the kitchen door wearing a red, green, and white Italian
neck scarf and shouting "mange, mange-eat,eat" to everyone and
everything, the illusion, or delusion, became complete. She then
considered her customers ripe for seduction. However, despite all

her efforts and pleas to try her calamari, customers stayed with her lunch staple-the cheeseburger and fries platter.

Ollie soon entered and walked hurriedly towards me. Suddenly, a burly forearm reached out and stopped him like a subway commuter smashing into a locked turnstile. Ronnie then nearly suffocated him with hugs and questions.

"When did you get back? And why didn't you write? Are you sure farming is what you wanna do?"

She fired the questions so rapidly, Ollie only managed to open and close his mouth and never answer anything she asked. When a customer called for a refill on the coffee, Ollie took the opportunity to escape and join me. He had a huge grin on his face.

"It's nice to be missed, huh?"

He thought a moment.

"But I wish I didn't have to go away first."

"Only for awhile. Then everyone is glad to see you."

He smiled.

"Yeah, I like that part."

"I bet you do. You milk it for all it's worth . . . . "

He laughed. Then I realized.

" . . . . And farmers know how to milk it, right?"

Ollie laughed again, nodding. I heard Ronnie scream into the kitchen, for everyone to hear,

"One calamari marinara!"

I looked for Blue, who apparently entered only a few minutes before. But Ronnie's attempts to start a stampede for that dish ended with Blue's order. However, she never stopped trying, and when I saw her approach our booth, I groaned. She looked at Ollie.

"Must be tough gettin' used to civilization after three months with the moo moos . . . . We probably seem like New York City to you . . . . "

She laughed. So did Ollie, whose loyalty to the joker often surpassed his understanding and enjoyment of the joke. Soon I laughed too, but at my own joke. I tried to picture a moo moose, and the recipes Ronnie would create from its body parts. She stared at me, my laughter still continuing after theirs ended.

A DROWNING IN SWANSON LAKE   233

" . . . . You're either in one heckuva good mood or I'm a lot funnier
than I think . . . . How about tryin' our featured selection? . . . . "
I stopped laughing.
" . . . . You like seafood, don't you?"
"It gives me blisters."
"I know it does, Ollie. But I'm asking Hal."
"Sometimes I like shrimp . . . . "
"This is better than shrimp . . . . and it's in tomato sauce. You
like tomato sauce on pizza, don't you?"
"I suppose . . . . "
I felt cornered.
"Try it, Dusty. It sounds good."
I glared at my supposed ally, then looked at Ronnie.
"But I never even heard of a calamari . . . . "
"It's Italian . . . . one of the many fruits de la mer . . . . And
it's delicious . . . . an excellent choice. And for you, Ollie?"
I refused to be sucked into the vortex Ronnie created with
hurried explanations that clarified nothing.
"Tomato sauce . . . . on fruit?"
"No, no . . . . fruits de la mer. It's French . . . . just a French
expression."
"Then what is it? . . . . in English."
She hesitated.
"Squid."
"Puke! That's what we cut up in biology . . . ain't it, Dusty?"
I nodded. Ronnie looked around before reprimanding Ollie.
"Hush up. You've never complained about my specials before
so don't be sayin' things about somethin' you never even tried. If
you didn't have the seafood allergy, I'd force you to try it . . . .
that's how sure I am that you'll like it."
"Uh-uh."
With Ollie's rebuttal completed, Ronnie turned her attention
back to me.
"So . . . . Ready to try somethin' wonderful."
"No, thanks . . . . I'll have the b . . . l . . . t, fries, and a cherry
Coke."

Ollie ordered the burger platter. Ronnie snapped the menus and walked off in a huff. I knew she felt more frustrated than offended. She had come so close to hooking a potential devotee, only to have me wiggle free at the end.

" . . . . Squid . . . . barf."

And then I stuck my finger down my throat to emphasize my point. Ollie laughed.

"Squid barf . . . . That's funny."

"I bet you ate lots of good stuff up there. Everything probably tasted better."

"It did. Mrs. Dietz baked everything from scratch, like Ma used to . . . . The bread was better than *Wonder Bread* and I ate rhubarb pies and milk that tasted better than Stan's . . . . "

"No *Twinkies*? . . . . "

He smiled, shook his head. Soon Ronnie returned with our lunches, saying nothing, but slamming the dishes hard on the table to show her contempt for our menu choices. Ollie didn't seem to notice and I didn't care. We began eating the fries on the tablecloth before getting to the ones on the plate. After a few minutes, I spoke again.

" . . . . Well, old man, another two weeks and you know what. It'll probably seem like prison after being out on the farm all day . . . . "

"I wish I could go back."

I thought I knew what he meant. Later I would realize I didn't, and would reconstruct every word of our conversation for clues.

"You will. One more year and you're a graduate . . . . I'm really proud of you."

Ollie looked serious.

" . . . . What's wrong?"

"How come the communists want to make us slaves?"

I chuckled.

"You've been talking to Stan again?"

He shook his head.

" . . . . They want to put women in houses and make them do bad things . . . . houses of ill . . . . something."

"Ill repute? Where did you hear that?"

"Mr. Dietz. He said the commies were going to take over all the farms, and kill children and animals, just for the heck of it."

I sighed. Of all the brains least able to resist washing, Ollie's had to be foremost. I wondered if Mr. Hockney or anyone else at the school knew all they should about farmer Dietz. I looked at Ollie, who began shredding his napkin and dropping the pieces into his coffee cup. I wanted to assure him the communists could never defeat us, and he did not need to let Stan's, Mr. Dietz's, or anyone else's paranoia upset him. But he had already become convinced of the truth in what he heard, and I considered it futile to even try and reason with him. After sitting silently for another ten minutes, I stood up to leave. To my surprise, Ollie remained seated. He then looked up just long enough to nod to a question I never asked, before resuming his napkin shredding.

When another week went by without Opal and me seeing each other, I began to panic. I feared the summer had put too much time between us. I wanted to speed up life, to resolve what had been gnawing at me for so long. I decided that by week's end, I would find out whether or not Opal Magnusson wanted to marry me.

I drew some courage from the fact that Opal had already accepted my marriage proposal. Eight years earlier, in the apple basket and makeshift hot air balloon that would transport us to distant continents, her enthusiastic "yes, I will" resounded through my head and transformed the back yard into a land of enchantment. I thought about that earlier promise and tried to see my latest proposal as a mere formality. But maturity knocked aside the naïve assumptions from my childhood as I soon headed into the great unknown.

I called Opal early one Friday evening and asked her to meet me at the pond. This time I used diplomacy, expecting the words "important" and "confidential" to convey my wish for privacy. We agreed to meet at ten the next morning. This would give me time to drop Dad off at the store before proceeding on to Brewman for the lavender gladiolus I planned to buy her. That night I tried to think of everything except what I would actually say to her. I didn't want my proposal to sound rehearsed. I would just say the words I felt, as I felt them, even as I realized my nervousness threatened to render me sufficiently incoherent.

The next morning I drove Dad to work. He kept looking at me, expecting me to provide details. Aside from telling him I planned to meet Opal and possibly go to Brewman for lunch, I revealed nothing else. Soon he grew tired of my expressionless face and stared ahead until we reached the store. Before closing the door, Dad leaned in.

"Worries are taking numbers. You'll get old before your time."

He appeared frustrated when I only nodded. But I felt sure he would have discouraged me, and maybe not without good reason. However, I did not want logic and reason to intrude. If my impulsiveness rarely went beyond a late night walk in the rain, soon I would dive blindfolded, not sure if there was water below and not bothering to ask. It felt exhilarating and I didn't want a few unwelcome details to ruin it for me.

The florist had three bunches of the lavender gladiolus and I bought them all. A few of the flowers had already bloomed, while most of the stalks had not yet opened. Those reminded me of long paintbrushes dipped into a lavender watercolor. I lay the flowers on the back seat so Opal would not see them when I drove up. On the way to the pond, my stomach erupted into a cacophony of noises, most of which sounded like popped mattress springs. I wanted to go back a day and erase everything I said and thought, afraid I had confused stupidity with courage. But I soon calmed myself with memories of how our love showed itself in the touches and looks we gave each other. I convinced myself only shyness kept us from showing more passion. When I reached the pond and saw Opal walking towards me, smiling, I had no doubt about the wisdom in proceeding with my plans. I stepped out of the car and looked around, half expecting Ollie to jump out from behind a bush.

"Ollie's not here . . . . Your hints were pretty obvious."

"I only wanted-"

A DROWNING IN SWANSON LAKE   237

"I know. . . . He wouldn'ta come anyway. Dad took him to buy some new clothes."

"So maybe it was meant to be."

I could not say why I expected a smile, but none came. She ignored my remark.

"What is this big secret? You said it was important."

"It is. . . . Well first of all . . . "

I opened the back car door and reached in to grab the flowers. I didn't care about the water stains on the seat I would have to later explain to Dad.

"Oh, they're so beautiful . . . . "

My body so stiffened from tension that when I extended my arms to hand her the flowers, I felt like a soldier presenting his rifle for inspection.

" . . . . These are my favorites . . . . "

"I know."

"That's very sweet . . . thank you."

She kissed my cheek.

" . . . . What's the occasion?"

I slid my trembling hands into my pants pockets. I took a deep breath.

"You know how much I care about you . . . . "

Her smile heartened me.

" . . . . and that I've loved you from the first time we met . . . . and I really care about you . . . . "

If I initially felt confident in expressing feelings not hollowed out by too much thought, now I wish I had rehearsed.

" . . . . and I think you care . . . love me, too . . . . I should have told you long ago how much you mean to me . . . . "

Her smile no longer seemed genuine, which I attributed to my long-windedness.

" . . . . So, anyway . . . . will you marry me?"

The seriousness of her expression, and her reluctance to respond, devastated me. Before I could try and delude myself into believing I misinterpreted her reaction, Opal spoke. Her words only compounded my despair.

"Why are you doing this?"

I gave a nervous laugh.

"Doing what?"

"Marriage . . . . You can't be serious . . . "

"Of course I am . . . "

She walked a few feet away, then turned to look at me.

"You know all that's goin' on . . . . Does all that get suddenly left behind?"

"Like what?"

'Like what?! Like takin' care of Ma and goin' to nursing school and-"

"Then we'll wait awhile . . . . and I can save up while you're in school . . . "

"I worry about Ma and I'll wanna spend a lot of time helpin' her . . . . "

She looked at me. I could only nod.

" . . . . I don't know if I can marry anyone . . . . "

"What does that mean?! Why can't you?"

Opal went and sat on a large moss covered boulder. I followed her. She stared past me toward the shed, before looking at me.

"Ollie needs lookin' after . . . . that means livin' with me . . . . "

I tried not to react. Opal smiled.

" . . . . Your face turned a shade lighter."

"I was just surprised . . . you know he's like a brother . . . . "

"But if he lived with us . . . in time you would resent him . . . We both know how exhausting he is . . . . "

I thought about the impossibility of supervising six uncontrollable brats in a perpetual state of the "terrible twos".

"It'll be okay."

"How can it be okay? You resent him even now."

"That's not true."

"Did you forget the last time the three of us were here?"

"I didn't mean it. I just wanted to be alone with you. We hadn't spent much time together."

"We'll always want to be alone . . . . and that might not be possible."

A DROWNING IN SWANSON LAKE   239

As much as I wanted to continue refuting what she said, I couldn't. I then phrased my next sentence very carefully.

"But you have a right to be happy . . . . don't you?"

She said nothing for a few moments.

"It's something I've thought about a lot, believe me . . . . But unless and until someone else can care for him, he's going to live with me."

I saw the crack of light and hope.

"Like Mr. Dietz?"

"Yes, if that's what Ollie wants and Mr. Dietz will have him."

"It sounds like they got along great, from what Ollie said."

"Yes, from what Ollie says . . . . Well . . . we'll see."

Ollie's words became inexact signposts to the reality he knew. Opal understood that, recognizing only time could reveal the accuracy of his perceptions. I had more to tell Opal. I wanted to reassure her I would never again feel or show resentment toward Ollie. But I could neither guarantee that, nor convince her to believe it. I said nothing. Instead, I resigned myself to the idea I could do nothing more to ensure our future together. As Opal and I each wrestled silently with our feelings, I thought about Ollie and Mr. Dietz, and how they were either the obstacles or answers to my happiness.

22

The first day of classes began without Ollie.

"Is he sick, Ope?"

"No . . . . He won't go back."

I knew Ollie's refusal, although it earned him an extra vacation day, would come at a high price once Mr. Magnusson returned home. I felt the need to apologize for him.

"It's hard after the summer and all he's done. It'll probably seem like boot camp until he's used to it."

Opal looked at me.

"No. I mean he's never going back."

I still did not understand.

"But he graduates."

She shook her head, the irritation in her face quite apparent. I assumed I had been the cause until she spoke.

"I thought so but he kept lots hidden . . . classes he didn't pass or never took. Dad didn't question anything. I guess I was supposed to know about that, too."

The diligence with which Mr. Magnusson pursued Ollie's summer school education evidently ceased once Opal returned.

"You're not his parent."

A DROWNING IN SWANSON LAKE 241

"No one else watches out for him .... only me ... That's what I kept telling you at the pond .... "

I tried not to sound self-serving.

"Well, like I said before .... maybe he's happier learning stuff on the farm .... without all the rules and without forcing him to do somethin' he's not gonna do anyway .... Can't your Dad see that?"

"He's not keepin' Ollie from going back. In fact, Dad wants him to learn something he can use .... He's long given up on him graduatin' and said the 'on the job' farm training is the best education he could get .... But Ollie's still not anxious to go back."

I felt disappointed, although I recognized its inevitability in the unrealistic expectations I had. Ollie's capriciousness had become legendary, and I should have realized his passion for farming would disappear as soon as everyone, especially his father, approved of it.I felt especially naive in thinking Ollie would return to farming and leave Opal and me free to marry. Then Opal added.

" .... I know he loves it .... I do."

"So why doesn't he just go? .... and do something he loves."

"Because of Mr. Dietz .... "

I suspected Ollie had, as Opal feared, misread the relationship between him and Mr. Dietz.

"I thought they liked each other ... and Ollie was a good worker .... "

"I don't think it has anything to do with that .... I'm pretty sure it has to do with his dog."

"Chestnut? .... uh, Chester?"

Ollie hated when I called his brown bulldog Chestnut.

"He ain't a horse so don't call him that."

As with the cold cuts in the deli case, his remark made sense in an Ollie sort of way.

"Mr. Dietz won't let him bring Chester. I overheard part of the conversation the other day."

At fourteen, partially crippled with arthritis and emphysema, Chester dared fate. Not only had he long outlived the veterinarian's prognosis, he escaped, with Ollie's help, Mr. Magnusson's recent attempt to euthanize him.

"So what's he gonna do?"

She shrugged.

"I told him I'd take care of him like I did in the summer, make sure nothing happened . . . . and that's not an easy promise to keep when the mutt runs away half the time."

"And that wasn't enough?"

"He seemed okay with it at first, but then . . . I don't know. Maybe he thinks Dad will trick me . . . . "

"What if your dad promises him?"

Opal chuckled.

"You think Ollie is gonna believe Dad?"

Mr. Magnusson had always chosen between apathy and harshness when dealing with his son. Ollie, in turn, either ignored him, or defied Mr. Magnusson to the point of questioning his parental legitimacy. From an early age, Ollie searched newspapers and magazines for men that looked more like him, and which he could claim as his probable father. From what he read about these men, he would create a biography less disappointing than the one he had. But when the genetic code kicked in, and he and his father became facial bookends, even Ollie recognized the futility in continuing the search. It did not, however, reconcile him to his father.

"Maybe if I talked to Ollie . . . . "

"There's no talking to him these days. He leaves when he sees Dad coming and he clams up when he sees me . . . . "

We said nothing more about it that day, and I neither saw Ollie nor talked with him over the next few days.

" . . . He'll call you when he's ready, Hal . . . . You can't push him."

I nodded. I had never known Ollie to avoid me, but the confrontation with his father and frustration with Mr. Dietz apparently overwhelmed him to the point of depression.

That Friday evening I heard Dad pick up his car keys. Once settled in for the evening, he rarely went out. I became curious.

"A late date?"

Dad looked at me, preoccupied.

"Adelaide Benton stopped in as I was closing up . . . . got me going about politics, and now I don't remember locking up. I'll be right back."

"I can go."

I liked driving the car at night, especially on cool, quiet autumn evenings.

"You sure?"

"It'll clear my head."

Dad gave me the keys and I drove into town, the windows rolled down to let the crisp night air smack me awake. Dad had, in fact, locked the store. On the way back I made a slight detour. When I approached the gravel road leading up to the half lit house, I shut off my lights, parked, and stared at Opal's room. A soft light came from her bedroom, and I pictured Opal lying on her bed. I grew envious of her pillow, her sheets, of anything that touched her. I wanted to lie beside her, stare into her eyes, and breathe in her breath. Suddenly, I heard a noise, a rustling in the grass near the side of the road. I had not intended my whisper to sound so desperate.

"Ollie . . . is that you?!"

No one answered. I would have welcomed his prank. When I heard the sound again, only closer, I quickly started the engine, turned on my lights, and attempted a quick getaway from the Bigfoot I imagined ready to pounce on me. My bravery never extended to things I could not see, and as I made a screeching U turn to escape one peril, I felt sure I created another. Despite my attempts to drive in the opposite direction from their house, I still believed the noise and lights from my car would alert Opal to the pervert who had been stalking her. No sooner had I straightened all four wheels, than I accelerated. Immediately, I recognized the cause of my fear. Chester froze, as I did, the light from my headlights reflecting off his eyes, emanating light like two smaller headlights, hypnotizing me, pulling me closer, and finally sucking me in like a bug in a flushed toilet. Soon a hard, hollow thud jolted me. I didn't stop and I couldn't look back.

When I arrived home, I felt relieved Dad had already gone to sleep. I did not want to talk, and I did not want to sort the real from the imagined in what occurred. Only Chester's death appeared certain, the circumstances surrounding it far more dubious. Whether accidental or deliberate, I knew my confession would do more harm than good. The time had passed for action and apologies, and my salvation lay with my silence and with the absence of any witnesses. I could only be sure about one.

Arriving at the store early Saturday, I divided my time between working and looking out for Ollie and Opal. However, as each hour passed without a phone call or a visit, I grew more confident I had not been detected. Still, when Opal stopped in around noon, her presence unnerved me until I realized she had not come to accuse me.

"I just left Ollie . . . he's been crying all night . . . . A terrible thing happened . . . . "

I went over to her.

" . . . . He found Chester on the road near our house . . . . Someone ran him over . . . . I even heard when it happened . . . "

My heart began to race.

" . . . Who would do such a thing?"

I felt myself relax, although I could only respond with a cliché.

"Accidents happen."

"Then why wouldn't someone stop to help it . . . or call for help . . . . It takes a really small person to do something like that."

I pretended to check some invoices. When she said nothing else, I looked up. I could not determine whether her eyes now indicted me or simply waited for my response.

" . . . . Don't ya think?"

"Of course . . . . but maybe they didn't know they hit him."

"He's a sixty five pound animal. You'd know if you hit it . . . . "

I wanted to suggest other possibilities, including how someone might have thought he ran over a tree branch or stone, but I knew the television detectives always became suspicious of those who tried too hard to explain away the events. I kept silent. Opal seemed preoccupied and her silence worried me. So did her sadness.

A DROWNING IN SWANSON LAKE   245

" . . . . We're going to bury him this afternoon."

I had an excuse planned if she expected me to attend.

" . . . . the poor thing . . . . "

I did not know if she meant Ollie or Chester, until she continued.

" . . . . He'll blame himself for Chester."

I couldn't listen anymore.

"I better get back to my work. Dad wants all his accounts organized today."

"Will you see him?"

"I can't today."

"Then tomorrow. It would mean a lot to him . . . . and me."

"I promise."

"You were always good at cheering him up."

I nodded, anxious for Opal to leave. I took refuge in the meaningless work I had yet to finish. I would go and see Ollie the next day and listen to his sadness and hear his anger over what occurred. But I would only listen.

Over the next few weeks Ollie and I had little contact with one another. I welcomed his unwillingness to see me or anyone else. If I regretted what occurred, for the sadness it brought him and Opal, I considered it the means to all our happiness. Ollie could move on to pursue his dream, and thereby let Opal and me pursue ours. But my sympathy for Ollie was soon replaced with frustration, then annoyance, and finally, with anger. It had been three weeks since Chester died, and he showed no inclination to leave home and go back to Dietz.

"He just sits quiet, moping like Mom used to . . . . Dad's given up on him . . . . "

I could not react to Opal. I felt stung by the realization Ollie would become a permanent fixture in our lives. But a few weeks later that situation changed, although not necessarily for the better.

As I waited for the school bus, Opal drove up. She came to a screeching halt.

"How come you're not takin'—"

"Get in, Hal . . . . "

The moment I jumped in Opal accelerated with the same finesse she displayed in stopping.

" . . . . Ollie didn't come home last night after his walk . . . . I'm worried sick . . . . Where could he be, Hal?"

"He's probably hiding out . . . . he's been wanting to be alone . . . . "

"But he's never done this . . . . that reckless fool. God knows what he might try or where he'll end up . . . . Dad's drivin' up and down the roads . . . . I'm checking the school . . . "

She saw my confused look when I turned to her.

" . . . . Well, I don't know . . . . Maybe he'll turn up at Mr. Hockney's . . . . "

"Does he know to call you if he does?"

"He can't if Ollie makes him promise . . . . That's what Dad said."

I did not know if guidance counselors had the same client confidentiality restrictions as other professionals, but it didn't matter. Opal would not trust someone else to do what she could do herself.

" . . . . and then I'm goin' to Brewman and . . . . "

She pulled off to the side and began to cry. I put my arm around her.

"I know he'll show up later . . . . "

I could think of nothing else to reassure her. I offered to accompany her to Brewman or anywhere else she wanted to look.

"I appreciate it, Hal . . . . but I still think Ollie could show up at school . . . "

I promised to check Mr. Hockney's office frequently, and make the rounds of the school and schoolyard. But Ollie failed to appear at the school, and Opal's hysterical phone call later that day informed me of his failure to return home. Then I heard nothing and I thought she hung up.

"Are ya still there?"

"Yes . . . I'm here."

"Listen, Ope. Maybe he went back to Dietz. It only makes sense. I mean where else is he gonna go?"

A DROWNING IN SWANSON LAKE   247

"He wouldn't do that without sayin' goodbye to me . . . "

"Suppose he had to because he didn't want to deal with your dad . . . . Maybe he figured it'd just be easier to leave . . . . and then call you . . . "

She became excited.

"That sounds like him . . . don't it, Hal? . . . . Hal, could you do me a really big favor . . . . "

She lowered her voice to a whisper. I strained to hear.

" . . . . I can't take the chance of talking here . . . . Ma still doesn't know about Ollie. Would you call Mr. Dietz and let Ollie know I'll call him when Ma's asleep?"

I agreed. She whispered the number and a few minutes later I dialed.

After three rings, a man answered.

"Mr. Dietz?"

"Yes?"

"My name is Hal Moffat. I'm a friend of Ollie's. And—"

"Oh, Hal, yes. Ollie's talked a blue streak about you. Said you were gonna marry his sister one day soon."

I became dumbstruck. Ollie and Dietz had knowledge I was not yet privy to.

" . . . . I didn't mean to shut you down. Don't tell me it's news to you."

"No . . . . it's just that I'm still workin' on it."

"Good for you. I asked the wife three times before she finally broke down."

His laugh provided the pause I needed.

"May I speak to Ollie?"

"You sure could . . . . if he was here . . . . "

I might have appreciated his humor under different circumstances, but now I only became upset. I barely heard his next words.

" . . . . Did he say he was comin' here?"

"Uh, no . . . but I just thought . . . . and you're sure he . . . ."

"Am I sure he's not here? If you hold on, I'll check under the bed . . ."

When he didn't laugh, I knew I had insulted him.

"I'm sorry . . . We're all worried about him . . . . "

"I understand, but if he's not here . . . ."

"Then when you spoke a few weeks back . . . did he mention anything that sounded unusual?"

"Unusual? Ollie?"

He laughed.

"Something that could give us a clue to where he might be."

"Nooo, can't think of what. We just talked about the usual stuff . . . ."

I didn't want to hear him launch into an anti-communist diatribe.

" . . . . and his dog. I told him he couldn't bring it. The Mrs. is terrified of them ever since one turned on her a few years back . . . . He was okay with that."

"I thought he was upset."

"Is that what he told you?"

"Well, actually . . . . no. His sister overheard the conversation."

"Now you see. There's that spyin' crap the commies do with their people. If-"

"Please, Mr. Dietz . . . . She only happened to overhear it and she said he sounded upset . . . . Was he upset?"

"Only for a moment. You know how he gets. Then cheerful as ever."

For the moment I could not think. Then I heard Dietz's voice again.

" . . . . You still there?"

"Yeah."

"I thought you left me hangin'. Say, maybe he's got himself a sweetie he's keepin' a secret . . . You never know with these quiet ones."

I had not considered that possibility, and I felt sure no one else had either. But I also knew that would be one secret Ollie could never keep from me or Opal.

"I don't think so . . . ."

"Never can be too sure . . . . but I'll call ya if he shows up."

I hung up. I dreaded calling Opal, fearing her disappointment over the news would extend to me, as well. She had looked to me for answers, and I had none to provide.

For me, Ollie's disappearance seemed like an extension of the *Ring'O'Levio* cat and mouse game we played as children. I still expected him to come dashing around the corner at any moment, crying "Ring' O' Levio" before he could be tagged out. But after a few days, when Ollie still failed to appear, Sheriff MacCauley organized a search party. If he considered foul play a possibility, then no one, including me, could be ruled out. He could consider the inevitability of Ollie living with me and Opal sufficient motivation on my part. And in his interrogation, I would confess to an occasional fantasy about "doing Ollie in". But despite the occasional sinister thought, I knew I could never hurt him. His disappearance distressed me far more than his presence ever did.

The speculation surrounding the vanishing ranged from the grotesque to the ridiculous. Some guessed Ollie had electrocuted himself on an overhead transmission line and would remain stuck to it, convulsing, until the power could be shut off. This had some plausibility, knowing his past exploits. But a check of the overhead lines within a twenty mile radius revealed nothing unusual. Others believed, as did Mr. Dietz, Ollie embarked on a brief odyssey that suddenly introduced him to a new love and a new life. I referred to them as "delusional romantics". I, on the other hand, did not want to speculate. I chose simply to believe Ollie had left and would soon return. I drew comfort in knowing even if he faced danger, "Cat" Magnusson still had many more lives to spare.

Weeks passed without any word from, or about, Ollie. Old bones and skulls were found, although none proved to be human.

"It's tough enough to survive with all your wits about you . . . . but Ollie . . . . the poor lad . . . . "

Doc stopped, shook his head, his words and demeanor echoing the distress we all felt. Opal considered each day the likely harbinger of tragic news, believing a discovered article of Ollie's clothing or one of his possessions would confirm what she had feared. My attempts to console her failed miserably. I knew she questioned my sincerity, perhaps even blaming me for Ollie's disappearance.

But I accepted her aloofness, confident time and Ollie's return would restore our friendship, and more. And I prepared for that day immediately.

Although she never said so directly, Opal expected me to be more than a hardware store clerk/junior partner. So I decided to explore alternatives. With permission from Mr. Hockney, I audited classes in everything from physics to theater history. I spent my lunch hours and study hall recesses in the library's vocational guidance section. I even added creative writing and advanced history to my curriculum, excelling in both. But after months of this, despite my small successes, I concluded that I was best suited to be a clerk in a hardware store. Everything interested me and nothing did. Part of me still hoped a bolt of lightning, in the form of a chance meeting or a moment of inspiration, would strike me and provide the direction my future needed to take. In the absence of that, I reconciled myself, for the time being, to a quieter, more humble, destiny.

If I felt frustrated in not finding a suitable career alternative, I at least felt comfortable with the career I had. But that all changed one afternoon. I had just finished stocking some new "glow in the dark" light switches, when I noticed Dad staring at me.

"Didn't you want them here?"

"No, they're fine . . . "

He continued staring.

"C'mon, Dad . . . . Stop givin' me the creeps."

"Listen . . . we held another board meeting in Brewman . . . you're gonna become eligible at graduation."

"You mean I should clean my rifle and march off to Nam?"

I laughed, hoping Dad would do the same and we could enjoy his joke. But he neither laughed nor smiled, and his somber expression frightened me. The war in Viet Nam had been escalating, although it never concerned me that much. Whether my naiveté allowed me to believe it would somehow miraculously end before I graduated high school or, probably more likely, I grew arrogant enough to think Dad's position on the local draft board would protect me, I dismissed the war's relevance to my life. I spit out the first thought that came to mind.

"But I . . . but I thought you could do something."

Dad paused before he spoke.

"And how would that look?"

"How would it look?"

"That's what I said. How would it?"

"It's done all the time."

He walked over to me, his expression never more serious. I half expected a slap across my face. He stopped within a couple of feet of me and spoke softly.

"You disappoint me, son."

"Why? Because I don't want to be a soldier?"

"Because you're turning your back on your country."

I wanted to tell him to save his patriotic rhetoric for Stan and Mr. Dietz and anyone else who cared to listen. I became angry. Then I said something that even surprised me.

"And maybe I'm disappointed in you. You're my father. You shouldn't be so anxious to send me over there to get killed . . . . or worse."

"But it's okay for other fathers to send their sons? It's okay that others die for you? . . . . "

I couldn't argue with that, and didn't. If I wanted direction for the future, I now had it. And the realization made my head throb. Needing some fresh air, I began walking toward the door when I heard words of deliverance.

" . . . Of course, there is something you can do . . . . something to keep the wolf from the door . . . . "

I turned around so quickly I became dizzy. I sat on his stool and waited to hear more.

" . . . . The government is still deferring full time students . . . . full time college students . . . . Nothin' wrong with takin' advantage of a bona fide option."

He smiled, and for a moment he reminded me of Satan. My instincts told me this might be a trap, to see if I thought myself too good to work in his store and too good to die for my country.

"I already mentioned college, but you laughed at it."

"I never laughed at college. I laughed at you . . . . because you just wanted to dive willy nilly into anything that would keep you from working here full time."

"You'll still want me-"

"Yes . . . . I need you. But you'll get your chance to study, I promise.

He chuckled.

" . . . And this time you'll have some real purpose in going. You'll teach the other students a thing or two about business . . . . This store's gonna give you lots of bragging rights . . . . "

Dad's solution began to lose more of its luster with each new comment. He had already limited my curriculum and my study schedule. I realized he had specific expectations for what I needed to learn, and they all had to do with the hardware store and his plan to expand. But that didn't matter. I felt grateful for the lifeline thrown to me, making sure I held on for as long as possible.

23

Doc came less and less frequently to the grocery, and when he did come, he remained uncharacteristically quiet. At first Stan welcomed the respite from Doc's badgering, but soon began to miss it. On this particular Saturday morning Doc sat, sipping his coffee, and staring out into the street. Stan watched him for a few moments before speaking.

"Anything exciting I should know about? . . . . "

Doc continued staring out, not answering. Stan walked over to him, tapping him on the shoulder.

" . . . Helloooo!"

Doc jumped, spilling some coffee on his leg.

"Goddamn you! What the hell are you tryin' to do?!"

"I was tryin' to talk to you."

"Get me some napkins, for God's sakes! . . . . "

Stan reached behind the counter to retrieve a couple of napkins. He handed them to Doc, who counted them.

" . . . One . . . Two . . . . Two. You sure you can spare them?"

Stan grabbed one back.

"Now that you mention it, no. And get your own goddamn napkins!"

Doc wiped his leg and tossed the damp napkin wad into the wastebasket. He looked at Stan.

"So? You already did the damage. What was so important? . . . . Or do you like pokin' people and scarin' them half to death?"

"It's a hobby of mine. Okay?"

Doc only grunted, then looked out towards the street.

" . . . . You waiting for someone?"

"No."

"You look like you're waiting for someone."

"It's a beautiful day. I like looking out at it. Is that okay?"

Stan shrugged.

"I don't care. Why should I care? . . . . "

They said nothing for the next ten minutes or so. Stan then purposely dropped a donut onto the floor.

" . . . Oh, my . . . . "

Once Doc turned his head to look, Stan picked it up and threw it back into the box with the others. He expected Doc to explode, even counting on his fingers the number of seconds before Doc's rage would erupt. When he ran out of fingers, he looked at Doc, who now stared vacantly in the direction of Stan and the donuts.

" . . . Oh, no. This is not good. Are you havin' a stroke on me?"

Doc then focused on him.

"What now?"

"You don't look good. And you're breathin' like you just ran the hundred in nine four."

I agreed with Stan. Doc's breathing had always been noticeable. Now it became intrusive.

"The weight's catching up with me . . . . Maybe I should drop a few pounds."

"A few pounds?! First cough up the person you swallowed. Then you can talk about a few pounds."

"And you wonder why I hate talking to you?"

I had absorbed as much baseball news as I could before Dad expected me back at the store. I returned the unwrinkled magazines carefully to the shelves and proceeded to leave. However, I had barely taken a step when I heard Doc mumble something that prompted a loud response from Stan. I picked up another magazine to browse while I listened.

"Are you serious?! You mean it?!"

"I wouldn't say it otherwise."

"But . . . . but . . . . you're toyin' with me. Right?"

"Nope."

"But how come?"

"I have my reasons . . . . "

Stan thought a moment.

"It's because of what I said about your weight . . . or the coffee . . . . That was the straw that broke the camel. Am I right?"

"You make it sound like it's punishment . . . . I don't understand you."

"No, I'm glad . . . . I mean if you want to, I'm glad. It's just so sudden, that's all."

"Here's your chance to finally get me off your back."

"But I'm finally used to you . . . . you know, like a bum knee or a bad case of hemorrhoids."

"I'm not leaving town. I'll make sure you still get enough of me."

Stan paused, before speaking again.

"There gotta be a catch?"

Doc laughed.

"You're incredible, you know that? For almost twenty years you drool over the idea of buyin' me out. And when you finally get the chance, you're making noises like you're not interested."

"So how much?"

"Fifteen thousand, cash."

When I heard nothing I looked up and saw Stan's jaw hung open, his expression suggestive of someone flashed frozen in stupidity. He blinked a few moments later, thereby activating his jaw and returning his ability to speak.

"I don't like being made to look stupid."

I waited for Doc to hit that one out of the park. But he continued as though he never heard it.

"I told you. Fifteen thousand."

"But it's worth twice that . . . . I mean, it's probably worth more than fifteen."

"Spare me. You know it's worth more than twice that . . . . Do we have a deal?"

"I don't know."

Doc blasted him.

"What don't you know?! I'm giving you the deal of a lifetime! . . . You're a damn fool!"

"I have to think about it."

"Fine. Think about it."

"It has to be cash?"

"That's right."

"How come?"

"Because I need cash. Do you think I'd sell this store to your sorry ass, otherwise? And at this price? . . . . I wouldn't look a gift horse in the mouth."

"Let me think about it."

"You're pathetic."

Doc stood up to leave.

"I'll give you twenty four hours to get me the money, or the deal is off. I can find someone else who'll pay me what it's worth."

He left. Stan watched him walk to his car and drive away. He then turned to me.

"Whaddya think, Hal?"

It seemed pointless to pretend I hadn't been eavesdropping. I felt flattered Stan wanted my opinion on something this important.

"Sounds like a good deal."

"He must be desperate . . . . You goin' back to work now? . . . "

I thought he might have resented the long time I spent reading his magazines. I came up front and nodded.

" . . . . Could you ask your dad to stop by?"

"Sure."

Although almost a half hour late, I understood why Dad hadn't called me. Sitting behind the counter, he appeared preoccupied

A DROWNING IN SWANSON LAKE   257

with a magnet and a box of nails. The slow day would give me the opportunity to hear even more.

"Stan asked you . . . and me to stop by. He wanted to talk to you about something."

"You know what?"

"Yeah, but I'll let him tell you."

Dad and I went next door. I remained a lookout for the hardware store while I listened to Stan repeat the story. I then waited for Dad's reaction.

"I don't know what to say. It's your decision."

"Of course it's my decision. I'm askin' your opinion."

Dad thought a moment.

"He's a shrewd one . . . "

"He can be . . . "

"So maybe the offer is too good for a reason."

"I knew it . . . . So you think something smells bad here?"

Dad averted his eyes to keep both of us from laughing.

"Could be . . . . I don't know . . . . And he didn't say why he needed the money?"

"Refused to say."

"He could just be desperate."

"That's what I think."

"But not stupid enough to try what he did last time."

I couldn't believe what I heard. The years had not erased Dad's suspicions about the fire. Stan seemed as surprised as I was.

"I thought for sure that was water under the bridge. You still don't believe him?"

"I guess not."

"So you think he's desperate but I shouldn't let down my guard?"

"That's my opinion."

Stan scratched his head ferociously, as though attempting to scrape away any barrier to his brain and the solution it might generate. However, except for the ricocheting flakes of dandruff, nothing else emerged.

"So what should I do?"

"Offer him ten."

"Ten thousand?! It's a steal at fifteen."

"So?"

"He said he'll find another buyer . . . I ain't ready to toss the dice with someone new."

"It's a bluff. Trust me."

At first I wondered how Dad could feel so certain and so cavalier about his advice. But I later realized he only told Stan what he wanted to hear.

Stan looked at Dad and soon began to smile.

"I like the way you think."

"Business is business."

I heard enough and returned to the store. If I had expected Dad to be more impartial, it was only because I had not factored in the years of lingering resentment he still harbored towards Doc.

School kept me from witnessing Stan's counter offer to Doc, although I later heard how Doc's yelling and cursing drowned out conversations a block away. Dad said he stormed out of Stan's, his face so red it seemed bloody. Doc not only rejected Stan's counter offer, he also spurned Stan when he finally agreed to pay the original fifteen thousand dollar price. He stayed away from town for over a week, and only returned when a ruptured tank ball forced him to.

"In case I forget how steeped in shit my life is, I got a broken toilet to remind me."

Doc paid for his purchase and left. Dad and I watched him approach his car, then suddenly fall to the ground. I felt sure he tripped. Dad and I ran outside to where Doc lay motionless, his face smeared with blood from the fall. Dad shoved him gently, then hard. It only took a few more moments to realize Doc had died before he even hit the ground. In a week we would also know what killed him.

24

With Doc dead, Ollie gone, and Opal doing all she could to avoid me, the familiar was disappearing rapidly and leaving me as unsure about the present as I was about the future. The world seemed bathed in a harsh yellow light of a semi-dream, making it treacherous to negotiate the steps in front of me. I still expected to hear Doc's snoring and the ritualistic arguments between him and Stan, and felt confused and astonished when I didn't. The same appeared to be true for Dad. He would stare into space, only to interrupt that with a shake of his head and a "huh!", as though overwhelmed in his struggle to come to some understanding of it all. But for Stan, Doc's death seemed to pose no such dilemma. He simply went about his business, remarking every so often that "it was a damn shame" and how he "missed the old Grizzly". I searched his face for more, anything more, but came up empty. Only when a newspaper article appeared a few days later, could we talk about Doc and bring him back into our lives. Unfortunately, the *Brewman Beacon's* story resurrected a great deal more.

PHYSICIAN'S DEATH CLOSES INVESTIGATION

The death of Swanson Lake physician, Dr. Henry Wyatt,

61, from a heart attack late Wednesday morning, brought to an abrupt end the two month criminal investigation into his medical practice, the County Attorney's office announced late yesterday. A complaint brought by the parents of the late Angela Vitale, a twenty five year old patient of Dr. Wyatt, who died of complications arising from a leg infection, prompted the investigation. An anonymous source close to the County Attorney's office disclosed certain irregularities had been discovered among the subpoenaed materials confiscated by the Sheriff's department. Chief among them was an inventory of medicines well beyond their expiration dates. The Public Defender's Office and the attorney for Dr. Wyatt, Michael Darby, refused to comment on this or on reports that the County Attorney had been looking into possible "involuntary manslaughter" charges.

Stan put down the newspaper and looked at Dad and me. No one could say anything, each of us waiting for the other to speak. I thought back to the time I saw Doc's office, and how it seemed a testament to neglect. Soon more and more began to make sense. Seeing Doc and Sheriff MacCauley that morning, the somber looks on their faces and the sheriff carrying the medical bag, and Doc's sudden decision to sell Stan his interest in the store—it all made sense. Yet we could be sure about very little. That didn't stop Stan and Dad from drawing conclusions.

"You don't want a public defender with all that starin' at ya. Fifteen grand can buy a heckuva lawyer . . . . or give you the means to make a getaway and disappear."

Dad laughed.

"You watch too many movies. We're talkin' about Doc. He could barely get to his car, let alone stay one step ahead of the law."

I had to agree with Dad. I remembered the time he walked with me to Ben Maxwell's bakery. We said nothing for a few moments before Stan asked the question we all wondered about.

"Do ya think it's true . . . . about the medicines and all?"

Dad waited a moment to answer.

"I could believe it . . . . He wasn't exactly at the forefront of medical knowledge. He probably couldn't be bothered updating his medicines . . . . no matter who it hurt."

Stan nodded. I could agree Doc was a physician of marginal ability, but I refused to believe his actions stemmed from mean spiritedness. Their pronouncements about his character only confirmed how little they knew about him. I could have related the many kindnesses he showed to Ollie and me. But I knew it would not matter. The contempt they had for Doc during his life, would not end with his death. Only a few people attended Doc's funeral, the newspaper article having much to do with that. Aside from Stan, myself, and Dad, the remaining mourners included Ida Du Page and a coterie of Sunday worshippers willing to risk the stigma of attending a "criminal's burial".

The words made me wince, but I heard them in town prior to, and long after, Doc's death. Ida conducted the service, asking those who wanted to say a few words about Doc to do so. Although I heard Dad clear his throat, he remained quiet. Stan said "Doc was a good friend" and left it at that. One of the worshippers, Maddy Carmichael, reminisced about meeting Doc for the first time after moving from Maine, and how his humor, tinged with a "definite gruffness", made her feel welcome. When she stopped speaking, we all waited for someone else to say something more. I opened my mouth, to no avail. Instead, I prayed silently and hard, and looked to Ida for help. Unlike years earlier when my prayers went unheard, this time, miraculously, she spoke my thoughts about Doc's compassion, his dreams for the town, and a crankiness that often belied his sensitivity. My mind became a kaleidoscope of images, from the time we found Ben Maxwell, to his Career Day talk. Then I remembered his words, "sometimes a person has to talk", and I wondered whom Doc talked to. Aside from the everyday banter at the store, conversations that skimmed above emotions like stones skipping across a pond, nothing much had been said. I sensed Doc needed that to distract himself from the silence that was his own life. I looked at the faces of the mourners and no one seemed genuinely sad for Doc. Not Dad, not Stan, and certainly not the others who waited impatiently for the service to end. I didn't expect them to pound their breasts in grief, but I expected more. Death disappointed me. I had always expected it to intensify and perpetuate Opal's love for me. But as I watched them lower Doc's body into the ground, I realized death could not be trusted to provide anything more than a few reminiscences and a smattering of hollow praises.

In the ride back into town, Stan referred again to the newspaper article.

"Considering all he woulda gone through, he was better off dead. At least it's over with."

Stan did not realize, and wouldn't until a few years later, the repercussions from the investigation. A civil trial found Doc guilty of negligence in the death of Angela Vitale, and the court's judgment against Doc's estate awarded her parents a controlling interest in the grocery. With one fell swoop, the grocery would be sold to satisfy the judgment, Stan would find himself unemployed, and a five and dime would eventually move in that competed with Dad and drive him out of business.

25

Despite my reluctance to see Mrs. Magnusson, I felt confident a visit would endear me to Opal and end her indifference. I picked Mrs. Magnusson a bouquet of mums at the pond and prepared myself for anything she, or Opal, might say. As I stood on their front porch I heard Opal's laughter and readied myself to hug her as soon as she opened the door. When she did, her laughter ended as abruptly as my numbness began. Opal stood before me, her hand tucked under the arm of a man I did not know and never saw. Her hand jolted as though to remove it, but she let it remain. And far worse than seeing her touch another man, was seeing her keep her hand there with me standing before her.

My skin sizzled, my skull splintered, at the image before me. I felt a pressure rising and spilling across my insides, suffocating me, and choking out the last bubbles of dignity. I muttered something about Dad and dinner, and left. My mind reeled in confusion and I understood nothing. I could not recall when I dropped or tossed the mums. I don't know if Opal called after me. I just seemed to walk through a jellied darkness that drowned out everything but the crashing of blood against the inside walls of my ears.

That evening I rehashed the moments leading up to seeing

Opal. Since I had not given her the chance to say anything, or had not heard anything she might have said, I considered the possibility I had made incorrect assumptions. Perhaps her laughter had been excitement over hearing about Ollie, the wonderful news brought by the relative she stood next to. However, the image of her hand under his arm shattered all illusions, and it took only a few moments for my skin to peel away and the onslaught of raw pain envelop me. Finally I understood what Opal had really been telling me at the pond. It's not that she did not want to marry. It's that she did not want to marry me. I vowed never to forgive her for her betrayal, and I wanted her to die. I wanted to die. I could kill and I could cry. But I did neither. I just closed my eyes and swore to God and myself that I would never again speak to her.

The next day Opal stopped by the store.

"I didn't mean for you to find out like that . . . . I didn't mean to hurt you that way."

"How did you mean to hurt me?"

"There was no way you wouldn't be . . . . once you found out . . . . But I didn't want it to be like that . . . . the way you looked . . . "

"Pretty funny, huh?"

"No, not funny at all . . . . I cried later . . . . "

I looked at her, not sure what she meant.

" . . . . your eyes . . . . the tightness in your face . . . . someone I love . . . "

"You love me?"

" . . . Yes. And someone I'll always care about . . . "

"But not enough to wanna be with."

"I wasn't looking to meet someone . . . "

"I don't get it. He's not handsome . . . . not even good looking."

"Maybe not."

"Sure, he's taller, but you gotta admit I'm—"

"Is that what you think is important?"

"Yeah . . . . kinda . . . . "

"Then you're shallower than Brewman creek."

"You tryin' to tell me he—"

A DROWNING IN SWANSON LAKE   265

"Peter."

"Pete isn't thinkin' about your looks day and night? You're too pretty."

If I thought I paid her a compliment, I miscalculated severely.

"Is that all you think I'm about? How dare you?!"

"I didn't say that . . . . but it's a big part of what you're about. What's wrong with that?"

Opal grew red in the face.

"What's wrong?! If you have to ask, then you're more immature than I even thought."

"So I'm shallow and immature. Anything else? . . . "

"You don't care about anyone but yourself."

"I see . . . "

She looked at me as though to rattle off a whole list of my shortcomings, but said nothing more.

" . . . . Well don't stop there. You're on a roll . . . . "

She moved to leave.

" . . . What is he, some fancy doctor you met at the hospital?"

I had hoped to draw comfort in discovering the playing field had not been level, recognizing I could not be expected to compete with the wealth and prestige of a medical degree. Her answer disappointed me.

"For your information, Peter is studying to become a pharmacist."

"A pharmacist. Ha! A glorified pill counter."

"It's pathetic how small minded you are . . . . and actually, if you want to know, I'm the fancy doctor Peter met . . . . I've decided to study medicine."

"Medicine? . . . . Yeah, right."

I laughed. Her glare told me she had been serious.

"Well, that's not a bad arrangement. Go into cahoots with him. You prescribe and he fills . . . . make a fortune . . . go off to some foreign country and—"

"You're getting smaller and smaller by the moment, Hal."

"Well, maybe you've gotten way beyond yourself . . . . Your roots are here, Ope . . . . and forgetting that . . . that's a sorry way to be . . . . "

She stared at me, then turned around to leave. Before she got to the door, I asked something I knew went beyond the bounds of our relationship.

" . . . . You don't have to feel trapped . . . . if you're in trouble. You know I won't let you down."

I could think of no tactful way to mention it, but I had to know and understand the desperate choices Opal appeared to be making. She looked at me.

"I'm really sad for you."

I expected her to say more, to admit or deny what I just said, but she left. As I watched her cross the street to Mrs. Crabtree's, I felt my insides become suddenly cold, then numb. I continued to watch Opal walk out of my life.

26

Despite all that transpired between us, I half expected Opal to return to the store, confess her wrongs, and ask for forgiveness. I would forgive her, laugh about the absurd turn of events that intruded on our lives, and discuss how we would once more become inseparable. I listened for every footstep, looked up at every sound, and watched the street for hours. But Opal didn't return, nor did I see her anywhere in town, and I became angry with myself for being so willing to forgive such an ingrate and worse. My insides blistered with rage and even though I said little to Dad, he knew enough to stay away from me. He took the opportunity to drive to Albany and spend a few days celebrating his mother's ninetieth birthday. I continued watching the street, if only to pounce on Opal and tell her what I thought of her betrayal. It was during one such vigil that I saw people running toward something. When I stepped outside, I could see a crowd swirling and expanding around someone in its center, like the formation of a giant ball of cotton candy. Although the voices grew louder, the words banged against each other and prevented anything coherent or understandable from emerging. I moved closer to the source of the commotion when suddenly, it all began moving toward me like the all consuming *blob* in a horror movie. I didn't know whether to run or hold my ground. I stayed and soon people began peeling away from the figure dressed in an army uniform. I could not reconcile the distinguished looking individual I then saw, with the one I knew. However, the soldier, upon seeing me, broke into a grin as wide as an elephant's butt crack, and a laugh as unmistakable as it was eerie. I stood dumbfounded and unable to move, even when Ollie charged and tackled me to the ground as though I were a straw football dummy. That amused the crowd, and even as Ollie pulled me up, I didn't know whether I would slug him or hug him. However, the decision became obvious when Ollie embraced me in a bear hug that kept me immobile and gasping for breath. When he backed away, I could not help but stare at the bronze star and colored ribbons adorning his jacket. It seemed as though we were again playing soldiers. Yet now I felt jealous over the uniform and decorations he got to wear, and for the adulation he received. The crowd again gathered around Ollie, and someone might conclude he single-handedly drove the communists from Viet Nam and preserved freedom for Swanson Lake and America. I could arrive at that same conclusion myself, knowing the exhilaration he derived from his death defying antics. A wise recruiting officer had to recognize this potential for heroism and overlook all other considerations.

"I'm back, Dusty. I'm back . . . . "

I smiled.

"I'm glad . . . I'm really glad."

" . . . Let's make a run for it."

Before I could respond, Ollie yanked me like a rag doll and pulled me into Dad's store. Once inside, he locked the door and hung the "closed" sign on it.

"Dad'll kill me if he finds out."

"For ten minutes . . . just for ten minutes. So we can talk."

Despite the obvious hints, the crowd remained in front of the store. Some tapped on the window, others peered in. Soon we heard a voice so loud it could splinter wood.

"Let them get caught up, for cryin' out loud! . . . . Show some consideration . . . Git! Git!"

A DROWNING IN SWANSON LAKE   269

We laughed at Ronnie Dawes's scolding, but she succeeded in dispersing the crowd. I could now be alone with my friend.

The ten minutes came and went a dozen times as we talked for hours. I learned that Opal already informed him about Doc's death, and I waited to hear if she told him about us, about the fight we had, and about Peter. I didn't ask and Ollie didn't say anything, which left me to conclude his sudden and recent arrival had not given him time to find out much. But if I felt disappointed he could not tell me anything new about Opal's feelings, I listened and became fascinated with what he told me about himself. It appeared Mr. Dietz's political beliefs made more of an impression than anyone, including Dietz or myself, realized. I regretted not taking more seriously his comments in Ronnie's, and not recognizing how someone of Ollie's mindset could become galvanized to act so fearlessly for his beliefs. He told no one, so no one would worry, as he explained his sudden disappearance and enlistment in the army. Although I suspected he told no one, so no one would try and stop him. But Ollie had not considered what his disappearance would mean to Opal and everyone else. It would have surprised me if he had. And as we leaned back against some empty tool crates, I stared at his face and uniform and tried again to reconcile the discrepancy between the two.

The next morning Ollie nearly pulled the hinges off the door as he raced to the counter, his face flushed with excitement at the news he was about to tell. While I waited for him to catch his breath, my heart began to race at what he might tell me about Opal. Ollie wanted me to marry Opal, something Dietz confirmed, and he would now be my advocate in the face of the sudden competition I faced. I could only assume his excitement heralded a strategic plan or other announcements of good news. "She broke up with Pete", "she only talks about you", and "Pete was only meant to make you jealous" are the expressions I hoped to hear. But they bore no resemblance to what he actually said.

"They're givin' me a parade . . . . next Saturday. Ronnie said so and she don't lie . . . . "

My disappointment in not hearing about Opal muted my reaction.

"That's great."

"No, really . . . I'm not lyin' to ya, Dusty. She already checked with Miss Du Page . . . She did."

"I believe you . . . . And you deserve it . . . . I mean it, Ollie."

I slapped him on the back.

Ida Du Page assumed the mayor's position after Doc's death, and approached its responsibilities the way her predecessor did. She regarded indifference as her mandate, and knew to leave well enough alone. But with a call to honor Ollie, Ida had everything to gain in officially declaring "Ollie Magnusson Day" and approving a parade. Swanson Lake's hero punched my arm.

" . . . . What's that for?"

"You didn't answer me."

"You didn't ask anything."

"Yes, I did . . . I asked you to guess what they're gonna call it."

I pretended to think.

"Ollie Magnusson Day?"

"That's right! You always get the right answer . . . . "

I smiled.

" . . . But I bet you won't guess who's gonna march next to me . . . "

I looked at him and thought of the possibilities. It could have been someone he fought with in the war, although more likely, Opal or his dad. Then I thought of Mr. Dietz and the critical part he played. Finally, I guessed Opal. Ollie laughed that hyena laugh.

" . . . Ha, ha, you're wrong. I stumped you . . . . "

I watched him hop around in a sort of mock Indian war dance before he stopped and looked at me.

" . . . . It's you! I want you to march next to me."

My jaw hung open, prompting one of Ollie's vintage taunts.

" . . . . Fish mouth . . . . you got a fish mouth."

I ignored him.

"But I haven't done anything special . . . . I don't belong up front with you."

"I can pick whoever I want .... It's my parade."

"You'll want Opal along side you."

"She's gonna march behind us with Dad .... "

Then he paused, and his expression became sad.

" .... Ma can't go .... She's not feeling good .... "

I didn't know what I could say to comfort him. But I didn't need to. He perked up immediately.

" .... but everyone else will be there."

I wondered if he meant Peter. Although I waited for Ollie to mention his name, he didn't. I tried not to read too much into that.

"And she wasn't mad? ... "

He looked at me, confused.

" .... When you mentioned me .... she didn't seem angry?"

He paused a moment before realizing what I might mean.

"Oh, no. She's not jealous she's behind me. She just said it's my parade and I can do whatever I want."

Ollie appeared satisfied that he had answered my question, and I satisfied myself that in her failure to say anything negative about me, Opal welcomed my presence in the parade. I accepted Ollie's invitation, which prompted a deafening hooray and a skull crushing "noogie".

The next few days saw a flurry of activity. Ronnie and Stan buried their personal animosities toward one another and became allies. To be precise, they took charge of the decorations, climbing atop ladders to drape red, white, and blue crepe paper over doors, windows, and anything else that would hold it. I helped with the "Swanson Lake's Favorite Son-Ollie Magnusson" sign which we placed above Stan's store.

"It's only right. The boy worked for me .... It was like a second home to him."

I didn't answer Stan, concentrating all my efforts on leveling the sign. I had hoped Opal would show up during the times I helped, but I saw neither her nor Ollie. I then heard Ronnie mention that Ollie went to see Mr. Dietz, and would return that Friday. By Thursday, with the decorations completed, the town readied itself for an unprecedented display of hoopla. Dad had called earlier in the week and I told him about Ollie and the parade. Not wanting to miss it, he promised to return early Friday. Former schoolmates and teachers, shopkeepers in Brewman—anyone who knew Ollie or knew about him were expected to line the streets on Saturday. It made me nervous to think about it. I suspected their eyes would look at the person next to Ollie and question my legitimacy, my right to march along side a hero. I contemplated emulating Ollie and doing my own disappearing act. However, I knew my absence from the parade would disappoint Opal and him. And then, suddenly, it all did not matter. I saw Peter and Opal leave Ronnie's, his arm draped across her shoulder. They did not see me, or rather, they did not see me see them. As much as I wanted to go home and just sleep and forget everything, I knew I couldn't. So I returned to the hardware store, and stayed vigilante at the counter until I could no longer tolerate the anger and despair flooding through me. I then went into the back storage area where I stepped over the mouse droppings and crushed cockroaches, found a corner between some empty boxes, and fell asleep.

Although I could not remember my dream, I had no difficulty recalling the nightmare that awakened me.

"HAL! . . . . "

All disintegrated into whiteness as I jumped up and saw Dad standing before me.

" . . . . I thought you were dead! . . . . And what in God's name are you doing here, sleeping in this filth? . . . . "

Even if I had not been groggy, I don't believe I could explain it to his satisfaction. I just looked at him and hoped he would either understand or drop the subject.

" . . . . I don't know, son. You're worryin' me . . . . a lot! . . . . "

I believed him. He did not even mention my leaving the store unattended.

" . . . . If you got somethin' to tell me, I'm listening . . . . "

I looked at him, my throat garbling the few sounds I tried to utter.

" . . . . It's the Magnusson girl. You're incoherent, glassy eyed . . . . You've got lovesick written all over you . . . "

Then he did the worst thing he could have done. He laughed. My eyes widened at seeing the devil before me, and I barely heard his words as I pushed him aside and rushed toward the door.

" . . . . It happens to all of us . . . . It does . . . . "

Then I heard him laugh again. I ran the next block, not wanting Dad to try and catch up with me. My head pounded from too much sleep, the sunlight adding to the agony. I felt sure brain worms had begun chewing their way from the inside out. I wanted to be alone, and only the pond or my home guaranteed that. But I worried Dad would return home to apologize for laughing, and I chose the pond. On the way there I realized what a simpleton I had beome. Opal loved that spot. She most likely took Peter there. They could even be there now. And if Ollie returned from Mr. Dietz, he might be skimming his stones across the pond right at that very moment. My mind raced with these possibilities and I slowed down to a walk. I didn't know where else to go without asking Dad for the car. I decided to approach the pond cautiously. To my relief, I saw and heard no one. I spent the next three hours sitting on a boulder, organizing pebbles and twigs into opposing army battalions, and watching two squirrels play tug of war with a candy wrapper. Suddenly, I felt a pair of hands on my neck. I refused to react, even though my heart rate doubled.

"What is it, Ollie?"

"How'd you know it was me?"

He sounded disappointed.

"I just kinda figured."

He came around to face me, dressed in his Swanson Lake uniform—black chinos, blue polo, and sneakers.

"Your dad said you might be here . . . . "

He began laughing.

" . . . . Look at you, Dusty . . . . "

I had no idea what he meant until I remembered where I slept.

" . . . You're a mop with arms and feet."

He laughed again. I felt the tangled tufts of hair that sprouted from my scalp like clumps of weeds.

" . . . . We gotta get to town."

"I'm goin' home."

"Just for a few minutes . . . . it's a secret no one knows about."

"Tell me."

"Uh-uh. But it's a good one."

I felt certain Ollie's secret would either not be much of a secret, or would be a secret about nothing much. But I did become curious, and so I agreed. I regretted my decision immediately after reaching town, and seeing Ronnie gallop towards us.

"There's l'homme celebre . . . . You mustn't hide, dear boy."

"I went to get Dusty . . . . so he could hear it."

Ronnie looked at me as though I was a source of foul odor, then looked at Ollie.

"You tell him, sweetheart . . . and then I want you to stop in."

She ignored me and left.

"Guess what Ronnie is gonna do?"

I had a hunch.

"You got me this time."

"Ha! I told you it was a good secret . . . . and even you can't figure it out."

"Tell me already."

"Ronnie's namin' an ice cream sundae after me . . . . And I get to decide what goes in it."

I half expected him to ask me what I thought it would be called, but he didn't.

" . . . . Vanilla and chocolate . . . . and strawberry topping, no, no, hot fudge and marshmallow cream with pineapple . . . . walnuts and coconut . . . . and . . . "

"What about the mayonnaise?"

He thought a moment, then laughed.

"I don't like that no more . . . . not on ice cream, anyway."

"Well, you work on it, Oll. I gotta go."

He looked surprised.

"Don't you wanna walk around?"

I smiled.

A DROWNING IN SWANSON LAKE   275

"You old showboat. Now that you're a celebrity . . . . "

Then Ollie did something I never saw him do. He blushed.

" . . . . Hey, this attention is the good kind, Ollie . . . . You don't have to maim yourself or scare a person half to death . . . "

I grabbed his throat.

" . . . . if you know what I mean."

He smiled.

" . . . . Now you have to admit you're enjoyin' bein' in the spotlight."

Ollie nodded, but he seemed preoccupied.

"Let's keep walking, Dusty."

"My head's splitting."

"Then you got two heads."

He grinned and I tried to smile, but my head hurt too much.

"I'm going home to bed."

Ollie's expression soured.

"You're getting sick on purpose."

"That's ridiculous . . . I'll be okay for tomorrow . . . . "

He didn't seem assured.

" . . . . Just let me go home and lie down."

I began to walk away when he called after me.

"We can ride up front . . . or walk. What should we do?"

I didn't turn around.

"We'll see tomorrow."

"Honest Injun?"

I stopped and turned around to look at him. I raised my right hand.

"Honest Injun."

His face remained serious, even a little sad. He knew I was lying even before I did.

I excused myself early that evening, Dad too exhausted from a visit with his mother to offer any resistance. Although he said little about the visits, his eyes always seemed puffier, his face more creased, when he returned. I never knew whether that stemmed from the unfamiliar bed he slept on, or from the stress in seeing her, but Dad always looked younger at the start of his trip than at the end.

I lay in bed, unable to sleep, and unwilling to think about Opal or the parade. When sunlight illuminated my room the next morning, spotlighting me and part of my bureau, I imagined the light intensifying until the heat cauterized the raw nerve fibers throughout my body.

I could hear Dad in the kitchen. Only a fear of heights kept me from leaving the house through my bedroom window. I took my time showering and dressing, hoping Dad would leave before I finished. But even after the hot water turned warm, then cold, and after trying on every shirt and pants combination I had available, I could still hear Dad moving about downstairs. I finally realized he had been waiting for me, and any further delay served no purpose. I entered the kitchen just as Dad put toast on the table.

"If it ain't Rip Van Winkle . . . . "

I grunted.

" . . . . Thought you should eat before your big day."

"*My* big day?"

"Not everyday someone gets to ride in a parade with a hero."

"Who told you?"

"The man himself. He stopped in."

I didn't say anything. Soon I noticed Dad staring at me.

"What's wrong?"

"You gonna wear that?"

"Since I'm already dressed, I guess the answer is "yes".

"Don't get snotty with me, Hal . . . . I know you're upset about Opal . . . "

"Now how'd you know about that?"

"Since you're in a piss poor mood, and since Opal is about all you think about, it don't take a suitcase of smarts to figure it out."

I knew he was right, but I said nothing. A few moments passed before he spoke again.

" . . . . I'm not the enemy. I had nothing to do with the way things turned out."

"Neither did I . . . . She just changed."

"Unfortunately, that happens . . . . there's not too much you can do about it."

A Drowning In Swanson Lake 277

I tried not to listen.

" . . . . Did you ever meet that Peter fellow?"

I hated hearing his name. I glared at Dad.

"I don't not want to talk anymore about it."

"Fine, fine . . . . whatever you say."

I closed my eyes and leaned back in the chair. When I opened them, I wanted Dad to be gone. But he not only remained, he stared at me.

"Now what?"

"I told you . . . . it's your clothes."

I had opted for dark green slacks and a red and green madras shirt.

"What's wrong with them?"

"Not dressy enough. This is a serious event."

"It's a parade."

"But all eyes will be on you. And Ollie's sure to be in uniform . . . . Wear a white shirt and tie . . . . "

Since I didn't respond, Dad continued.

" . . . . and, of course, a sport jacket and matching pants . . . . "

I stopped him there.

"I'm not wearing a suit."

"Then a sport jacket and more dressy pants."

Dad liked wheeling and dealing. He only mentioned a suit to get me to agree to the sport jacket. When he felt satisfied I would change my clothes, he put down his coffee mug and prepared to leave.

"Carry yourself proud, son. No one's parading in Hanoi."

He left me with words intended somehow to motivate me. Then I walked to town in the clothes I had been wearing.

When I arrived, it appeared Brewman had already emptied its population onto Swanson Lake's streets. I recognized many familiar faces, although I only nodded, not stopping to say hello to anyone. I soon saw Ollie in the *Cadillac* convertible parade car in front of Mrs. Crabtree's. A small crowd descended upon him, and I could see him try to answer their questions as he searched the crowd for me. I still did not know what I planned to do. At least that's what

I wanted to believe. But just as I began to raise my hand and call out for Ollie, I instead ducked quickly behind a trash dumpster. I remained there, using it as my vantage point to see and not be seen. Opal and Mr. Magnusson made some last minute adjustments on the car's decorations. Stan and Peter stood off to the side, talking and laughing like two long lost buddies. I only needed to see Dad squeeze between them and befriend Peter, to complete the picture of betrayal. But Dad seemed too preoccupied with finding me. I could see him shade his eyes with his cupped hands as he looked around for me. I crouched and I peered, knowing I would not be detected. Ten years earlier I employed those same tactics when Dad enrolled me in an after school foreign language program. He had listened to Stan, who championed the idea that a knowledge of Russian provided just the edge we needed to uncover the Soviet spies in our midst. So every Monday and Wednesday afternoons, Dad brought me to Mr. Hinson's house, a history teacher whose knowledge of Russian earned him a few extra dollars a week. For almost an hour, five of us squeezed out some vowels, pounded out consonants, and contorted our faces in an attempt to speak in a foreign tongue. However, after two weeks of sounding like a chorus of Russian chimpanzees, I grew weary of the class and declared Mr. Hinson a failure. Thereafter, I hid inside some empty boxes left outside of Ronnie's cafe and waited until the lesson hour elapsed. Dad never had time to search for me and despite his anger and resulting punishment, nothing would deter me. Only when Dad discovered he did not have to pay for the remaining lessons, and when Stan began questioning his own wisdom and convinced Dad a history teacher who "just happened" to know fluent Russian might be a "communist plant to brainwash young minds", did Dad relent. As I now watched Dad and Ollie turn and strain to find me in the crowd, I knew neither would have time to search for me. When I heard the roar that started the parade, I began my slow walk back home.

Dad refused to talk to me for the next few days. I considered that far more preferable to the tongue-lashing I deserved and anticipated. But I did not expect Ollie's reaction. The spigot of

A DROWNING IN SWANSON LAKE   279

forgiveness had finally run dry, and even my previously reliable ice breakers failed to work. My attempts at humor, or an invitation to harmonize in a song they way we used to, were either met with a cold stare or ignored altogether. And even though I never expected to hurt him as much as I did, I still couldn't be sure I would have acted differently, given the opportunity again. I retreated and waited for a more appropriate time to approach. But after a week of not seeing him in town, I assumed he had simply chosen to avoid me. I could not believe he would disappear again.

"No, no . . . . he didn't disappear . . . . He went away . . . . nothin' to keep him here . . . . "

Stan looked at me as he spoke those last words. He knew they stung.

"Did he say where?"

"Went back to that farmer . . . . Said he was proud of him. Hell, I said I was proud of him . . . and I offered him real money . . . "

I couldn't imagine Stan being able or willing to pay Ollie, and I couldn't see Ollie back behind the meat slicer again. Stan laughed.

" . . . . You'd think I'd offer him that? That would be an insult to him and his uniform . . . Oh, no. I'm talkin' about a good, clean job . . . "

Once Stan used "clean", my mind rejected any and all work with the grocery. Stan continued.

" . . . . A greeter . . . "

He looked at me and waited for a reaction. I might have given him one if I knew what he meant. He repeated it louder this time, in case I was deaf and not stupid.

" . . . . A greeter, a greeter! Ollie would just hang around the store and talk to people and shake hands, sign an autograph or whatever . . . . He'd be the draw to get customers shopping here . . . like they do in the Las Vegas Casinos with Mickey Mantle and Willie Mays . . . . "

The idea seemed both brilliant and ridiculous, and something I could see Ollie doing. But the chance to return to Dietz had to be an easy choice, even for Ollie. Soon animals would replace people, and his world would again become both comprehensible and habitable. Within a year, despite Stan's refusal to accept the inevitable, the litigation against Doc's estate was complete and his property sold to pay the judgment. The national five and dime that soon gutted Stan's store carried an inventory of gardening supplies and small home appliances Dad could not compete with on price or selection. When he closed down eight months after Stan, Dad never again mentioned the hardware store and I knew never to discuss it. However, both he and Stan found new careers in a relatively short time. Stan became the produce manager for the *A&P* in Stilton, and Dad sold cars for a struggling *Buick* dealership outside Brewman. We rarely saw much of Stan, and Dad's erratic hours made our dinners together an even rarer occurrence. Once I showed up unexpectedly with a sandwich and malt, and watched unnoticed as Dad and another salesman looked out upon a sea of emptiness and searched the distance for something, anything that might deliver them from their imposed exile. I left without giving Dad his dinner, choosing to have him go hungry than to see him humiliated. When he collapsed a few months later, the diagnosis seemed irrelevant. Myocardial infarction stopped his heart and ended his life.

Dad's death left me with a sadness and a shoebox of odds and ends. But amongst a tarnished silver hair brush and a host of official documents, lay a signed Joe Dimaggio rookie baseball card. It did not surprise me that Dad squirreled it away without telling me. But when I sold the card to pay for my tuition, I knew he would have admired my initiative and practicality.

I considered leaving Swanson Lake soon after and moving a hundred miles north to Braxton or another scenic town on the Canadian border. The Sunday newspaper always touted special places to move to, making each place sound more wonderful than the next. But Dad had warned me about trusting their descriptions.

"It'll always be foreign to ya . . . . You'll feel like you're looking through pop bottles and sidesteppin' puddles made by the sun . . . . nothing'll ever seem quite right."

The more I thought about that, the more I accepted the possibility it might be a mirage. So I remained in Swanson Lake,

comfortable and confident in my decision. I spent my days trying
not to think about Opal or Ollie, and always did. I half expected
to be called or smacked from behind, and became disappointed
when it didn't happen. Only Stan seemed to know about their
brief and infrequent visits to their parents, although my trips to
the Stilton *A&P* often proved futile.

"Did you come to see me or grill me?"

"Both."

He returned to unloading a case of apples. I assumed he had
ignored me and I began to leave.

"If you're concerned about them, they're doing fine. I called
Ollie the other day—"

"He won't accept my calls."

This time Stan ignored me.

"But I can't tell you more than that. Opal told him to make
me promise . . . "

Then he stopped unloading and glared at me.

" . . . . And *I* keep my promises."

If Stan had not been my only link to the Magnussons, I might
have pushed him into his apple display.

"So Opal's okay then?"

Having just proclaimed his oaths of allegiance and secrecy, I
expected Stan to provide no more than a one word answer. To my
surprise, he divulged a number of specifics.

"She's doin' great, to hear Ollie tell it . . . . Almost finished
with that medical school in New Paltz . . . . to treat people like
her mother."

"A psychiatrist?"

"I suppose . . . . Ollie didn't use that word."

I wondered if that meant she would return to Swanson Lake.
Stan laughed so hard, he nearly knocked over his display and the
one holding oranges.

" . . . . You really are in the dark . . . . "

He then proceeded to give me more specifics than I wanted.
Macy Magnusson had made a sudden and almost complete recovery,

even cooking again, and he thought everyone knew she and her husband had moved to Long Island.

" . . . . evidently there's a mega building boom out there."

Then Stan made a "slip of the tongue", as he said afterwards, about Opal's marriage to Peter. My face must have blanched white because he told me to sit down before I fell. I should have expected his news, but I always hoped Opal would tire of Peter and attempt a reconciliation with me. Stan's smirk, although he tried to hide it, let me know his "slip of the tongue" had been intentional. Apparently, despite his often harsh treatment of Ollie, Stan cared enough about him to despise my act of betrayal, and me with it. I left Stan, both of us knowing I would never return. As I walked to my car, I felt glad the Magnussons moved away. I could now assure myself I would never see Opal or Ollie again.

Over the years I worked at the department store in Brewman selling sporting goods, then later, as an inventory manager for a new house wares factory. I kept track of the number of scouring pads and cast iron frying pans, but of little else. I remained as unobtrusive as the co-workers I barely recognized, and rarely spoke to. I focused on the hour to hour, minute to minute details, still expecting the bolt of lightning that would rescue me from the drudgery and steer me in a new and exciting direction. But nothing ever did, even when I attained my community college degree, and completed another year beyond that. I settled in to the short and long factory buzzes that punctuated my days, and I stared at a time clock that assessed my value. If I toyed occasionally with a mutinous urge to direct shipments to the wrong destinations and wreak havoc on that well oiled machine, I only had to remind myself how much I needed, and depended on, the weekday buzzes. But lightning did finally strike one brisk autumn morning, and it threatened to undo the fragile peace I found.

The nearby town of Garvey had become the mecca for shopping, and each week I drove the twelve miles to buy groceries. In the burnished gloom of one November Saturday, I had just finished packing them into my trunk when I heard laughter from Betcher's furniture store across the street. I looked up and saw a woman emerge, her back to me, pointing to someone or something inside the store as she continued laughing. I smiled at the silliness of it all, and was about to turn away when I saw Macy Magnusson. She had become beautiful again, looking the way she did when I was eight and watched her cook her special dinners. But the Magnussons moved away and the woman seemed too young. Then thought and pain merged as I stared at Opal. My eyes zoomed in on her face like a telephoto lens, everything and everyone else around her a blur. My feelings erupted, and then fizzled into confusion and disorientation. Her pure and perfect laughter echoed in the cold air, and crystallized all that I felt and didn't want to feel over the years. I wanted to call out, then I wanted to scream at her, but finally I just wanted to run to her, hug and kiss her, and never let go. I called her name over and over. She did not turn around and she did not look up. My calls had remained inside my head where her name rose and exploded like so many skeet on a shooting range. She waited for Ollie, she always waited for Ollie, and I became exhilarated at the prospect of surprising them both and daring them to chase after me. My excitement ended abruptly, however, when I recognized the figure who soon emerged from the store. A middle aged stocky man, Peter's thin lips and Roman nose made him easy to identify. He held a small gift wrapped box which he then handed to Opal. She slapped him playfully on the arm, and they both laughed. My eyes followed them to their car. I still expected Ollie to appear and follow them, but he didn't. As Opal and Peter drove away, I heard her laughter long after she disappeared, and I knew I would hear it for a few lifetimes after that.

BVG